WICKEDLY ABLED

SCI FI, HORROR AND FANTASY BY DISABLED AUTHORS

Edited by

SUMIKO SAULSON

Contents

ISBN:

This is a work of fiction. Names, characters, places, and incidents either are the product of author imagination or are used factiously, and any resemblance to actual persons, living or dead, business establishments, events, or locales, is entirely fictional.

❀ Created with Vellum

To Flynn Keahi, with love.
You're in my system, babe.

ACKNOWLEDGMENTS

Thanks to everyone who supported our Kickstarter! Rachel H Sanders, Erin Diaz, Anaïs Noa, Fester L.D. MacKrell, Robin Hill, Thea Flurry, Alphanzaı, Ellie Yee, Mark Durrheim, GM Coates, Krypton Radio, Finn Evans, Hog and Dice, Oliver Lauenstein, Ember, Natalie Ward, Brynn Reiff, Jessica Enfante, Abi Godsell, Jessa Willson,

Cover Image by Lillian Rose Asterios
Cover Layout/Formatting by Mimi Heft
Editing by Sumiko Saulson
Editing Assistance by Seruus Ualerium Tristissima Liber
Proofreading by Ran Reiff
Interior Formatting/Layout by JA Clement

CONTENT WARNINGS

This is a book written by and for people with disabilities, including some people who have serious mental health issues and suicidality. It also contains detailed descriptions of physical health issues, caregiver abuse, bodily fluids and functions. It has vivid depictions of hallucinations, suicidal ideation, suicide and suicide attempts, voices and other symptoms that may trigger readers. Since this is an attempt to give voice to the disabled, the realism in some stories may be difficult for some to process.

"*Magpies*": Animal death, child sexual assault, death, suicide, sexual assault.

"*Believe*": Child sickness.

"*Bloodstock*": Mention of sex, alcohol, blood.

"*The Other Side of What If?*": Caretaker abuse

"*Tannenbaum*": Brief description of animal abuse.

"The Last Book": Genocide, child death.

"Secundum": So-called corrective procedures, blood.

"Tapestry of Sentiment and Sunset": Religious prejudice, homophobic speech and violence.

"How Pace Wilkens Died": Gore, alcoholism, domestic violence, animal and child death, gun violence.

"Image Monster": Graphic homophobic violence, death, alcoholism.

"Her Eyes Were Blue in Lebanon": Gun violence, war.

"Blood Loss": Drugs, blood, emotional and implied possible physical abuse, incest.

"The Secret Life of Randolph James": Racism, homelessness, classism, child sexual abuse, incest.

"Aduality {0≠2;1=108}": Graphic sex involving an escaped (genetically-engineered) sex slave.

"Dark Djembe: Drum of the Damned": Racial violence, child sexual abuse, incest, pregnancy/childbirth.

"Pallas' Sword": Poetic death imagery.

HOPE, AGENCY, AND HORROR:

BY SERUUS UALERIUM TRISTISSIMA LIBER

There is a statistically significant correlation between Autism and not identifying with the birth assignation given to one by the doctor who aided in their birth. I start with that to underscore immediately just how complicated speculative fictions are for me as an Autistic genderqueer. Science fiction, fantasy, horror, and other speculative fictions have provided me throughout my life with the ability to imagine worlds in which I was possible. In which I was right when I asserted my gender identity. It also told me that people like me (mentally ill, Autistic) or people like my mother (who walked by means of a crutch and braces my entire life and now uses a wheelchair) were dangers, victims, or burdens. That we were wrong.

Wickedly Abled is Sumiko Saulson's effort to resolve that painful paradox, and I am beyond grateful to help hir with it. In the stories in this book, we bring the agency we experience in our own life into the imagined worlds we love. Here, we are heroes, point-of-view characters, and just people interacting with the fantastic like any other. And, yes, here we are victims sometimes, as well. However, the monsters which terrify us in these stories tend to be the society able-bodied, sane, allistic people built for themselves, the very environment that disables us.

Take, for example, Felix Flynn's absolutely chilling "Secundum," in which Lacy's parents and the larger society pressure her into accepting a monster of a device to "fix" her Autism. Felix's descriptions of the Aut-Implant's effects call to mind any number of horror and science-fiction stories in which some horrible thing removes the ability of the main character to decide upon their own actions, makes them a prisoner in their own body. Rather than some exotic Other like a ghost, a possessing demon or alien, or mind control, however, in "Secundum" it is the idea that allistic ways are the norm which everyone else must change themselves to fit that is the monster.

In a similar vein, Sumiko's "Tapestry of Sentiment and Sunset" offers hope amidst a stark depiction of the ways in which different cultures understand similar underlying experiences. What Chloe calls a religious experience, Dr. Robbins—and the institutions of white, so-called "sane" society which she represents—calls mental illness. We often discuss the social-ecological model of disability as it concerns the society in which we live, rather than to imagine (or remember, as the story asserts) other societies that don't disable us. Sumiko shows us the ways in which this disabling, this harm and even murder, rhymes with the ways that white society harms and murders people of color. In this way, hir use of Sara Baartman as an example is eloquent.

Yet, s/he also gives us hope not only that it is and has been different in other contexts, places, and times, but also that we can build our own new societies that meet our needs. Jo, Bethany, and Chloe realistically show the ways we find to dispel the spell of disability, to see each other's value in all our diversity. I hate the term "high-functioning", as its metric always seem to be the value system of abled, sane, allistic capitalism, but/and it is small groups like these that allow those of us lucky enough to have built them to define it ourselves and build brighter futures for ourselves than we are offered.

Carolyn Saulson's "The Secret Life of Randolph James" shows the problem with the idea of "high-functioning" even more clearly, even as it shows more resonances between sanism and racism, adding classism to the mix as well. Randolph's life is consumed by his efforts to pass, as white, as sane, as upper-class. There is a subtle horror here, one that resembles that in "Secundum" the way a trickle of liquid down the back resembles a catastrophic tidal wave. Carolyn shows here how we must harm ourselves to be treated as people by a society that refuses to think of us as such. The horror of how we must turn our own agency upon ourselves as a weapon, cutting off love, putting ourselves into the social equivalent of a pile of razors, lurks throughout this tale.

Furthering the themes of oppression and the hope to end it is Kat Fury's "The Other Side of What If?". Disabled, mentally ill, Autistic people are abused at a rate far higher than that of the general population, often by their caretakers. This story, like many in this volume, details an example of this abuse. Its victim is drawn to an act of desperate magic that provides the story's premise and allows Kat to describe both the terror engendered by the idea of losing one's hard-won life to a return to the abusive situation as well as the strength offered by speculative fictions themselves. Sometimes all we need is the faintest idea that things can change, can be better. Fantasy can provide the destination and with the destination comes the strength to endure the difficulties of the journey.

I have felt the pain of that haunting paradox I mentioned earlier ease as I have edited this tome. These are worlds in which all of me can exist, in which my queerness and my Autism and my depression and my anxiety and my executive dysfunction, in which my damage and my justice, are real.

WHY WICKEDLY ABLED?

BY SUMIKO SAULSON

Like many disabled writers and fans, I have grown tired of future worlds that are so-called utopias, where disabled people such as myself have been erased by eugenic scientists. Hereditary disabilities, such as my own bipolar disorder, are often bred out of future populations. Not all disabled people feel that they need their allegedly disabling condition bred out of the human population. I am bipolar, and bipolar disorder is associated with increased creativity. Like many other disabled people, I find fictional future worlds where people such as myself are, as a group, eliminated from the population through genetic tampering or abortion. Futures we aren't a part of are represented as utopias. To some of us, they seem like dystopias.

The social-ecological model of disability suggests that it is neither physical and neurological differences nor inherent biology that disables the individual, but social and institutional structures that fail to accommodate us. This sort of narrative shows up often in *Wickedly Abled. Wickedly Abled* turns the Othering of mainstream dark fiction over on its head.

The title *Wickedly Abled*, coined by author Serena Toxicat (one of the seed authors who helped me develop the project idea in its early stages) is a play on the now-outdated term "differently abled." It was popular when she and I first met some 25 years ago, but is now widely considered to be a condescending artefact of concern-trolling abled-savior narratives. *Wickedly Abled* is an attempt to take back the phrase. With the subtle sarcasm that informs the writing of the gloriously dry-witted Ms. Toxicat, it pokes fun of the phrase. It brings back those days in our childhood when we imagined disability to connect us to superhuman powers. Like the *X-Men*, and the kids in Professor Charles Xavier's *School for Gifted Youngsters*, we were being persecuted for being different. We are not disabled, we are authors and artists who are wickedly *able* to write, draw, perform and more.

We reclaimed the term and made it our own in the spirit of our elders and mentors. Such as Patty Overland. a lesbian poet, suicide survivor, and self-identified crip who is paralyzed below the waist since her suicide attempt at eighteen years of age. She took back the term when she cofounded the *WryCrips Disabled Women's Theatre Group* in Berkeley, California with two other disabled queer women in the Summer of 1986. The group is working on *Wry Crips Occupy*, a historical play about the 504 protest in 1977, when disabled activists took over the federal building in San Francisco.

Elders in the disability rights advocacy community such as Patty, and my mother, Carolyn Saulson, who exposed psychiatric abuses with the Citizens' Commission on Human Rights on a radio program with Mickey McMeel in Los Angeles in the late 1970s, paved the way for modern advocates. Patty spoke at my mother's funeral, and people like her fought for disability rights in Berkeley when I was still in diapers. In the early '70s, Michael Pachovas's guerilla act of civil disobedience was to pour concrete and create a makeshift wheelchair ramp on a Berkeley sidewalk curb. He and other wheelchair users were threatened by police. But they forced the architecture to bend to their will. In 1972, the City made it first official ramp on Telegraph Avenue.

I was 22 years old when the Americans with Disabilities Act (ADA) was signed into law by President George H.W. Bush on July 26, 1990. It guaranteed that all government structures would become wheelchair accessible. It meant that I, who have bipolar disorder, PTSD, and have had chronic pain associated with endometriosis since I was a teen, could work. The fight for basic civil rights for the disabled has been long and hard, with much major ground achieved during my 51-year lifetime. When I was a child, people with inheritable conditions like Down's syndrome and schizophrenia were regularly forcibly sterilized. Eugenics are still being practiced against the disabled. Down's syndrome has been virtually eliminated in Iceland. It was done by testing in vitro and aborting affected fetuses.

At the same time, "disabled" has itself become a dirty word. The root of the social-ecological model of disability is one where the environment should change, but how do we discuss it without using the very word that is attached to legislation protecting our civil rights? The spectre of eugenics frightens many people with inherited conditions listed as disabling. Avoiding the label allows the high-functioning to disassociate from groups of people who lack economic privilege and are often trapped in the foster care system. As adults, many of us are forced into group care homes, lose our rights due to conservatorships, and are incarcerated in mental hospitals against our will. As a result, groups of people with inherited conditions often choose to self-segregate and fight their battles separately in safe spaces with like-minded others.

The stories in *Wickedly Abled* are on the whole, dark and horror-leaning. *Wickedly Abled* is a dark speculative fiction anthology designed to challenge well-worn tropes depicting disabled persons solely as villains or victims by promoting darker-themed works of fantasy, sci-fi and horror by authors with disabilities which feature disabled protagonists. Since the hero of a horror story or dark fantasy epic is often escaping the victim role, our victimization is depicted in many of these pieces.

Tristissima, Serena Toxicat, and the rest of our seed authors dreamed of science fiction that does not create so-called utopias for the able that are dystopian nightmares for those of us who are disabled. We were sick of horror stories where mutation, mental illness, and deformity were signs of inherent evil. The common societal biases against disabled people show up everywhere. Tropes such as *Mental Handicap, Moral Deficiency* define people like Stephen King's Mr. Toomey in the Langoliers as evil. Not to mention tropes like *Evil Albino*; *Depraved Dwarf*; *Eunuchs Are Evil, Evil Cripple*, and more, which are pretty self explanatory. You get the picture.

Kat Fury, who has Ehlers-Danlos syndrome (EDS), a physically disabling condition affecting the connective tissues, often speaks of how triggering Anne McCaffrey's *The Ship Who Sang* is for her as a person with mobility challenges who uses a wheelchair. The book treats the bodies of the disabled as useless garbage, and disposes of them, depriving the person of tactile and other senses in order to enslave their brains.

We are interested in dissecting the ways in which old tropes about disability informed the oldest of fairy tales and camp-side stories. We want to demystify disabilities that have been considered by the able-bodied as signs of some sort of curse. We wish to challenge the ableist and sanist realms which have plagued world-building in fantasy, horror, science-fiction, and fairy tale mythologies since the dawn of mankind.

This anthology flips the othering narrative on its end by creating worlds where the horror comes from the normative. Allistic society forces a monstrous allegedly corrective device on neurodivergent protagonist. The dominant paradigm tells a witch her contact with elementals and ancestor spirits is a mental illness. Rather than regurgitate tired old tales about the dangerous lunatic, abuse at the hands of sane, able, allistic caregivers is taken to task here.

MAGPIES

BY OMEWENNE

"One for sorrow," I say and we salute the black and white bird perched on a wind-slanted tree stretching out of a hedgerow as we drive past on the South West motorway. Colin is driving as it isn't something I can do. Colin is my husband, for only a few months now. We are on our way to visit his parents—my first time with them. My emotions run flat with fear at the possibility of something going wrong.

"Tiding."

"What?"

"Tiding is the collective noun for magpies. I looked it up online."

"Oh. I thought, perhaps, that you were wishing me a Happy Christmas which is odd in that you don't celebrate the same as me."

"Yule Tidings!" I answer. It was somewhat of a shock that I had married a Christian since I had been abused by so many Christians in the past.

"You're going to die on this road unless you see a blackbird," the nasal voice says. I ignore it but feel the fear rise in my head close to bursting. My voices come and go and I can do nothing about it.

"I'm sorry," I say.

"Nothing to be sorry for," Colin says back to me, a real voice from a flesh and blood being.

"They're going to do the same thing families always do," a smooth female voice says.

"I'm no good with families, you know," I say.

"Don't worry. It'll be fine," says Colin.

"I know my family is not your family, but the damage is done."

"They're looking forward to meeting you."

"Well, I'm scared to meet them."

"He's going to touch you. He's going to touch your breasts!" a gravelly voice says.

"Please don't leave me!" I cry softly.

"I'm never going to leave you! You're my world!" Colin says looking at me clear in the eyes, his beautiful maple syrup eyes glowing back at me.

A tasteful room but not to my taste. Comfortable, yellow, green, and beige with cream, but all covered in plastic. Marissa, immersed in her recliner by the fire, my mother-in-law. She speaks with a thick Italian accent and smokes perfumed French cigarettes.

Albert, the father-in-law, overweight, balding in a chair facing Marissa with a charming smile. Bright-eyed.

Marina, in her fifties, sits in a wooden chair close to her mother, looking at me with sad longing in her eyes. She had given me, a moment ago, a black scarf for Christmas. We had not bought her a thing. I am embarrassed.

There is a tense silence.

Colin and I got married in the States and because Marissa is bad with planes, they were unable to come to the wedding. They didn't come nor did they know anything about it. A whirlwind romance? Not really. Colin and I had met online while he was in Sarajevo working with the Red Cross in communications. Ours was a slow-bake romance through emails and then phone calls, then suddenly there he was in San Francisco and we were married. He had felt very alone at the reception without his family. Now, here, they seem very impressed by me but without a thing to say. Marissa seems to hold the reins on conversation. I have always been very shy so it is difficult to start a conversation or even join one. But silence...I feel all my voices all at once and cannot understand through the cacophony.

Another time, a memory: fear, absolute. My father is carving the turkey while my mother stares down at her plate, visibly upset but holding it in for dear life. My sister and I have the same lopsided sour look on our faces. We know we are about to be punished even though we've done nothing.

"What the hell were you thinking, Gwen?!" he yells at my mother, furiously.

"I'm sorry, Jay."

"Where's the *goddamned* stuffing, huh? What is this? What's wrong with your *goddamned* brain?!"

A tunnel of darkness opens before my late teenage self. A tunnel of voices shouting chaos. I scream in this memory. I scream.

"Anything we would've seen?" asks Marissa and I am back in the present.

I realize she must be asking me. "Oh, no, probably not. They're all arthouse films, nothing big. They just play festivals."

"Well, you'll have to show them to us sometime," she says through puffs of smoke.

"Of course. They're not anything I'm that proud of. Independent films leave you at the mercy of some rather twisted writer-directors who have chips on their shoulders." I try to explain about my short-lived life as a film actress.

Silence.

"I'm much better on the stage."

Silence.

Colin then launches into old family memories and the chatter begins. Laughter but with a remoteness for me as I am left out.

Later, I am coming out of the loo when the plump Albert corners me with shining eyes and bright false teeth.

"You are so very beautiful, Annabelle."

"Oh, thank you, Albert. I always thought I was plain. Especially without make-up."

"No, very interesting. Very." Then leaning towards me, he places his right hand on my breast. I want to back away but there is no room. I freeze, horrified.

"You must kill yourself!" an angry voice shouts and continues over and over at me.

I am relieved when Albert moves away, his fat hand no longer on me, his boozy breath releases its pong on me. Albert goes down the stairs to join the others. I think of Colin knowing what his father has just done to me. I cannot tell him. He'll leave me.

"He's going to leave you," the smooth voice says.

"No, please, no!" I whisper to the air.

I remember in a flurry a series of people's fathers who had sexually assaulted me or made sexual overtures towards me. I feel sick.

"You're a whore," the gravelly voice says.

I do not tell Colin about what his father did. I have not yet shared my voices with him either. I have gone into a trance, rejoining the others. Marissa is in the kitchen still, with a cigarette hanging from her lips. We all sit at the table. I try and sit as far away from Albert as possible. The turkey arrives with stuffing! Marissa's long red lacquered nails maneuvering around the platter. Cigarette smoke whirls around the table, laboring my breath.

I lean over to Colin and whisper, "I'm sorry." He squeezes my hand.

"Colin tells me you are psychic? So do you see anything for me with your psychic powers?" Marissa is smirking. I know she is teasing me but the flash before my eyes of what I have seen for her isn't worth repeating.

"No...I mean I haven't done any of that for a long time. Rusty, I guess..."

She bugs her eyes out, "Ooh, I seee..." Everyone laughs but me. I feel myself sinking.

Back at our new/old home in Cornwall, far away from Albert, Marissa, and Marina, I want so much to tell Colin what his father has done...But did Albert really do that to me, or was it my imagination? Was it some repressed memory superimposed over my reality? I cannot trust myself.

"I think I'm getting bad again."

"What do you mean?"

"Please don't leave me!"

"Why would you think I would leave you?"

"Because I'm crazy."

"You're not crazy."

"You know what I mean."

"I love you no matter what, alright?" he says gently.

We're watching television. The phone rings. Colin goes to answer it as always. No one ever calls for me. Leo is on the phone. Leo is Colin's son from a previous marriage—a marriage that ended with Colin having a breakdown and Leo being very young. Now Leo is twenty-five. They are close. Leo likes me despite myself. He even knows about my illness.

Once the three of us visited Tintagel, the supposed birthplace of King Arthur of legend, but I couldn't handle the openness of the area, the wide bright sky, the height, the endless fall to the ocean. I began to talk to myself to calm down, to stare fixedly at the ground and hug myself. Leo held my arm and led me back over the frightful suspended bridge back to the car park. He is very kind. Leo attends university in Cambridge. Colin works hard to put him through university. Leo is a scientist, a neurobiologist. Colin is very proud of him.

"Your husband hates you. Everyone knows you let his father touch you," the nasal voice says.

I am disgusted. Disgusted by myself. If it was real, I should have stopped Albert. It's my fault. I'm not strong enough. Or maybe it wasn't real. Maybe...

Memory: Dr. King is staring at me. I have just explained to him that I was sexually assaulted on a bus after coming back from visiting my sister in Northern California. Here I am only twenty. I am wearing heavy black eyeliner and mascara, my skin painted white. My hair is dyed black. I am wearing a 1940s white ballgown.

"You know what I think, don't you?" he says, rolling his tie in his fingers and then flinging it outwards.

"No. I don't."

"I think you wanted it."

"No, I didn't! I promise you I didn't!" Bells began to ring in my ears. Image: My father reaching for my crotch. I am a toddler and I cannot tell what age I am but I cannot speak. I remember the feeling. FEAR.

It is many years later. Colin and I are attending his mother's funeral. Colin is very quiet. I hold his hand. Marina stoops over the open grave, the coffin beneath. Her face is solemn with none of the glamor that Marissa had. I can remember Marissa's impeccable make-up, her nails, her silver hair piled up upon her head. Marina blames everyone for the death of her mother. A lot of Italians are present, relatives of Marissa. A feeling of oppression. The sound of weeping weaves in with the pitter-patter of raindrops. Albert has slow tears running down his face—or is it the rain? Black and blue umbrellas are everywhere. Yellow roses are thrown into the grave by those closest relatives, even I receive a rose to cast into the grave. I will miss her.

Albert is now frail and in a home, with brain cancer. It is only a matter of time. Colin and I take him back to the home afterwards. Colin goes to order us some tea. I am left uncomfortably alone with Albert. He has lost all of his hair from his chemotherapy treatments. He stares at me smiling, his eyes shimmering.

"You are very interesting. Very." He reaches out towards my breasts in front of everyone in the main room, all of the elderly people asleep in their chairs, their mouths slack and open. No one sees him, but this time I am able to pull away. "Bitch."

"You dirty whore!" the gravelly voice mutters.

Back down in our Cornish village, I wait for Colin to come home. He is working with the church-goers at the Community Centre again. He is always working these days, outside of working at the telecommunications office just alongside the village in an upcycled tin mine. He is a Christian and I am not. I pray to many gods, he prays to one; although if he were honest his is a trio: the father, the son and the holy spirit. A lot of women swarm around him at his workplace, at church, and at the community centre. Colin always tells me their troubles, but seems to ignore mine as though I am not struggling as well.

I begin to suspect that he is sleeping with an older woman from his church, a Welsh woman called Cerys. She is a very nervous woman but overly devout. I sense an imperiousness about her. Colin is always at her house after church for her instant coffee and stale biscuits to "help her with her computer."

"You're sleeping with her aren't you?"

"What?!"

"Everyone is taking advantage of your good nature, your politeness and manners!"

"I am not sleeping with Cerys—how could you think that?"

"Everyone wants to take you away from me!"

"You're not worth anything to him," says the smooth voice.

"Well, they can't! I'm only for you. You should know that!"

"I'll go back to San Francisco or maybe L.A.. You can divorce me and marry her. I know I'm worth nothing to you. That's what she wants. She told me she wants you herself!"

"Well, she cannot have me. It's harmless anyway. There's nothing going on."

"It's not harmless! Look at what it's doing to me." I grab the scissors from a small vase with assorted pens poking out of it. "I am going to kill myself!" I begin to rake the scissors over my wrist. Colin snatches the scissors from my hands. I break down. He holds me.

"Please don't leave me!"

"I will never leave you. You are my world." His arms around me, looking at me with his dark eyes.

"Liar! You don't love him. You love no one. You cannot love," says the nasal voice.

This "procedure" repeats itself often over seven years. Colin still regularly visits the elderly Cerys. I am still jealous. Then a strange thing. While watching *The English Patient* on television I am seized by a grander, greater sense of self, euphoria. I begin to write more often. I see a better place for myself. I cannot get enough done...but none of it is any good. I begin to curse and spit at Colin. I become obsessed with becoming a writer but see myself living in the U.S.A. rather than in Cornwall. I fly into rages at Colin. And in my rages I am filled with a perverse joy that lifts me up towering over all my problems where I am merciless and cruel.

"Why are you being like this?" he pleads.

"This isn't good enough for me anymore! You don't care! You're asleep when you're with me and when you're not, you're with other women! You're probably fucking all of them!"

"No, no, I'm not! I am not doing that! What's come over you?"

"It's over. I am going to leave you! I am moving back to the States!"

Colin is helpless but to oblige to my heightened state. My rage. I get back in touch with friends from San Francisco who now live in Portland, Oregon. I decide quickly, feverishly, that I shall move there. All arrangements are made, and an apartment is secured through Colin paying my first year's rent upfront. In fact, Colin takes care of everything for me, giving me over half of our savings. Without a thought for him I take it along with our white cat, Delphine, leaving our rather delicate black cat, Damselfly, to stay with Colin. Colin comes with me and Delphine to Gatwick Airport and we board the plane for Portland—all three of us. Colin comes because I need him to help me...I need him? Want him? What am I doing? Too late. Mania ensues.

"You must forget about me and pursue other women."

"I don't want anyone else."

"Well I am going to see other men. You should see other women. You've got all these other women anyway."

"What?"

"What about Cerys?"

"Don't be ridiculous! She's an old woman, Annabelle. I don't love her. I love you. I don't want you to go."

Colin helps me settle in Northwest Portland only blocks from downtown. Sadie and Cordelia are there waiting for me. Old friends from San Francisco now re-situated in Portland. Sadie is also in the mental health club with bipolar disorder. Cordelia has never been diagnosed—but certainly she has some oddness about her rather controlling, forceful nature but charming all the same. Cordelia seems more responsible of the two. Sadie is more of a sister to me than my own but she distrusts Colin. She distrusts any man in a relationship with me.

When the time comes and all is as settled as it can be for the time being, Colin and I go to the PDX airport and I bid farewell to him... sobbing. Sobbing!

“You wretched bitch, look what you've done now. Crying, you sad cunt,” taunts the nasal voice.

“We're going to die...” whispers the smooth voice.

“Die! Die!” screams the raging angry voice.

I watch Colin disappear into the crowd of queues for departure. I am weeping all the way back on the tram. 'What have I done?' becomes 'What will I do?'

Back at my lonely one bedroom apartment with my new furnishings bought by Colin, I remember holding onto Colin's hand in Cornwall. I remember begging for him to help me through my move to Portland.

Delphine is a very pushy cat. Older, set in her ways, she does not like life without Colin. But Colin has Damselfly who is devoted to him. He doesn't need me. He doesn't want me. I am brokenhearted at having left behind Damselfly, and Delphine misses her too. I compartmentalize her in my head in my mania, along with Colin. Almost immediately I go out to late night coffeehouses to write.

At these late night coffee bars I attract men who are interested in what I am writing, or who use it as a barrier breaker to starting up a conversation. Though I am in deep with my story I oblige them. The worst of it is when I put up an ad on Craigslist for a boyfriend who's interested in horror fiction (the kind I write).

A series of men pass through my bedroom. A self-obsessed drummer wants to keep me down and maintains vulgar control over me. I feel nothing, gain no pleasure from the experience. I find him quite unattractive. I dismiss him.

A hair stylist who wants me to change my hair, my whole look, putting me down. He goes on to confess to me about his incestuous affair with his long lost sister. They were unable to keep their hands off each other. He says he suffers guilt. I am the understanding older woman.

These young men either know I am forty-five or think me younger. Another is a younger man barely in his twenties who comes in a cab in his pajamas for one night only in which I still am unable to have any sensual pleasure. My lady parts are useless. No passion. Really there isn't any sex, just lying together. All of them.

All of this time, in-between all of these men, I am in video conversations with Colin wherein I reveal nothing of my deep shame. I have become the thing some of the voices say I am and they are never-ending in reminding me of this. And all of this time Delphine is growing more sluggish. I buy a small set of steps for her to climb onto the bed. White cat, white duvet.

Then one morning I find a deep red stain, a gash across the white bed, over the white carpet. And there she was on the white kitchen floor. Her beautiful snowy white fur sopped up the blood. Did she die in the night? So lovely she is as though still alive! But I put her into a shoebox, my little baby, tears flooding my face, and take her to the crematorium. I bring back a little wooden box with her ashes within.

"You did this to her. You savage," says the gravelly voice.

"You feel nothing, do you?" asks the nasal voice

"Count to ten before the kettle boils or your building will burn down," says the smooth voice.

At this point The Sun seeks me out trying to strike me down. I hide from The Sun. Can only go out on overcast days. I see many faces in The Sun. Faces like my voices. I feel the hammering of its rays. It wants to kill me.

I find a psychiatric nurse at a cheap health clinic who sees me dressed up like an old Hollywood moviestar in pale Shiseido make-up, deep orange lipstick and nails. He has to laugh at me. But he appreciates my beauty in the way that some gay men love old Hollywood and has a sensitivity to my kind of mental health trouble.

"What about the schizophrenia?"

"Well, there's that too," he adds, "Take the medication. If it's not enough then we'll build it up. Come see me in four days." He has prepared the room for me by pulling down all the shades and blinds to hide me from The Sun. His name is Oliver and I am so grateful to him.

With my umbrella in full sunlight and on medication I retreat back to my apartment alone. Sadie has left calls for me. She cannot come to visit me in my distress, for she is afraid to cross over the big bridge in her old car. Cordelia phones me later and takes me, zombie-in-tow, for sushi. I am lucky to have friends. But I am insane.

"Why are you with so many men?"

"I don't know."

"Don't you think it's destructive?"

"No."

"You're being ridiculous! You should be alone for awhile. It isn't time yet."

When I return to my empty apartment there is no longer Delphine. Delphine who doted on Colin and who greeted every one of the transient men that came through my bedroom. I would have to tell Colin about her passing. He would find it hard going.

Then a message on my answering service.

"Hello Annabelle, it's Leo here. I'm so sorry to have to tell you this but it's Dad. He's been killed. A boating accident in the Balkans. Could you come back?"

"Please don't leave me," I said.

"Self fulfilling prophecy. You said you didn't want him to leave you and you were so scared of him doing just that, which drove you to leave him in a manic state. Now he's really gone and you have to face yourself. All this time it's been about grief. For the grief of the death of your relationship. Grief that now takes it to a new level," Oliver is holding my hand. I am dumbstruck.

Sadie and Cordelia arrange to have everything packed up for the shippers. On heavy medication I am going home, my world crumbling down like an iceberg into the arctic. A terrifying new world beneath its waters. No Colin.

Leo meets me at Gatwick and he drives us down.

"One for sorrow," he says, we salute. The black and white bird flutters across the road. Suicidal bird.

"Colin and I always saluted magpies. You must have picked that up off of him."

"I don't remember. I must have been young."

"Oh look, another! One for sorrow," we salute again.

We stop at Colin's father's care home first. I ask Leo to wait for me in the car. I am worried about what Albert might say or do.

Inside the home with its many white furnishings and stale smell, I am led by a care-worker to a snug room where Albert sits staring out of a long, floor-length double-glazed window. Outside the trees are bare. It is the beginning of winter.

The care-worker says, "Look, Albert, it's your daughter-in-law come all the way from America to see you!" Then she leaves us alone, disappearing down a corridor. I wish she would stay. I am afraid.

Albert perks up and smiles at me, his eyes twinkling.

"Albert, I have some unpleasant news...Albert?"

Albert is staring at my breasts. He slowly looks up to my eyes, his eyes shimmering. "Annabelle, looking lovely, my dear!"

"Albert," I sit next to him and put my hand on his shoulder, "It's Colin. There's been a terrible accident. He's gone...he's dead...I'm so sad. I'm sorry to tell you this."

"Well, now you and I can be married, yes?" He begins to grope my breasts. I pull away weeping. "Marry me, Annabelle. You were always meant for me." My voices rise in my head, making me foggy. I resist.

"No, I am not meant for you Albert!" I rise violently, shocked. I begin to back away, "How could you?" I flee down the corridor of clinical white. When I get to the car outside, Leo is reading a book. He sees that I am upset.

"You alright?"

"Could we just go on to Cornwall now?"

"Of course, certainly."

"You whore! You loved it," the gravelly voice says.

At the funeral are all of the women who had swarmed around

Colin, including Cerys and another, Therese, from Sarajevo with whom Colin had once had a long-lasting but troubled relationship. I recognize her from photos I'd once found in one of Colin's photograph books. How had these women found out??

Cerys approaches me, "You know, if he had been my man I would have taught him how to speak more clearly." She pats me on the hand. I want to spit at her. All the other women shun me. But then I had left him.

Beside me are Leo, Marina, and Marina's children whose names escape me. I feel as if I am holding in the whole world of voices from spilling out, a whole ocean of sobs from bursting forth. I must hold it all in. Not here, not in front of these people. The music is what Colin wanted. "The Liebestod" from *Tristan und Isolde*. Was this passionate music about him and me or him and someone else?

Afterwards the funeral moves to the headlands where I scatter Colin's ashes over the headlands' edge with white roses.

"You didn't love him. You used him to prop up your insanity!" says the gravelly voice.

I collapse.

Leo is reviving me, helps me back to my cottage where Colin and I lived for many happy years. Damselfly is thrilled to see me and it dawns on me that I have had a manic attack. An episode which dragged me from Cornwall to Portland. Then psychosis, but...does the mania mean I am bipolar as well? I am drowned out by terms and all I want is to curl up into my bed...Colin's and my bed...and sob. I had turned my back on Colin, yes, but also on little Damselfly who weaves against my legs. She will wonder where Delphine is...now just a small wooden box in my luggage. Damselfly remembers me and loves me still. We grieve together. I ask Leo if he could leave me alone for now although I know he is hurting. He does have his mother and girlfriend to look after him so I do not feel so guilty...well, I do. He heads back to his hotel. Tomorrow he heads back to London for his job in a neuroscience lab.

"Take care, Leo!" I say to him with a hug. "Thank you. I'm so sorry."

As I see him leave in his car, a tiding of magpies are suddenly in the front garden chattering. I count seven. Seven for a secret never to be told. No need to salute them as there are more than one. The garden is wild, overgrown as it has always been. Colin was never much of a gardener, nor am I. What would I do with the cottage?

"You used him to soak up your misery," says the nasal voice.

"I didn't! I love him more than anyone!" I protest aloud even though Colin is gone.

I think of Colin. "Please don't leave me!" I whisper.

I take the bus into Truro to see my old psychiatrist who, when I had fled Cornwall, was only too glad to have seen the back of me. Now the madwoman returns.

Doctor Stringer's young, sallow face turns to face me, and his large, cold, watery eyes look up at me. I feel his displeasure and begin to cry. He pulls tissues up from a box and hands the box over to me. I drown myself in tears.

"How am I going to take care of myself?"

"You managed in America."

"You know nothing! I was *psychotic* there. You should have *kept me* here. I was manic!"

"I know it is easy in these difficult times to look for someone to blame—"

"Blame? I blame myself. But also *you* for not listening to me, for not knowing better than me."

"Your very thorough psychiatric nurse in America has stated that he was treating you for grief."

"So?"

"What would you like me to do for you?"

The session is useless. I leave no better off than before. The cacophony of voices in my head is so bad that I have to cover my face from the other passengers on the bus on my ride home to the village.

For months, I live a recluse's life in the cottage. I have food delivered from online for Damselfly and me. October rolls in and so do the spiders from outside. I am overwhelmed by them and go about with a book of nursery rhymes crushing them in terror.

My widow's pension comes. It is meager.

"Please don't leave me."

I grow fearful of neighbors trying to shoot at my head from outside so I stay away from windows. Magpies are in the house, many of them. They must have come down from the two chimneys. Their chatter fills my head. Their chatter turns into voices.

"You've let yourself go. Better count to ten or the killers will get you!" says one of the magpies with a smooth voice. I count to ten. They grow large, unfold their wings and I see that their faces are like Botticelli angels. So tall are they that they must bend over to fit in the lounge. They follow me wherever I go.

"You've got to kill yourself!" an angry man's voice rages from one of the magpies, disgruntled.

I call Leo.

"What? It's 3 a.m., Annabelle, what is it?"

"What was he doing in the Balkans?"

"He went there with, well, with Therese. He thought you were divorcing him so he did what you told him to do. He moved on. I know you didn't want him to."

"I'm troubled. That's why I left. I hurt him but I never meant to, I never meant to leave him. I messed up."

"I know. I'm so sorry, Annabelle. Look, it's late. Why don't you call me tomorrow after I get out of work, around seven?"

Seven for a secret never to be told.

Therese. He went back to her. He loved her more dearly than he loved me. I remember when I caught him emailing her just after we'd got settled after our wedding. He had claimed they were only friends. He had truly left me. Now I am alone. Damselfly would never forgive me. She has been left behind. The magpies crowded around me.

"What am I to do?"

"You've made a mess of your life!" the nasal magpie says.

"I have."

"Count to ten before you die," the smooth voiced magpie says.

"One—two—three..."

"You're a whore. You whored around on him," the gravelly voiced magpie grumbled.

"Kill yourself now! You must do it now!" the angry magpie screamed. I weep.

It begins to snow. There is a knock on the front door. Colin is there. Colin is leading me over the hills towards the sea to Chapel Porth, a small cove. Colin wanders out into the water. My breath is labored. He is beckoning to me. I am shivering.

"Please don't leave me."

All around me are the magpie angels in the bedroom eating spiders off of the walls. Damselfly is nowhere to be seen.

The phone rings. It is the sexual abuse group offering me an appointment with Jo. I go the next day but she is dismissing everything I feel as sexual abuse side effects. Even my mental illness. She is a dog person. She says she cares so much about her dog but it is locked up in her car as we speak. Jo smells of sausages, garlic, and dog stink.

As I continue to see Jo she offers to take me to the spiritualist church which I reluctantly agree to do with her. In the sparse church are a scattering of lonely people, all with longing in their eyes. I am acutely aware that I look strangely like an old silent movie star in an eighties chick flick. Lonely people are facing forward towards the medium, a middle-aged woman wearing glasses and standing at a podium. After a mumbled and off-key rendition of Rod Stewart's "Sailing" which makes me want to run out of there, the medium calls out to me and says, "You have lost someone very close to you...You were also hurt badly as a child, by someone you had no choice but to trust...Someone named Colin is saying he loves you, that he'll never leave you." I burst into tears and thank her but really all I feel is immense guilt. When Jo and I leave she invites me for a drink at the local pub. She says it will be good for me to "have a laugh."

I am revolted by her.

I remember my father reaching for my crotch again and begin to cry. We are in the pub in a booth and people are looking at us.

A fat middle-aged woman with an orange face says, "It's not so bad love! Give us a smile!"

I hiss at her.

"Suit yourself!" she grunts back.

I order a brandy and then another, and another. Jo drives me back to my cottage. I trod back to the door through the snow. I will not be seeing her again I decide as Jo drives away. Damselfly is there looking at me with a worried expression on her face. I feed her in the kitchen. Around me suddenly are the magpies. Their usual insults surround me. White pieces of flaked paint fall, from the walls? The ceiling? They fall all over me, stuck to me. I cry out and run upstairs to the bathroom. The magpies are with me, giant and overseeing all that I do with their angelic faces. The bathtub is filled with cold water. The magpies push against me shouting:

"Kill yourself!"

I fall on the floor and find a pair of scissors. Into the cold water I slip shaking, the dress I wear drinking up the dead weight of the water, pulling me in. As I lay there I make the first incision on my left wrist. The blood flows down my arms and dyes the water in a plunge of crimson. It is beautiful. I think of Delphine. I slice my other wrist. The blood flows. I am very cold, slowly growing colder. Damselfly looks over the edge of the bathtub at me mewing helplessly.

"Goodbye darling. You'll have to go out the cat-flap to find what you need now. I have failed everyone."

The phone rings and rings until the machine picks it up. I hear a voice, "Annabelle, it's Leo. Just worried about you. Dad wouldn't want you to suffer. Er...I'll call you later. Hope all is well," he rings off.

I sink into the water after what seems like an hour. I am numb. The water is red. My hand left over the side of the tub bleeds onto the white tiled floor. I hear a deep yowling...Delphine? I feel someone's hand in my own. A magpie? I look up through the water and see Colin sitting there with Delphine in his lap. Damselfly is still looking down at me. Colin looks sad, his eyes tearing as when he listens to powerful pieces of classical music.

"Please don't leave me!" he says crying, and I am lost in the forever water.

BELIEVE

BY STACY SCHONHARDT

Heather tried to watch the walls breathe, but her view was obscured by the thermometer stuck in her mouth. As the mercury in it rose, she could hear her mother's anxious voice somewhere behind her, in the kitchen. Soft footsteps, and the thermometer disappeared. A sigh, and a cold, wet washcloth, carefully folded, was laid across her forehead. The light sheet covering her was tucked under her little feet.

"Rest a while, baby girl," her mother said. Heather nodded and watched the walls. In and out. In and out. White walls, with a raised stucco-y swirly pattern, rough and sandpaper-y, and slate-blue Berber carpet. The TV set was on, but she couldn't really focus on it. It was huge, at least 20 inches across, and big brass buttons scrolled across the bottom of the wooden frame it sat in.

She could listen, though. Cartoon voices, women's voices, men's voices, news, weather, soap operas, they all were thick and taffy-like to her. Across the room was the big front window. The drapes were open and she could see part of the clear, blue sky from her position... part of the sky, and part of the tree across the street. The leaves were just starting to turn a spotty red and orange.

Voices of the other kids that lived nearby, as they walked home from school. She wished she were there instead of here, on the couch, with endless thermometers, washcloths, popsicles, and cold baths. She wasn't hungry at all—her throat was sore, and her tummy hurt. The rash had spread from her neck and was around her armpits as well as her private parts. Clothes hurt. Even her underpants hurt her delicate skin. Her mother had placed soft towels under and around her, and draped a cotton sheet over her for modesty's sake. It smelled nice.

She lay there, hour after hour, half awake, wondering if she'd get well or die. She had been to the doctor a few times already. The nurses didn't like it when a child her age could watch them draw blood without so much as a whimper. They gave her lollipops for "being so brave". She didn't want them. Sucking on them hurt her tongue. Her mother made her a lot of powdered breakfast drinks in milk. Even swallowing hurt, but she knew she had to eat something. These meals were followed by cold baths. A few times, her mother doused her with calamine lotion, and once she was pretty sure Mom had put rubbing alcohol on a sponge and rubbed her all over with it, to try to lower her fever.

Her tummy hurt. The doctors looked at her mother through their thick glasses and mustaches and said things Heather didn't understand, but they made her mother cry. They made her pee in little cups, and examined her wherever the rash was. She was embarrassed and blushed, turning even redder. The nurses had to take more blood, and she had to visit them a couple times every week.

The spotty leaves turned dark and began to fall. A classmate brought Heather's homework to her every few days, and took the finished work back. Heather spent a lot of time on the couch reading, propped up with pillows. She took a walk in the backyard, finally getting some fresh air. She was so weak she could barely reach the fence.

Heather lay there on the couch. Her mother said she'd be back in "just a little bit" and walked away. She could hear her talking on the pink phone in the kitchen. The cord wouldn't quite reach her in here. She continued to watch the walls.

Then.

Something moved. From behind her, or off to her right, or maybe her left, something flew over her head and across the room. It glowed. A small ball of light. It was maybe the size of Heather's fist. It moved around—first to the right, near the window, then to the left, where Heather was, then back and forth and toward the television. Heather thought maybe it was a reflection. It moved closer. Heather held her breath.

It was a tiny woman with wings. It looked a bit like her mother, if her mother were blonde. She had pink skin and yellow hair, and big, shining eyes. She wore a long grass-green dress that floated around her ankles, and wings that shimmered so fast that Heather couldn't quite see how big or what shape they were. The tiny creature flew very close to her, until Heather was sure of what she was looking at. There was no doubt in her mind. The little woman hovered about a foot in front of Heather's nose for several seconds, or minutes, or hours. She carried a tiny wand in her right hand. The wand had a point of light on the end. She waved it at the sick child. Almost as if it were a story, golden sparkles floated down gently over the girl. With that, the tiny fairy flew away. The window was closed, but she moved through it as if it were open.

Heather blinked.

"Mom! Mom! Come here! Mom!" She rarely cried out, even during the exams, and this brought her mother very quickly. She told her mom all about the fairy woman—what she looked like, what she did, and pointed to where she had gone through the window, hoping she'd left some residue of golden dust behind.

Her mother smiled enigmatically. "Mommies have a way of taking care of their little girls when they are sick," she said. Heather would remember that for the rest of her life.

Heather grew well, but the memory of those few minutes on the couch never left her. She read everything she could about fairies, the paranormal, ghosts, and the list went on and on. She looked at her mother with suspicion, noting the time she found a single Tarot card in a drawer, wondering constantly what, how, her mother had comforted her. What hand she had had in it. As she got a little older, she asked. Her mother remembered that day, too. She smiled and promised to tell her when Heather was grown and had children of her own.

The years went by, and Heather continued to wonder and study and learn. She noted a few other strange things about her mother and her mother's side of the family. She wrote stories in her head about the fantastic things she may learn one day. She noted the unusual names of family members a few generations back. A family reunion, and she met her great uncle Merlin. She could tell, by looking, whether someone was a relation by blood or not. She noted that her grandmother could tell who was calling before she picked up the phone.

Heather got older, and hadn't married, hadn't had children. She had dark moments, but always through it all, she held onto the memory. The promise. She lost herself to all things strange and wonderful, the fairy tales and stories of kings under hills, fish that could talk, and things that lurked in the night. She turned to art and writing, and was hailed as a most imaginative painter.

"I'll tell you when you're thirty."

Then, "I'll tell you when you're forty."

Heather still remembered it all, with crystal clarity. She begged her mom, during long phone conversations, to at least write down the story. Write down the secrets. Just in case, heaven forbid, something should happen—she said she would go crazy if she couldn't know.

Unbeknownst to Heather, her mother would always smile when asked about it. Long ago, she'd written down a single word at the bottom of a sheet of blue-lined paper, underlined it three times, folded the sheet crisply and put it in an envelope with the words "For my dearest Heather, I love you, Mom" written on it. She'd licked it and closed it up, and put it with the family's important papers. Just in case.

When Heather turned forty, her mother sent her a card. In her mother's beautiful handwriting was a test. She claimed that Heather's fever had been so high she'd been hallucinating. She'd been worried sick about her little girl, and tried everything to entertain her while she was ill. Mother knew Heather couldn't focus on the television, and that she wasn't allowed outside while so sick. Finally, she resorted to something that had worked in the girl's not-so-long-ago infancy. She found a mirror. Sneaking around the corner, she'd flashed the mirror around, catching the light and shining it around the room. What Heather had seen, the fairy, was a figment of her imagination.

Heather knew the gentle lie for what it was, and waited.

Her mother had Skyped her, so she could watch Heather's reaction. She watched her daughter's face fall, and said, "I'll tell you when you're sixty."

BLOODSTOCK

BY KAREN JUNKER

8:30 PM, OCTOBER 15 - PIONEER SQUARE, JUST OUTSIDE THE ENTRANCE TO THE SEATTLE UNDERGROUND TOUR

Camille LeBlanc shivered in the borrowed woollen overcoat, wrapping her knitted scarf a little tighter around her neck and lower jaw. Even after the past week's unseasonably chilly weather in Seattle, the day had been surprisingly cold. She'd left their hotel wearing her usual jacket, but as they'd stood out in the frosty night air, she'd begun to shake so visibly even the normally impervious Braeden Kelly noticed it and insisted she wear his coat.

She couldn't believe she'd forgotten to bring her meds with her earlier in the week when they'd flown into Seattle from LA. They'd done this trip dozens of times with her careful packing and checklists and double-checking the lists. Had she skipped the final review? Usually so compulsive about taking her meds, she really wasn't sure what could happen if she went without them for too long. Her muscles were already cramping and felt as if they were on fire. A psychotic break could come in lots of flavors, and she was the last person who might realize she was having one. And she couldn't let

Braeden know. She needed this part time job as his research assistant to pay her bills.

She watched his eyes scan the passing crowds, mostly frat boys in stiff new leathers. Their tough looking outfits were no doubt meant to make them pass for hip, Underground regulars. Occasionally one of the street bums made an attempt to con them out of some money—to buy enough gas to get to a job interview or just to get something to eat. She might have given them something, if their breath hadn't smelled so much like the dregs of cheap beer and tobacco. She sniffed, searching her jeans pockets for a scrap of tissue in vain. Finally, she waited until she was sure Braeden was focused on someone further down the block before she sneaked a corner of her scarf from under the overcoat to wipe a tiny drip from her nose. She hadn't had a cold in over two years, but with working around all the street people for the past nine months, she was sure her immune system had to be taxed to its absolute limits. If Braeden knew about her health issues, he might fire her from the research project. She couldn't risk losing her stipend, but it wouldn't surprise her if she caught pneumonia, standing around in the freezing cold. She shuffled her feet, her knees rubbing together, as if even that small amount of friction could generate enough heat to get her warm again.

"Braeden."

It was no use; he couldn't hear her. He'd spotted something interesting and there was no way she'd get his attention until he'd made contact with the subject. Maybe he'd be a talker and they'd get what they came for and get out of there before she perished from the cold.

"Don't be such a big baby."

"Look, I'm not complaining." She twisted her neck out of its wrap as if to prove the point. "I'm just saying. We haven't seen anything that even remotely resembles a vampire in over an hour. Can't we just give up and go back to the hotel?"

"You don't have to stay, you know."

"But what if one comes? I'm not sure you'd find our way out on your own, once you get inside their lair."

"Well, then. You'd better not leave me alone out here." His eyes sparkled, glossy obsidian-blue in the halogen streetlights. A neon beer sign flashed streaks of green and red across his weathered face.

~

9 PM, Monday, October 15 – Waxing Gibbous Moon

"Simone, wake up!"

In the light of the rising moon, Simone could just make out Vincent's profile. Naturally, he wouldn't have gone for a doctor or even troubled himself to splash a little water on his old friend's face. No, Vincent Charles sat gloomily on the only really comfortable chair in the room and lit a cigarette, while Simone squinted at him from the floor.

"Give me one of those, or I'll cast your immortal remains into the outer realms of darkness forever," Simone said to the vampire in the armchair.

Vincent's platinum hair shimmered in the moonlight as he shot Simone a sideways glance.

"Too late, by about a century, old girl."

"Well, give me one anyway, you dolt. I've had a hell of an evening."

"Sounds exciting." Vincent threw her a gold-tipped cigarette and drew another long drag off his own. "I'd very much like to hear all about it, absolutely love to really, but there is magic afoot and you're needed at the old homestead."

"What's the old man up to now?" Simone asked. She lit the lavender cigarette with an old piece of magic she'd left floating around the house. She drew the smoke deeply over her tongue, tasting its savory warmth as the nicotine entered her bloodstream. The feeling started to return to her feet in icy needles and she longed for the days when she enjoyed that kind of thing.

"It seems that some jackass, and by that I do not mean an actual were-donkey, but a jackass in the figurative sense, has performed magic in front of an entire stadium full of mundane. Your father is of the opinion that something must be done."

"Are you talking about the football game?"

"The very one, Simone, my precious." He opened one orange, cat-like eye a tad wider for effect.

"What does he think we can do?"

"That, my lovely, is entirely up to you, he said. He merely wants it to be handled, and quickly. Before containment is breached, or words of that nature."

"Isn't there anyone on site?"

"Oh..." Vincent flicked a nonexistent ash from the knee of his patent leather pants. "Well, I suppose if you mean a Jester, like the one in 1977? Then, no, I don't think so. He seems to want you to go down there and do something, anyway."

"Since when are you my father's messenger boy?"

"No need to be rude, Simone. I merely happened to be in the neighborhood, so I told him I'd come by and tell you. Believe me, it would have been far more convenient had I simply gone my way and heard about it later, when we were all being burned at the stake."

"You disgust me. I'm thinking of making you Chief of the Naga after I'm crowned."

"That's so typical of your kind, Dracul. Revenge, revenge, revenge, for the slightest imagined insult." He punctuated his words with little cigarette stabs, as if preparing for a fencing match. Smoke eddied in tiny streams around his face. The feline slits of his eyes disappeared behind snow-white lashes as he gave a small yawn.

"Well, I've told you what you need to know. I'll be on my way." He rose with the grace of a delicate, imperious dancer. "Do stop by and tell me how things came out later, will you? I'll be at the J&M. My usual table."

"Bite me, Vincent."

"I don't waste wyvern breath on the undead, you know that." With a squeak of his vinyl jacket, he slammed the door behind him.

"How did he get in here, anyway?" she asked, looking at no wyvern in particular. None of them answered her, which didn't surprise her in the least, since they don't know how to talk. Even if she believed, as some of the weaker clans do, that wyverns could speak if only you took the time to train them enough, she wasn't the sentimental type who talks to fetches, anyway.

It took a fair amount of willpower to keep from swatting the scaly little half-cat, half dragon fuzzballs across the room as they stole out from their hiding places. In less than the time it took her to open a can of disgustingly foul cat food, she found herself willing to forget about their stupid tricks. They were, after all, nothing more than creatures fashioned from bits of her own blood and bone, mixed with a charm that predates Stonehenge. She couldn't stay mad at them for long, anyhow, especially if they were all going out hunting for the evening. As she scraped the greasy mush into a crystal bowl on the kitchen's hardwood floor, the three wyverns gazed at her with what looked like genuine affection, then scampered up to be fed. She glanced at the antique Japanese wall clock on the far side of the apartment; its well-oiled works ticked in a gentle rhythm in counterpoint to the lapping wyvern tongues. If she got there before the third quarter was over, she could get them flapping their arms over their heads in the famous Seattle 'wave' and be back on the streets in no time. With any luck, she'd be able to catch the last Underground tour as its innocent tourists shuffled their way down the urine-soaked cobblestone entrance to Doc Maynard's. Her father needn't have sent Vincent Charles to summon her. The old man was capable of using a phone, especially for a task as simple as this one. Any half-rate vampire was capable of raising enough magical power to make forty thousand screaming fans forget they'd just witnessed something most of them didn't believe exists. No, the old man was up to something. Maybe after she'd had something to eat and a drop of the vein or two, she'd stop by and find out what scheme had been unleashed.

"I promised your wife I'd stay with you until you're back safe off the plane in LA. But have some mercy, will you? I'm only good to you alive." The cold was starting to feel as if it were killing Camille.

"Maybe I could use you as bait. You know, if you get any whinier, you're as good as a snack for one of them, anyhow."

"How do you know that?" She pulled the collar up around her ears. "I don't believe you."

"That's why you're so good as a research assistant, my dear." His eyes narrowed, focused on something behind her. "You broadcast all the right vibes to attract a hungry shapeshifter."

"Well, I'm not sure which I prefer. Death by bloodsucker or at the hands of Maura Kelly, if I don't return you to her safe and sound on the red-eye."

A stream of pedestrians emerged from the general area of the Seahawks stadium. The night was suddenly warmer, the air more alive with smells and sounds. Police whistles shrilled at the intersections while hordes of SUVs lined up at the traffic lights, engines snarling with aggression as the foot traffic impeded their hasty retreat from the historic district. Thousands of lawyers, programmers, insurance agents, and their kids poured out into the streets and parking lots along Seattle's once-seedy waterfront district. Drug deals went down as a whole new world of potential customers thronged around the bars and cafes of Pioneer Square. Too bad the coffee shops didn't stay open this late; they'd make a million in hot chocolate tonight, alone. She wondered when Braeden had last eaten anything.

"I'm going to go over to the J&M and grab a sandwich or something. I'm willing to bet you didn't eat dinner before you left the hotel."

He ignored her, his silver head swiveling in the path of the oncoming crowds. He was blissed out; she knew that much from working with him in the past. He always said he could tell when he was going to find a 'live' one, though that was a slightly ironic term for something that was technically undead. At the change of the light, she crossed First Avenue and headed for the only break in the row of Harleys lined up outside the front of the bar.

There was a doorman on duty, checking IDs and patting people down as they entered. She knew she looked younger than her age, but at twenty-eight, she was still pleased when someone carded her.

In the warm gust of air that shot out from the bar, she smiled at the bouncer as he handed her back her driver's license. For a moment, she thought he might be flirting with her, but then in an instant, he was chatting up the next group. Or its female members, at least.

Food at the J&M had always been a crapshoot. Since it served food late-night, they'd eaten there a lot over the years. But nobody ate there expecting anything worth writing home about. The sandwiches were a safe bet and big enough for two people to share and still have leftovers for breakfast.

Steam roiled from the huge cookers along the back wall of the café's kitchen. She could make out the aroma of grilled onions and over-fried potatoes. Back in the card room, a man with platinum hair leaned fully back in a spindle-backed captain's chair, the front legs lifted up at an angle she felt sure could only end with him sprawled out on the floor at any moment. But he was balanced there, a thin cigarette unlit in one slightly effete, slender hand and a glass of some dark liquid in another. From clear across the bar, a space of more than two hundred feet, his eyes made tangible contact with her body. She could feel, more than see, his imperious gaze as it swept over her like scorching molasses. The overcoat was too warm in the stuffy bar. She wriggled her shoulders out of it, letting the bulky wool fall in a cascade at her side. Just for a moment, as the waiter took her order, she thought she felt something slide across her throat before she coughed a small, polite cough, hand to her mouth. When she looked back to the card room he was gone. But there was no mistaking it. She would swear on a stack of Bibles that he had glowing, orange eyes.

Simone strode along the alley behind Occidental Park. The moon reflected back at her from brackish puddles amidst the cobblestones, the stench of human urine burning her nostrils. A meal or a fuck, anything to calm this nagging desperation. The stadium had filled her for a moment, the unleashed power of those thousands of souls, bearing down on her in anguish and ecstasy, on the edge of their seats for the final quarter, despondent when their team had ultimately lost the game.

Tonight was easy, in a magical sense. She had started with the closest beer vendor, gotten him to get the crowd in his section cheering and throwing up their arms, then the next section down, then the next. It was the classic Seattle Wave, an elementary form of magic first used during the 1977 Sonics basketball finals when someone had accidentally used some magic to transport a player across the court for a three-point field goal. Forty yards of free flight wasn't something you could just let the mundane think they'd actually seen, so a quick-thinking vampire dragged the beer guy behind a hot dog stand, snapped his neck and took his tray out to the crowd, then got them started by waving his arms up to show them what he wanted them to do. They took to it like lemmings to the sea. After they'd raised enough energy, he directed it, got them all in somnambulistic state and erased the image from their collective and individual minds in nothing flat. He took to moonlighting as a beer vendor after that. Power surges were addictive, after all.

Simone never got that much out of it, herself. After the first couple of times, she felt irritated just being around them. They were mindless sheep, too brain-dead to do anything but suck up overpriced beer and holler at overpaid athletes.

The scent of a hadiyon female shot up her sinus passages on a burst of salt air. Any one of the half-vampires, half-humans could be her soulmate, her twain noctu. But the chances were infinitesimally small this was the right one. She'd been in Seattle for most of the last couple of centuries and unless someone was a visitor, she'd already sipped their blood and ruled them out.

They were downwind of her, not far away. Adrenaline coursed through her veins as she tightened her pace, headed for the open space between the waterfront and First Avenue. A little food would calm her, a shot of whiskey would dull the edge of her annoyance. If the hadiyon was pretty enough, Simone'd buy her some nice champagne, get her a good meal and then drink from her 'til dawn in her underground lair.

They loved getting seduced by a vampire, those halflings. They always thought they'd be the one who'd set Simone straight, love her 'til she could love herself, give her back her soul, those who even knew of the hadiyon legend. But they couldn't. Not for lack of trying, but because her soul was always bound to another. Another hadiyon she hadn't yet met. One she hadn't yet partaken of, or attempted to charm into being her mate. She spat onto the pavement, thrust her fingers through her tangled hair. If this hadiyon woman harbored any delusions about being her twain noctu, Simone'd snap her neck like the worthless prey she was and leave her body in the warren for the shicksters to devour.

She was young; Simone could tell that much. She was drawn to her as to a bitch in heat, her nostrils flared, blood engorging the core of her body against the tight fabric of her jeans. She knew better than to take the hadiyon before eating some real food—it would be a waste of energy and she might not stop at merely killing her. If she let the wyverns at her, she might not remember feeding her, but she'd be left a vampire. There were too many vampires in the city already. She didn't want any more power hungry competitors, even if they didn't stand a chance.

Her scent was strongest in the street outside the J&M. When the swinging doors were open, it hit Simone in the gut, compounding her need. The hadiyon was fully ripe, redolent in her season. And this hadiyon was hers.

"Where to, Simone?"

She snarled at the voice, her lip curled up over lengthening fangs. Vincent Charles. Of course he was here. He would make it a point to challenge her, pretending to be a rival. Vincent's platinum hair gleamed in the pale moonlight, neon flashing in his flame-colored eyes. He'd picked up her scent and would stalk her until one or both of them had her that night. But Vincent didn't like to feed from females. He only liked males. Still, he'd make it harder for Simone to get to her, if she did indeed turn out to be her twain noctu.

"Nowhere you'd need to know about."

"Don't be coy, my sweet one. We both know I can smell the silly bitch."

Simone throbbed with the urge to mate. If Vincent wanted blood, he could have it. But not before she'd taken the woman someplace safe. She fought the passions that assaulted her nature, forcing herself to speak calmly, as the true Daimonos Prince she was.

"This isn't the time or place, Vince."

The younger vampire turned away as if struck in the face, his grimace exaggerated by the flashing neon lights in the bar windows.

"Darling, haven't I asked you not to call me that in public? You know how I feel about using my pet name on the streets."

"Out of my way. Or your life is forfeit, vampire."

"Don't be so melodramatic. You know I don't want her for myself." His hot coal eyes flared in the shadows. "But I wouldn't mind watching you, if that's alright."

"No, it is not alright." Simone shoved him against the crumbling plaster façade. A pair of drunken street tramps stumbled out of their way, broadcasting sherry fumes and bodily decay. "Go get yourself something to fuck and stay out of this."

Vincent's face showed no sign of fear, but he leaned back against the building. He regarded Simone with a flirtatious sideways glance, all eyes, all body English. His tongue flickered in and out, grazing against two-inch incisors.

"I'll be waiting for you in my apartments when you've finished with her. I'll give you a nice rubdown and a hot toddy."

"Very tempting." Sarcasm dripped from every word. "But don't wait up."

Blues mixed with jazz in cacophonous bursts as the bouncer let another couple through the brass hinged swinging door. Her scent reached out to Simone, reeling her in like a siren's song as she followed it into the noisy bar.

The woman stood at the marble-topped bar adjoining the kitchen, skin glowing through the smoky haze. She looked tired, her face showing signs of stress, dark circles under her eyes. Not a bad-looking little thing for a hadiyon. Simone'd definitely be up for fucking her after dinner. As for mating with her, that would take some planning if she was going to get it right.

With deliberate slow motion, she approached her prey as the woman simultaneously sensed her and turned to face her. Plates clattered over servers' shouts, laughter of half-sloshed legal assistants mingled with muted saxophone and a century of cigar smoke. The sweet smell of grilled onions held a bottom note to her overwhelming shock as she locked onto Simone's energy. With a slight twinge of regret, Simone allowed her to see herself as vampire Prince without illusion. If she mated with her, it would never be the same with other hadiyon women again. They'd know she was using them. It would take out all of the fun.

The woman didn't look at her eyes, but focused in the distance, pretending to be waiting for someone behind her. She'd seen it a million times. They want you, but they don't want you to come on to them, either. This one was more conflicted than most, but that wouldn't be an obstacle. If she was going to mate with her, it had to be by mutual consent. That was the way it worked. A twain noctu must mate with her soul mate willingly. If it were nonconsensual, the quickening wouldn't take place. The only way a vampire could regain her soul is if it is given to her willingly by the woman who carries it for her. The giving has to be sharp and clear, or the soul simply merges with that of the hadiyon and never separates, never enters the vampire's body. You couldn't steal your immortal soul from an unwilling partner, it had to be a gift. This one would be easy to win over as a source of blood, but the mating would not be easy. She was small, slender and looked as if she was about to jump out of her skin.

"Is this spot taken?" She skirted the leather barstool, took a stance inside her personal aura. Definitely a pushover.

"I'm waiting for someone, actually."

Perhaps she misjudged her. Her voice was strong. Her chest filled, pushing Simone back a fraction of an inch into the ether.

"Do you mind if I join you while you wait?"

"Who are you?" Her brow made a gentle furrow. A blush rushed to her cheek, she held her thick wool coat between them, as a shield. "Have we met?"

"I don't think so." She caught the bartender's eye, murmured something into her ear that she hoped would be taken for an offer if this one didn't work out. "If we had, I would remember it. Vividly."

She began the ritual seduction.

"My name is Simone. What's yours?" the woman asked.

"Camille."

"Enchanté, Camille."

With a deft move, Simone brought Camille's free hand to her lips, brushing them lightly over the skin on the back of her fingers. Heat emanated from every part of her body. It took Camille by surprise—she'd never felt herself so immediately attracted to a stranger. If Simone really were a vampire, that would explain it. If she wasn't a vampire, she could certainly play one on TV, any day of the week. Too bad Camille didn't believe in vampires. But this woman, Simone, if she was a woman and not a vampire standing before her, was swiftly changing her mind.

Simone's breath was cool, sparkling almost, with pinpricks of something Camille could only imagine was magic. She'd never seen such an enormous vampire, that much she could say about her when she described Simone to Braeden. If she didn't try to remember every detail so she could report about this one to him, he'd kill her later. If the vampire didn't kill her first. At least they were in a public place, lots of people around. Surely they didn't kill their prey in the middle of the J&M café.

But what if she wasn't really standing there? What if she was a figment of her imagination, a delusion? Could a few days off her meds cause her to see someone who doesn't really exist?

"Did you just come from the game?" Camille finally asked Simone. She'd never been any good at small talk.

Simone's eyes bored into her, full lips curved into a pleasant, but lethal-looking smile.

"So I did. And you? What brings you to Pioneer Square this frosty fall evening?"

"Actually, I'm with a friend. We're hunting vampires." With the same level gaze she used at her day job in LA as a social worker for explaining to bad parents that she'd been sent to take their children back to foster care, she allowed Simone's eyes to lock into her own. The truth works, when you can't think of anything to say.

"You don't believe in the supernatural." Simone stated it as a fact, not a question.

Camille brushed a stray lock of hair from her face, shaking her head. "Not really. But my friend does, and I'm tagging along to keep him company."

It was almost the truth.

The meal they'd shared wasn't the kind of thing Camille would normally eat at home. But half a burger and some fries washed down with a couple of beers would warm her up and hold her over until breakfast when they got back to LA.

The noise level in the bar was deafening, so they'd shouted a few words at each other while Simone fed Camille fried, limp potatoes, one at a time and watched her chew each bite slowly until she'd tried to swallow. But with gathering nerves, her throat seemed to slowly close in on itself. She'd made up her mind that Braeden would want her to find out as much as she could about the vampire before she got spooked away. He wouldn't mind waiting out there; he was too busy looking for a good one to even notice the passage of time. Funny that she, a mere research assistant, seemed to have actually found one. But like all male professors always, he'd be sure to take all the credit anyway when the time came.

Simone was trying to seduce her, that much she knew. Whether it was the legendary vampire ability to seduce through glamour, or that she simply found this woman the most amazing, charming, gorgeous and sexy creature she'd ever seen, she neither knew nor cared. She was going to follow Simone wherever she chose to take her.

But wait: what if it was all because she hadn't taken her damn pill? If she were having a relapse, that gorgeous vampire could be a heroin addict after her money, or she might not even be actually in the room at all.

Braeden would be able to let her know.

The seduction was going reasonably well. Simone felt that if she led Camille out into the street and down to the entrance to her lair, it would be the work of a moment to get her to agree to the bonding as she drank. A hadiyon mate of this complexity, this beauty, was not a thing she'd be likely to find in Seattle again, even if she searched for decades. And she was loathe to relocate. The weather here suited her. And she was surrounded by water, so fewer vampires wanted to move in to make a bid for territory.

No, it was going well, and the night was still young. If it didn't result in a mating bond, at the very least she'd have a nice meal of her.

But the bond had to happen soon. She needed to get her soul back so she could ensoul all of her progeny. Because an army of human vampires with souls could easily take over the world in her service. And Seattle was nice. But it was not enough. She would send her bitten children out into the nights of every town in every nation on the planet, to do her bidding and make her the ultimate Daimonos Prince of all the world. Or maybe she would style herself Emperor. Yes, Emperor, Emperor of the World.

Simone's boots clicked on the cobblestones as they walked over to find Braeden. Camille had convinced her to come along and take her friend, Braeden, a sandwich to go. She needed Braeden to see the vampire, and confirm that she existed, and then she would break free from the glamour and Braeden could take over. He claimed he'd dealt with the charms of a real vampire before and knew how to stay on guard and not let himself be taken as a meal.

They got to the doorway to the Underground Tour and Braeden wasn't there. He just wasn't there at all. She felt frantic as she turned around and around, looking in all directions, to see where he could have gone.

Simone finally put a hand on each of Camille's shoulders. "Maybe he's cold and went inside one of the bars. Let's go to my place, it's just over there around that corner. We can warm up and have some nice wine."

The look in her eyes frightened Camille. First, because she was not all that experienced at one-night stands. Second, because she was thinking she just might take her up on the offer. And third, because she might not be real. And that was a reality she had to take into consideration.

Okay, what could she do to stay safe? She was in a town she'd only been to a few times. She knew no one who could vouch for Simone, or tell her if she was even actually there. Or if she were, or were not, an actual vampire. But gods, she wanted to have sex with this woman!

If only Braeden believed in cellphones. But he was a Luddite, and he didn't even have email. How he'd managed to become the top professional in the field of cultural sociology, she would never know.

Her mind raced. Okay, slow down. It's probably fine. She could just be a nice, but amazingly good-looking woman, who simply wanted to have a hot date. Role-play. That was a thing for some people, wasn't it?

No, wait. Wait. She couldn't go on. She couldn't. She had to take care of herself. And gods knew, if she didn't find Braeden and take care of him, he couldn't take care of himself at all and he'd probably miss his plane. But herself. That was the important part. She had to make sure she wasn't acting on unverified information to do something dangerous, and possibly fatal.

Or worse.

***

The little hadiyon bitch was getting skittish. It was time to pull out the artillery.

Simone allowed her incisors a quarter of an inch reveal. She licked her lips as she gazed into the eyes of her prey.

"Please. Let me kiss you," she said, with all the force of charisma the unnatural gives a Daimonos Prince. She smiled her most winning smile.

"I don't think so," Camille said.

"What do you mean?"

"I mean, I don't know you, I don't know anything about you, and for all I know, you might not even be real."

"Oh, I'm real, all right." She narrowed her eyes to tiny slits. "And I can take you, here and now, if I want to."

"But you won't."

"What makes you think that?"

"Because if you are a vampire, and you didn't drink from me immediately, that means you want to mate with me. And you think I'm hadiyon, and that I might carry your soul." The tiny woman took a deep breath. She appeared to intend to continue her delusional rant.

"But even if I might, I am not going to go with you, I am not going to mate with you, and more importantly, I am not going to give you anyone's soul, ever. Because I know what you want to do with it. And I'm not going to be the one who is responsible for the end of the human race."

A man wearing only a light sweater over his shirt took the hadiyon by the arms, turned her, and led her briskly away.

It was not the last she'd see of this vampire, Simone thought.

Not the last by a long shot.

THE OTHER SIDE OF WHAT IF?

BY KAT FURY

Pain rolled through her body like lightning, dragging her into morning. She never let herself make a sound waking, silence ingrained after years of survival. It didn't matter that Cassandra had escaped her torment years ago. The fear was always there. Showing any signs of pain would end with more. Her mind echoed with her mother's voice. *'I'll give you something to cry about!'* She couldn't remember when she had last cried out. Tears fell in her life as rarely as rain in New Mexico. She felt the familiar pop of relocating joints, her body's inevitable dislocations working in place of coffee to get her body moving. Palpitations set in from the sheer amount of pain but to get relief she had to move. She had to grab her glasses and stumble to the kitchen, and down a handful of pills with milk. The start of every day for the last decade. This process could take up to an hour. It was the part of the day she dreaded most.

Her hand hit air instead of her laptop, perched on a desk beside her bed. She always worked, watched TV, and met the world from her bed in the small Santa Fe apartment she liked to call her cave. She didn't hear her cats. They weren't calling for their food, the elderly one more demanding with time. All that met her eyes was color. She was blind without her glasses, barely sighted with them. There was always a sense of urgency when things were knocked over, but it wouldn't be the first time that she'd taken out her desk with a bad dream. It wasn't *if* she would have nightmares but *how bad* the nightmares would be.

Forcing herself to stand, she felt no cool tile beneath her feet but the crunch of papers. She hadn't had clutter like this since she was back there with Mother. Her heart raced as she felt around. The bed was wrong. No hospital bed to make her breathing easier. It was flat. No wonder she'd struggled so much to get upright. The bed explained the way her spine rolled within her flesh, crackling with every shallow gasp, the pain making a properly deep breath at least an hour away. Her search for her glasses ended as a shrill cry came, "Cassandra Lessmore, get your ass out of bed now!" *Mother*.

How had they found her? Her worst nightmare was real. Panic, rage, and dread swirled through her but she knew to survive she'd have to press on. Play along. No excuses or be killed. No asking about her life. "I can't find my glasses!" Cassandra replied.

The scrape of flimsy metal on wood and stone confirmed her dread. "You could find them if you cleaned your room once in a while." She felt rough hands press her too-fragile glasses into her hands. "Thank you, Mother." The slap came like lightning. She almost dropped the glasses. She had used the forbidden word.

"How *dare* you!" It was going to be a difficult day.

"Sorry, Mommy." She made her voice extra sweet, remembering too late that Mother was a word akin to fucker in this twisted world.

"I want breakfast on the table. We're late." Her mother's voice was almost chipper. Abigail Lessmore was not a woman who would easily show what she was, her voice always kindest with company over or just before they traipsed into town. When she was younger, this meant another round of druggings. Why was she here? No ropes, chains, or other bondage. There was just that familiar and brutal start to her day. She knew there was no reprieve from the agony of her dislocated body here. No asthma inhaler, just unending pain.

Putting her glasses on, she studied her room, trying to prepare for a day of agony. She couldn't think about how long it might take her to escape again, just today. The word "room" was generous. She had spent much of her childhood in a shed in the backyard; baking under the heat of the New Mexico sun or freezing in winter. As the Bad One she could never do anything right, thus she had to earn a room in the house. She never had managed that. It had taken years to escape and learn she had done nothing wrong. She was simply born. The only dark-haired child amid a sea of blondes she wondered for years if she was the product of an affair. DNA testing might reveal that answer but it could also put her in danger.

The mess of the room was a tactical one, meant to stop the fumbling midnight predators. Her body was scarred and twisted from poor genetics and abuse. It was also wrong. This wasn't...*HER*...body. Where were her tattoos? Why did she have hair again? She'd been shaving her head and wearing wigs if she felt like it for years after she'd noticed she was trying to comb over three bald spots. She'd grabbed a razor and ended that mess without regret. It freed her.

The body she wore now bore more scars than when she went to sleep. There were fresh cuts hidden on the thigh. She was cutting again? Had her freedom been a cruel dream? Sick with fear and pain she forced herself to the dresser. It felt miles away. She would have to find a way to survive this. Pulling open the top drawer she found the same panties she'd worn ten years ago, with another ten years of wear and tear. They were stained rags that were more hole than cloth. There was a note folded haphazardly atop them, a drop of blood on the corner. She unfolded it, seeing her own handwriting.

I am sorry,

You didn't ask for this. Then again neither did I. I just need out. I can't do it myself. You aren't real. You won't suffer the way a real person would. Sam told me the spell would work; in case it does you need to know you will see Doctor Smythe at noon. You take Gabapentin. 6200 mg of Gabapentin. I wrote that twice. Sorry. I have to do something or kill myself. I am there again. This time you become real. I imagined you so many times, Galena. You are stronger than I am.

Cass

She recoiled from the letter as if she had been slapped. Gabapentin had been a medication that created nightmares for her. She had learned after stopping the drug that gabapentin ate away the brain, wasn't actually an antidepressant, and possibly was the cause behind her epilepsy. The drug stopped the renewal of brain cells, creating a neurological decay and increasing levels of rage. This drug had stolen her peace of mind, self control, and the ability to think for too many years. She felt her body shaking as she tried to comprehend the dose. It was too high, over the legal limit. She had spent so long trapped in a cycle of rage and suicidal thoughts because of this drug and the abuse. If it was all madness then Lily, Hope, and the other people who mattered in her life did not exist. She never needed help feeling anger or wanting to die—the pain and abuse was plenty—but Mother hadn't allowed her to stop any of the medications. She wasn't perfect, and thus had to take as many pills as Mother wanted. If she thought she was fine, her Mother would emphasize every error she had made and Doctor Smythe would write another prescription. She'd always had health problems, but they went untreated while her mind was destroyed.

"Cassandra! Stop wasting time!" her grandmother screeched, adding to her fear. There was no one worse than Grandmother. Unlike Mother, Grandma Lessmore had stopped pretending not to be a monster long ago. She bragged to strangers about beating Cassandra as a toddler, laughing as she described how far her small body had flown when hit hard enough. Most laughed along with her, though Cassandra had always hoped it was because they didn't want to put her in danger. The reality was that Dustville was just as bad as her family. A small New Mexico town full of dust and the worst of humanity.

Dustville lived down to its name; there was only dust and hatred for miles. The sun was already far too hot and bright at eight in the morning. She forced her feet into the too-small shoes and ugly, too-small dress. These clothes were what she had worn since she became a teenager. The closest thing that fit at the thrift store, in fabrics that irritated her skin. The colors were worse; nothing flattering existed in her wardrobe, just what she was assigned. If she liked something, it wasn't allowed. The clothing covered the necessities but no one would look at her and see a functional adult. She braided her hair; the ratty ends needed a trim, even if half of it hadn't fallen out from the excess medications and untreated ailments.

As she processed her day, she knew next came The Pills. If she never tapered off the medication, she could have a seizure if she quit taking it now. She would have to endure the rage and the way her thoughts sank into oblivion. Familiar steps that had haunted her nightmares for years led her forward into the house. It had fallen into greater disrepair since her escape. The windows were thick with dirt, the roof full of holes, the stench of mold tickled her nose. There were no repairs made; her Stepfather who built houses neglected his own. She wondered if Mother was still married to the same man. She'd gone through many husbands, few lasting long against the onslaught of her abuses. She stepped over piles of shit; Mother's pet cow was left free to roam the house. The creature was emaciated and seemed to suffer as much as Cassandra. This was the reality of life with Mother and Grandma Lessmore. Everyone else suffered, and if they had a moment of joy it would be destroyed.

She managed to make it into the kitchen, her legs trembling from the effort. Sitting at the table were Mother and Grandma Lessmore. Mother's blonde hair was curled in a pile on her head; in the eighties, the look had been trendy, but it had been thirty years. Unblended blue shadow, blue mascara and blue eyeliner adorned her eyes. Too much blush and hot pink lipstick completed Mother's dated look. She was a visual time warp. Grandma Lessmore was another story. She wore a similar outfit to Cassandra, her hair in a long braid, the same style Cassandra wore. Any changes to her appearance had always been copied. Grandma Lessmore wore a too-pale pink lip, the color seeping into the crags around her mouth. Her nose dripped snot, no effort to wipe it made. As always Grandma Lessmore simply believed in free-range mucus. Cassandra made herself smile, "Good Morning Grandma Lessmore, Mom. How do you want your eggs?"

The pair sat at the table her grandfather made. It was the only nice thing in the house, though it too had scars. Gouges in the wood from dinner tantrums. She tried to avoid the green arrows that were her mother's eyes as she turned to heat up a pan, gathering the eggs and bread. She wasn't supposed to eat gluten but she knew there was no safe diet. There was only survival. She would endure that pain as she did the rest. Flies buzzed about, the filth drawing them in. She hated having her back to the room and could feel her Mother's gaze on her twisting spine. She tried to hide the way her hands shook, pushing the wish for her wheelchair out of her head. There was no comfort here, no need met. She was home.

She'd learned to walk to survive, her body grinding away on dislocations. Helplessness was death and she had paid a heavy price for her survival. This version of herself had never had relief and this made certain things worse. "Scrambled," the verdict came at last. She whipped the eggs with cream cheese, the only way she could make herself eat eggs after decades of the same breakfast. Mother's favorite? Nearly burned toast, scrambled eggs, and bitterness. She set a plate before each of the older women, refilling their coffee before she sat down and made herself eat.

She didn't hear Ronald, her older brother, coming. She felt the stab of his finger in the most twisted part of her spine, stifling the cry of pain and urge to push him away. That would make it worse. She felt her eyes watering, and suppressed the urge to flee. She kept her eyes as dry as New Mexico, reminding herself to be a drought of emotion. She set an appointment for bedtime tears in her head. Ronald scowled, "Where's my eggs?" He took her plate. She made herself retrieve another plate.

Mother interrupted her thoughts, "Do you remember what today is?"

Cassandra paused, "I see Doctor Smythe." Mother was pleased. This was too rare and usually meant more trouble later.

"Did you take your pills?" Mother asked.

Cassandra shook her head, "Eating first." Mother seemed to approve. Cassandra forced herself to eat. She never ate breakfast after her escape. She had a lot of medical issues that this version of her would have endured without care. Gastroparesis from medical neglect, Ehlers-Danlos Syndrome, and much more. Eating too early in the day would fuck over her body for weeks but it was better than being force fed. The food was coming either way. So was the pain. She felt the echoes of the past trauma seeping into her thoughts again. This was not her body and the damage from being drugged and denied medical care was felt with every breath. She felt as if she was a spark away from being an inferno of rage.

Mother bit into her toast, the crunch seeming to echo too loudly. "Grandma Lessmore has given me the time to take you today." This meant another medication increase.

"Thank you, Mom, Grandma." The rituals had to be completed. The fake smile that no doubt still showcased her rage. Cassandra forced herself to swallow the eggs.

"Aren't you going to have toast?" Grandma Lessmore asked. She wore a look of smug satisfaction, well aware that Cassandra would feel worse if she ate it.

"Oh...there's not enough for me to have toast and Ronald too; I thought I should wait until he had his share." She looked to her brother, he glared at her as he bit into the toast.

"What do you want?" he asked. Kindness in her family always came with strings.

"Nothing," she said with a small smile, knowing that this would bother him for days.

"How generous," her mother said, her voice dripping with suspicion. Could they even know she wasn't the same Cassandra? They had never managed an iota of awareness of who she truly was before.

She watched Ronald pick at a dark spot on his arm; it looked a lot like skin cancer. She'd had a few. Did this body still have them? She wasn't allowed doctors and thus she could only guess. She tried to not think about the alternative to having the cancers removed. She chewed her food, ignoring the pop of her jaw and the stabbing pain. This at least felt like her own skin. Ronald kicked her under the table, and she dropped her fork, a bit of egg landing on the table.

She reached to pick it up, Mother slapping her. "If you're going to waste food, maybe you shouldn't get any!" This was not shouted but said in an overly cheerful way, the way someone might greet their lover.

"I'm sorry Mommy," she said as she picked up the egg and forced herself to eat it. The filth couldn't matter. No accusations of being kicked meant no recriminations most of the time. She made herself clear her plate, no food left. If she left any behind she would not be allowed to eat for days. She would need strength to survive this, even if that came with more pain.

As she cleaned up after their breakfast, Cassandra tried to suppress the urge to die. It was hard to survive when you just wanted to die. Her mind whispered it was the only way out, that the guns weren't far away. One magic bullet could cure her pain. It was a thought she had endured often enough. She took a breath, reminding herself she had escaped. This strange magic was perhaps a vivid nightmare, but if not she would escape again. The version of herself that left the letter had intended to summon Galena. Galena was an imagined version of herself, strong enough to leave. Yet Cassandra and Galena were nothing alike now. She couldn't quite figure out why she was here, the ache in her head growing.

"We are now late. You don't appreciate me, do you, Cassandra? I'm a bad mother. That's why, isn't it?" She was interrupted from her thoughts and the task of the dishes, then. Looking to her Mother, she took a breath. This was a song and dance as old as Cassandra herself. One of her earliest memories was a failure to appease Mother.

"Of course I appreciate you, Mommy, you made such a nice breakfast. I just wanted to help with the dishes." She'd be accused later of doing nothing around the house. She was already exhausted emotionally and physically.

"Then get in the car. We're going to be late. Everyone will think it's my fault!" Cassandra lowered her head as she walked to the car. There was not a single book in the house. This was something she missed immediately. No book meant nowhere to hide. No reprieve. Her mother had banished books when she was sixteen. It seemed this world was still a book-free zone.

She walked towards the car on wobbling legs. The familiar wood-paneled car with its battered frame, cracked windows, and dents had gotten worse since she had escaped. It sat with cracked windows and rust in its usual spot. She struggled to open the door, which screeched as it moved. The cacophonic symphony serenading them as Grandma Lessmore took the wheel. Cassandra sat in the backseat, where there was limited leg room. The stench of gasoline and oil told her the car was leaking and likely didn't have the exhaust fixed. She had to breathe that in the entire ride. There was no seat belt, leaving her floating free in the back. This was no surprise as the house and the car were always neglected in her family. Nothing important was maintained. If her mother was married to a mechanic their car would be the worst in town. Somewhere, whomever Mother was married to would be failing to repair something. Mother's type was desperate, dim, and lonely.

The car rattled down a dirt path that cut through weeds which choked the lawn leaving remains in patches of brittle yellow. The front yard was full of broken cars and appliances. Peeling paint and filth made the house stand out in the area, the sagging structure seeming as depressed as Cassandra felt. The car swerved into oncoming traffic causing chaos and adding more damage to the car. The interior was an abyssal space of garbage, McDonalds cups and old food giving the car its unique odor. If she cleaned it, she would be punished. If she left it, she would be punished. There was no appeasing these people, just small moments of juggling their expectations. Eventually she would fail, because success with a monster was simply being alive.

She spent the ride trying to figure out how to return to her life. There had to be a way, and perhaps she could even talk to this version of herself. She could help them escape. It was her job. Cassandra had managed not only to flee the abuse but to become a lawyer. She still wrote her stories on slow days, but she'd become a defender of the weak, protecting the innocent from Mother Monsters.

Mother filled the silence with music from the radio, the buzzing and static-filled speakers making the songs almost impossible to hear. All that was left was a tinny voice singing about a truck, a dog, and running off with someone's wife. The familiar road towards Town added to her worry that she'd lost her mind and had never left. Town was a slightly larger place fifty miles from Albuquerque. It was the nearest place to find a doctor. The village was small enough the selection was down to whomever was desperate enough to live there. The doctors were never skilled, and the psychologists were never helpful.

Town had barely changed since she was here last. There were two gas stations that sat side by side, their signs saying simply Gas. The roads were all dirt, and every building was made with adobe. A hand-painted sign indicated they had made it to Smythe's Mental Health. A smiley face was their logo. The fee was low, a five dollar copay reminding her of the actual value of this psychologist, if he had any at all. She sat, surrounded on either side by Grandma Lessmore and her Mother. The scent of Mother's perfume and Grandma Lessmore's old coffee and urine scent blended with the perfume ads tucked in an old Sears catalogue. The other alternative was a *Highlights* magazine. Nothing of substance was allowed. The chairs were bright orange and hard, rejects from an old school. The twist in her spine made her feet tingle as she sat, her eyes on the way her toe poked through the seam on her left shoe.

She didn't remember the nurse, though the woman bore a miasma of sorrow. One did not live in Dustville or Town to be happy. It was where the worst hid, and if you were not a rapist, murderer, or other monster you were their victim or enabler. No one thought good things about Dustville; if they even knew it existed. It didn't merit a mark on the map. Not even on a map of Torrance County. As the nurse muttered her name she stood up, following her down an overly narrow hall that went on forever. It was lined with mediocre art from a local artist who couldn't make it in Taos or Santa Fe. Bad copies of landscapes, failed attempts at being Georgia O'Keefe or Frida Kahlo her only reprieve from the bland yellow desert scenes. Somehow the sky was even bland. These paintings didn't serve as windows to what might be, or imagined worlds. They simply hung on white walls.

She entered the office. The door creaked as she stepped inside. There was a folding chair for the patient. It sat before a large metal desk. The blinds had layers of dust and the leather chair behind the desk was ripped, clearly broken. Doctor Smythe had not fared well over the years. The office had barely changed since she had declared her independence years ago. It had been ten years. In her reality, Doctor Smythe had been stripped of his ability to practice psychology, her malpractice suit bringing to light years of abuse. Here he was still free to harm.

She sat on the folding chair, awaiting her sentence. She could hear Mother's voice in the hallway, describing every sin, outburst, or feeling she had. They would be magnified until she was a monster. One did not feel in Mother's house. One obeyed.

After what felt like an eternity, the door opened and Doctor Smythe entered. This was not the man she knew. There was no hopelessness in his face as he raged at her for ruining his life, eyes clouded with bitterness and drink. This man had sharp golden eyes, too sharp. There was an aura of power that Doctor Smythe did not bear. She said nothing as he closed the door. "Cassandra Smith...pen name, M. Barlow. Can I have an autograph?" He held out a copy of one of the books where a short story was published. From her world. This book could not exist here, as the people who had encouraged her to write did not exist in her life. She reached out, hands shaking and touched it. The story in the book could not exist, as Mother had burned and buried her computer in the desert, threatening to bury Cassandra along with it if she ever wrote again.

She took the book and turned the pages, looking up at the golden-eyed man periodically. It was her story. She held proof her life wasn't a lie. Tears threatened to spill as relief and rage warred within her, but she pushed them back. She held the book out and said, "No." No autograph.

The man looked amused and said, "You don't know who I am?" He gestured around them as if this was a strange paradise and he was Lady Gaga, surrounded by adoring fans.

She snorted, "I would say Satan but we both know that's not true." He looked slightly offended for a moment.

"Clearly you've forgotten your own stories. It's *me*. Sam." He smiled, his teeth bared. Sharp teeth. Sharp eyes.

She stared at him intently. Sam. She'd written stories about the adventures of Samael the Archangel and his life balanced between Heaven and Hell. She did not let herself scream or shout but simply studied him. If this was indeed Samael, had he done this to her? "What did you do with my life?"

He walked around her in a circle. "Nothing. You did it." He waved a hand, "You can return to your life if you give yourself what you need."

"What I need?" she snarled, then paused. Perhaps it was a play on words. What did this her need? This her had tried something as a last ditch effort at survival.

"You can survive this." Samael said. He grumbled softly, "This skin is not comfortable. You must be feeling worse. I'll fix your drug problem and let you think and solve the puzzle. If you die here, *you* are dead." He put his hands on the chair behind her, his voice soft, gentle. "You are suffering more because this body has had no medical care, no relief. Every time you make a decision there's the question what if...this you never got a second opinion. This you never got out. Most of your Ifs are dead." She knew what this was now. This was the reality in her nightmares.

After a bad beating she had been approached by a golden-eyed shadow, offered a bargain. She would help everyone she could, and he would help her survive. She'd found out later her neck had been snapped but healed well enough she had lived. Her heart raced as she remembered what it was to lay dying alone. "I do help everyone I can." She said quietly, "That was the bargain."

Samael moved in front of her, smiling a little. "So you will help yourself?"

She studied him intently, "Is it helping her 'escape' or is it something else?"

Samael shrugged and said quietly, "You figure that out." He laid his hands on her and she felt some of her pain ebb away, the cobwebs of rage that networked through her thoughts easing, and the foreignness of her body lessened. "For one day you will feel your own pain, not hers."

Cassandra frowned asking, "Why not no pain?"

Samael smiled, "You don't know what that is." She knew he had a point, knowing what it was to live without pain might make her own life unbearable. She frowned at Samael as he wrote out the same prescription, opening the door where Mother waited and holding it out, "I will see you next week, Cassandra."

She rose and moved towards her Mother, trying to figure out what she was supposed to do. Her mind turned to her loved ones. Lily, who struggled with her own escape. Hope, who had found her name too much to live up to with her own Mother Monster. Then there was Dana, who struggled with subtle abuse and loss. Each of them had saved her, but she had saved them too. Were they even alive in this world? Lily was the most likely to be dead. She knew she couldn't find those friendships. This Cassandra would have to find others. She would have to find someone like Gloria, her caregiver. All of these people meant the world to her, they were her family.

"Was it a good session?" Mother asked and Cassandra nodded. She would consider the deal and how to help herself on the drive home. "I want steak for dinner," Mother said. Grandma Lessmore's violent turns of the wheel left them skidding along the road. Soon enough they were back at the house.

She moved into the kitchen. Poison? Would murder be the way out? She shook her head and pulled the steak out of the freezer, just the one. The rest of them would be allowed the side dishes. While the meat thawed she peeled potatoes, and listened. She could hear Mother on the phone. "I don't know why Doctor Smythe didn't up her dose. She's been such a little bitch. She actually was crying when she came out!"

Cassandra put water on to boil, cutting the potatoes into cubes. She then walked to her room. Finding a plastic garbage bag she dumped her clothes into it. Digging in the secret spaces where she hid the few treasures that she had. There was the stuffed dog that had been handed down to every Cassandra in her family and a pile of stolen change. This Cassandra still stole coins and small bills, but it would be enough for a bus ticket. The nearest bus stop was fifty miles away. She'd need food. Debating what was in the pantry she took canned beans, a hand crank can opener and a few spoons. She wrapped up the cheese and found some canned peaches. Taking a blanket, a pillow, and a few more plastic bags, and a few containers of water she had all she knew she could carry.

She walked out the door and began to walk not towards Town but the highway. It was a longer route but Mother would look towards Town. It was the easier path. Her legs burned with every step. Her own pain was still debilitating. Her legs still didn't work right. She made certain she was away from the road. She didn't stop as her knees buckled, she just pushed on. She could walk on dislocations. Each step felt as if it were her last. She would remind herself of an achievement with every step. Her first job. Her first apartment. Meeting Lily and Hope. Adopting her cats. Her husband. Her books. Her degree. Her practice.

She didn't keep track of time as she walked, the heat of the sun burned her skin. This was proof that she was moving at least. She was far enough from the road no cars could see her though she could still hear them. It was nearly sunset when she heard the familiar screech of Mother. She ducked into a bush. "Cassandra!" She could hear Mother calling. Her heart raced. Had she been spotted?

The car rattled on, the echoes of her name punctuating her hurried steps. Now she would go bush to bush. The scratchy barbs of desert foliage making her burned skin bleed. It was dark by the time she let herself stop. She curled up on top of her bag of supplies, tucked into some of the scrub brush. She had miles to go. Her legs burned, her flesh burned, her eyes burned but she wasn't with Mother. She would die if she was caught. This kept her half-awake as her body demanded rest.

She let herself eat some of the beans come sunrise. She knew it was safer to move at night but she could ill afford waiting for sunset and had been too weak to keep going. Thus she made herself keep walking. The sun was high in the sky when she saw the road, the strip of pavement danced in the heat. She crossed the highway, seeing the sign. Leaving Torrance County. She'd almost made it.

Hours went by, her skin blistered. Mother didn't allow sunscreen, it wasn't the first time she blistered. Her water was low so she didn't let herself drink much. A mouthful here and there. She was crawling now, dragging her bag after her. She could hear Lily and Hope speaking. She saw Lily's gap-toothed smile as she laughed at a joke. Hope's loud laugh echoing after. She was too dehydrated to cry. She didn't want to die. She wanted to see them again. She wanted to feel her lover in her arms.

Her knees had no skin left, bloody raw shins and palms were her prize for crawling over burning sands. She ached and wanted to die. Death was easy, however, and Cassandra would not give in. She wouldn't give up her life. Her water was gone. Had it been days? Hours? She couldn't remember. The desert danced around her, mirages of the life that she had fought so hard for tormenting her. Her cats rubbed against her face, soft purrs filling her ears.

She didn't hear the truck as it pulled up nearby. She didn't register the voices of the people as real. A low drawl in her ear, "Darlin', are you alive?" The man was definitely Texan. She couldn't fathom more. "Get the blanket from the back of the truck." Another gruff voice. Older. She couldn't open her eyes. She couldn't make herself move. She could only breathe. Pain overwhelmed her as they wrapped her up and her mind slipped into darkness.

In that darkness she found herself. The other her stood in the void, crying. She felt a bolt of rage. *This woman had taken her life.* "I'm sorry!" the other Cassandra cried out.

Cassandra took a breath, keeping her voice soft. "We always are. Why did you think it would be Galena who came?"

The other her looked confused. "I couldn't ask for someone real; she'd be strong enough to survive. I'm not...why do you look like me?"

Cassandra paused and realized why Samael hadn't told her what happened. Her anger evaporated. "I am you. The other you. If you had made it out. I came because unlike Galena I am real. I survived. My life isn't perfect, but I am safe."

The other her stared at her, "That's impossible. We're too bad to be safe. We don't *deserve* safe. Mother knows that. She'd never let us go."

Cassandra nodded, "I know. I didn't give her a choice."

"Mother's dead?" the other Cassandra asked, shocked.

"No. I weaned myself off of the pills with the help of one of Doctor Smythe's nurses. She kept my secret. I got better because they weren't what I needed. Anger and sadness are normal. You are being hurt constantly; of course you're angry. Once I could think I documented everything, and went to a shelter for abuse victims. I got a lawyer to help me sue Doctor Smythe for malpractice and get a restraining order against Mother."

"Why are you killing me then?" the other her asked.

"We'll make it." Cassandra said this quietly. "If you give up now, it's too late. When we wake up, if it's you, ask for help. Tell them what's going on. Tell them about your dose of medication, about the shed. Mother can't fix the house in time. Ask for help."

"*I can't!*" the other Cassandra said this with panic. The fear was real. Cassandra had never forgotten the fear.

"If you never ask, no one can help you." She stepped forward, her voice soft. "I am angry you summoned me, but I understand." The anger she'd felt over the situation left her. What would she have done if she had been denied help? If she had been made to go back? She couldn't know if it would be the same, but surviving had always come at a cost. No survivor was free of the bad things done to survive. She held a hand out to herself, "If it's me when we wake up, I will get you free. Just remember, you're also me. You *are* strong enough. You don't have to wait to live until Mother dies."

The other Cassandra reached for her hand. The moment they touched, they imploded, pulling both versions of Cassandra into one another. The darkness became radiant color, filling her with every memory she had, both painful and full of joy. Her pain. Her scars. Her life. She would live it again. Cassandra wondered if the other her felt the same. She hoped she would make the right choice, but Samael's words echoed in her mind. For every choice there was "what if?". Familiar pain echoed in her body. She reached for her glasses, as a voice called, "It's time to get out of bed!"

TANNENBAUM

BY JEF ROUNER

9 December 2016 – Friday
Merriam-Webster Word of the Day: daedal

Eden's lunch bag contained two cheese sandwiches, a bottle of lemonade, a bag of hard pretzels, an orange, a small snack cake, and to her dismay, about a dozen pine needles. She quickly zipped the bag shut again after getting her food out so that neither Pru nor Isha sitting beside her would have a chance to see and ask about them. It was the last day of school, and usually the needles wouldn't appear quite this early. She knew she should check her sandwiches to make sure none of the needles had ended up inside them, but rather than risking it she decided to eat very slowly and carefully, drawing as little attention to herself as possible. Next year, she vowed to make her own lunch or buy it from the cafeteria the final week before Christmas.

She'd been looking forward to the weekend. Both Mom and Dad were off, and Dad had gotten his Christmas bonus early. That meant early Christmas shopping, which also meant early Christmas presents since Mom was always too excited to wait until the day of. Dad actually had to hide presents from both of them just to make sure they had something to open under the tree sometimes. On top of that, they were planning a day at the museum and the zoo, complete with a train ride and one of the guided tours of the mummy exhibit that was Eden's favorite. Eden was going to ask if she could invite her best friend, Tessa, along.

Now she was glad she hadn't gotten around to it yet. The needles meant Dad's Bad Time was starting up again, and in all likelihood there would be no trip this weekend. She dreaded pick-up this afternoon.

As it goes, she was right to dread it. Dad wasn't there at the door with the other parents. Eventually all the rest of the third grade was picked up and it was just Eden standing alone and embarrassed with Ms. Zvan. Ms. Zvan took her up to the front office, and she sat on the couch while they phoned Dad. They told her that Dad was on his way. She nodded and said nothing. They gave her paper and colored pencils to occupy her.

Dad was there in about ten minutes, and to Eden's relief, he looked normal. It was cold outside, so he was bundled up everywhere except his hands and face. He hadn't shaved, and his voice was already getting slow. The ladies in the office didn't notice it, but Eden did, the way his Os and Ys in "sorry" went on just a little longer than they should. She could also hear the wooden creak in his arm as he signed her out and picked up her backpack. It was never like this so early. Furiously, she continued to draw, and Dad had to ask her three times to get up and leave. She threw her pencils down and stalked away out the door. Dad trudged after her with an apologetic backwards glance at the school secretary.

After they were gone, the secretary got up to look at the picture Eden had drawn. It was a Christmas tree, with a woman and little girl standing next to it. For an eight-year-old, Eden Pannell had a deft hand, and the secretary liked the picture so much that she decided to hang it on the staff bulletin board, lamenting that no one would likely see it with the school shut down until January. Busy to be on her way out the door and home to a quiet end of the first semester, she didn't notice the curious arrangement of ornaments on the tree, almost as if they formed a face.

10 December 2016 – Saturday

Merriam-Webster Word of the Day: objurgation

The day was grey, but not so cold. Eden refused to wear her jacket, but at least deigned to drape it over her arm as they walked through the cobblestone streets of the zoo. Mom walked beside her, holding her hand at an angle that became more and more awkward as she grew up. Behind them, dad dragged a red plastic wagon. Eden was far too old for rides in such a baby toy, but it was a handy, rolling carry-all for souvenirs and picnic lunches. Also, for coats when Eden would finally be able to ditch hers without objection from her parents.

Dad was mostly okay this morning and proceeded to prepare the family for the outing in the quiet, meticulous manner he always did. Eden noticed him changing the bed linens, going out onto the balcony to shake the needles from the sheets, but everyone pointedly avoided watching him do it and went on with the brushing of teeth and eating of breakfast. Mom made a big fuss of telling him how much she appreciated him getting everything ready and leveled a pointed look at Eden to encourage her to do the same. Dad accepted her hug passively, but warmly.

The zoo was fairly crowded, it being both a nice day temperature-wise as well as the first day of winter break. The more popular exhibits were packed with families and strollers. Some, like the lively sea lions, were all but impossible to get close enough to see, and it was putting Eden in a terrible mood. Mom wanted to visit her favorite, the tigers. Eden whined because she wanted to go in the reptile house, which was all the way on the far side of the large complex. When Mom asked Dad what he wanted to see, he gave a smile and just replied he was happy with whatever they wanted.

So the day went on, visiting animals and eating overpriced food while drinking sodas without lids. By noon, Eden was ready to head to the museum, fed up with the crowds and constant negotiations on what would be next. Mom insisted on a last stop at the small mammal house, where Dad always wanted to go. Dad offered to just move on since that's what Eden wanted, with Eden trying to voice loud support for this option, but another hard look from her mother sent her into a sullen silence.

Inside the exhibit, the ceilings were low and made to look like trees. For a time, Eden entertained herself crawling through a Plexiglas tunnel that passed through a bayou aquarium, until Mom finally made her stop after roughly the fourteenth trip.

Dad stood alone on the other side of the big room in a low-lit area. Ahead of him was a soft, dark rainforest exhibit full of trees and a soothing waterfall. It was the home of the zoo's slow lorises, small nocturnal primates and Dad's favorite. He could, if allowed, stand there and watch their tiny alien faces and languid movements through the trees for hours. He even seriously contemplated trying to get one for a pet until he'd read up on the corrupt and dangerous trade practices that made the species endangered. Eden made the mistake of asking him once why he never watched videos of them online anymore, which was something they used to do together. His blunt response about teeth-pulling and other atrocities designed to make them seem cute and marketable gave her nightmares for a week.

Now he just enjoyed seeing them in as close to their natural habitat as he was likely to get. Eden sat on the wagon in a snit. Her mom was over looking at the bats after telling Eden to not get back in the tunnel a single time more or she would deeply regret it. Instead of finding some other creature to learn about, she just stared angry holes in Dad's back as she impatiently waited for him to get his fill of what she now thought of as one of the world's most boring creatures.

She finally got up and walked over to him, each step an angry stomp. She managed three whole seconds of silence at his side before asking if they could go.

"Sure," said Dad. "We can go."

"Eden," said Mom from nearby. "Let Dad watch the lorises. He hasn't gotten to pick all day."

"But mom," said Eden. "He said we could go-"

"Eden-"

"Besides, they're stupid!" said Eden, her voice rising. "Stupid tree things that don't hardly move!"

She turned and slammed the flat of her hand on the glass loudly.

"MOVE!" she shouted, before feeling Mom's hand on her upper arm, dragging her out. Looking back, she saw Dad grimly pick up the handle of the wagon and follow after them as other families tsked and admonished their children to never act like her.

The car ride home was quiet except for the occasional rebuke from Mom. They skipped the museum. Dad said calmly that the parking lot was full anyway, and that meant it was probably even more crowded than the zoo. Eden grasped onto this fact like an unusual pebble found while exploring, turning it over in her mind in her room when they got home. She held it up against the backdrop of the morning, convincing herself that it absolved her of any real wrong in the day. It wasn't her fault everywhere was crowded and the lorises were stupid, endangered tree things that were boring.

It wasn't her fault, except for the times she was worried it was.

11 December 2016 – Sunday

Merriam-Webster Word of the Day: fillip

"Can I?" Eden asked.

"You know he doesn't like doing this before Christmas," said Mom.

"But please?" she asked. "It's nice outside. And-"

She dropped her voice to a low whisper.

"The sun helps sometimes."

Mom sighed and finally said, "Okay, go wrap it up. He might say no, though."

Eden sprinted to her room and rummaged under her bed. There in an old cardboard box was where she kept the presents for Mom and Dad. Certain good behaviors earned her currency at her school, and it was a tradition for students to go shopping for little gifts for family at the end of the year. For Mom, she'd picked out a small candle that smelled like cookies. For Dad, she'd gotten a kite. It was a massive, plastic thing adorned with a castle beset by dragons. She knew it was a Dad gift the second she saw it and wasted no time grabbing it before anyone else could.

Her wrap job was about a C- for an adult but a solid B for an eight-year-old. With the bundle behind her back, she plodded into the living room past Mom. Dad was sitting in his chair, watching television. His face was already taking on that immovable quality, and Eden's heart began racing. Bravely, she stepped between him and the TV to ask if she could give him something. He turned off the set and waited.

"It's your Christmas present-" she began.

"Wait for the tree, please-" Dad started.

"Hold on!" she said a little more forcefully than she meant to. Mom frowned, but stayed quiet. "It's a present that only works on nice days, and we don't know how many nice days will be left before or after Christmas. So I want to give it to you now so I can make sure you can use it. Okay?"

Dad looked at Mom.

"I promise we will all have presents under the tree, Chase," she said.

Dad sighed and resigned himself. He nodded and obediently closed his eyes when prompted. Eden placed the package in his outstretched hands, ignoring the bark-like growths that were cropping up between his fingers and down his arms. Smiling, Dad opened it. He made a happy noise when he saw the kite. They hadn't been flying in years. Just hadn't gotten around to it for a while. It used to be one of their favorite things to do. Dad even kept a picture of Eden flying a kite right above his computer in his office at work. He admired it for a moment before responding to Eden's pulling of his shirt sleeve. Everyone put on shoes and went out into the mid-December sunshine.

In the small grass courtyard across from the apartment where Eden and Dad often played a modified, two-person version of baseball, Dad assembled and prepared the kite. The wind was brisk, and the sun bright enough that no one needed a coat. It took two tries, but a combination of a good breeze and precise timing from Dad finally got the kite up into the air. Eden slowly let the string out while she positioned herself so no trees would tie up the string. Eventually she got it to its full length, and watched as it danced in the sky.

Dad sank down cross-legged, alternating looks at Eden and at his present cavorting on the wind. Eden happily sat down in the little nest formed by his legs, and they took turns holding the string. Little tugs would create loops, and their skin grew warm in the afternoon sun. Mom left for a spell, returning with three cold cans of lemonade and some apples. They snacked and chatted, nothing to distract them but the wind and whimsical physics above. Mom leaned her head on Dad's shoulder. Dad thanked Eden for a lovely present. She nodded, but kept her eyes on the sky.

Later, as they packed the kite up for the day, Eden asked to be carried home on Dad's shoulders. He muttered something about "his life as a pony," but obliged to kneel down so she could clamber up. He kept his arms crossed behind her back for safety, while mom carried the kite and garbage. Eden ran her hands up and down his forearms. The bark had retreated until you almost couldn't feel it anymore.

12 December 2016 – Monday

Merriam-Webster Word of the Day: Methuselah

The day opened with a terrible rain. Eden spent the morning on the porch looking it at it while watching a movie on her tablet. Every half-hour, on the dot, she would go into Mom and Dad's room. Mom had gone to work, but Dad was still sleeping. He took most of Winter Break off to take care of her, though he usually did some work in his home office in the afternoon. She would shake him and ask if he was getting up. By 9:30, he finally gave in and got out of bed.

The plan had been to put out the Christmas lights on the railings and over the garage. The rain stopped that, but they could still decorate the inside of the apartment. Dad hauled up the five foot Father Christmas who stood in the hall corner watching over the family. Eden thought he was creepy, but Mom loved it. There were stockings and garland and the tiny tree that would sit in Eden's room. They even found an old can of fake snow to cover the windows in.

Finally, it was time for the bells that would sit on the high shelf in the living room. There were sixteen left out of an estimated original twenty-four. The fragile, porcelain bells were adorned with angels, and hung on an elaborate wooden tree. Mom's great-grandmother had bought it long ago, and it had passed down through the generations to them. Each generation took its toll on the heirloom. One would be found broken in a move, another would meet death-by-cat, and some simply vanished to whatever strange world beloved Christmas ornaments disappear to sometimes.

Dad set the wooden tree on the dining room table and laid a towel around the base (no bell had been lost or broken under Chase Pannell's watch). One at a time, Eden and Dad took turns hanging the bells. As she held the last one, Eden imagined all the ringing it had done over the course of a hundred years, and she wondered if her own great-grandchildren would hear the same ringing when she was gone. Would the bell she held still be there, or would it become one of the lost? The thought made her sad as she hung it.

Dad carefully and slowly picked up the little wooden tree and carried it to the shelf where it would overlook the living room. When the heat would kick on, there would be just enough of a gust from the nearby vent to set them ringing, and sometimes, Eden would hear them in the night, the high, tiny and ancient sound of almost-Christmas.

13 December 2016 – Tuesday

Merriam-Webster Word of the Day: hors de combat

Skittle was a dog, but what type of dog Skittle was would probably require significant genetic testing to determine. He was grayish, bigish, had a long tail, virtually no ears, and his coat looked like an awkward middle school boy trying out long hair for the first time. He was also cataclysmically stupid. Sometimes he would fall over while peeing, and he had a habit of being startled by his own farts. Still, he was sweet. He had followed Dad home one day after a walk, came in through the open door like he had always lived there and promptly fell asleep on the couch. Eden could just remember a time before the shaggy idiot was a constant presence at their sides, but saw no reason to do so.

She was especially grateful for him at the moment. He rested his head on her thigh, casting sad looks up at her as she ruffled her hands through the fur on his head. They'd been at the dog park for an hour now, and Eden was trying not to think about it much. She had her book, a sandwich, and her dog, and every reason to be outside enjoying a bit of fresh air.

Eden and Skittle had been playing fetch when Dad went Tree. One minute he was standing quietly, watching them play with his hands in his pockets, and the next, he was still and immovable. Thick bands of roots had snaked out from his jeans and dug deep into the wet ground. You could just barely see his sneakers underneath them. His back had arched, and he spread his arms out wide. Sticks ripped holes in his sweater as they pushed out and broke into needles and leaves. Bark-growth distorted his face until his sunglasses fell to the ground. His eyes stared unblinking into the sun, dripping sap-like tears down his face.

Eden knew there was nothing to be done. The tree-phase would pass when it passed. It rarely happened outside and during the day, but sometimes it did. They were alone in the park. People almost never came there on weekdays, and the leasing office was aware of his condition. Still, she worried about leaving him. Sometimes he got confused when it was over.

So she'd walked very carefully back to the apartment, made herself a snack and grabbed *Charlotte's Web*, and now she sat with her back against the tree that was usually her father. He swayed gently in the wind, covering her with shade from the sun. If she put her ear to his leg, she could hear the low beating of his heart from deep inside the Tree. She eventually fell asleep like that, and the sun was just about to start going down when Dad was able to shake enough of the Tree from himself to carry her inside. Skittle followed, not a care in his doggie heart now that Dad was moving. His skin was uncomfortably rough, but Eden pressed her face against it anyway. Back inside, Eden had leftover pizza for dinner. Dad didn't eat. His face branches made chewing too hard.

14 December 2016 – Wednesday

Merriam-Webster Word of the Day: kapellmeister

Eden sat at the kitchen table writing and singing softly to herself.

♬ Jingle ♬ Jingle ♬ Bells are here

♬ Christmas time ♬ is very near

♬ But no one here ♬ will play with me

♬ No one here ♬ that I can see

"Eden," croaked Dad from across the room, slowly picking up the collection of dolls and board games she'd been playing by herself with since morning. "Can you help me with your mess? Dad doesn't feel well."

Eden got up and starting picking up toys, singing her song pointedly a little louder as she did so. Dad's twig-like fingers curled into a ball, and wood shavings fell on the carpet from where he was grinding his teeth. He said nothing, though, and the living room was soon reasonably neat.

"I'm bored," said Eden. "Can we go play mini-golf?"

"Sweetie, I really don't feel up to it," said Dad.

"Well, can Tessa come over?" she said.

"Eden, can't you find something to do?" asked Dad. "Please."

Eden made a disgusted noise and went to her room. She lost herself in Disney showtunes for a while, singing at the top of her voice. She heard dad when he knocked but pretended she didn't until he gently removed her headphones.

"Sweetie," said Dad. "I called Paw Paw Terrence. He said you could come over and play at the ranch. Cousin Jake is there. You could ride the electric cars and spend the night. Is that alright?"

"Yeah," said Eden, desperate to get out of the dark apartment where Dad had taken more and more to standing still at the window doing nothing.

"Okay, he'll come pick you up from here in an hour," said Dad. "I'm going to lie down until then. Pack warm jammies. Love you."

"Love you, too," said Eden, and escaped back into a world where there were more princesses and fewer parents.

15 December 2016 – Thursday

Merriam-Webster Word of the Day: jubilee

Paw Paw Terrence's ranch was a ramshackle affair sprawling over a few dozen acres. It had previously been part of a large cattle operation, but Terrence Pannell just raised a few chickens these days. There was enough woodland on the property that he could usually find himself a deer to shoot every November, and it was quiet.

Eden loved the sprawling, uncoordinated house that had been added to over the course of a hundred years before her grandfather had bought it after retiring from the military. It seemed like it always had one more odd room or closet hiding around the corner. She could get happily lost in the halls for hours, emerging with a pocket full of weird knick-knacks to ask her grandfather the history of.

Today they were playing with sparklers. Dad didn't let Eden stay over with Paw Paw very often because her grandfather was somewhat lax with things like basic safety. It had been nearly six months since her last overnight trip, when she had proudly shown off the snake skull she had found behind the chicken coop, which is where her grandfather often tossed the corpses of opportunistic predators intent on baby chicks for dinner who had met untimely ends at the barrel of his shotgun. Eden was pretty sure that fireworks, even those as benign as sparklers, would probably fit in the same category and made a mental note to lie about it.

Night was approaching, and Paw Paw sat on a bench next to the fire pit, drinking iced tea and watching Eden. He had the expression many older Texan men manage to acquire late in life: that of being supremely confident he had done all the caring he was obligated to do in the world and every bit of concern someone got out of him at this point was a bonus they should be grateful for. He wasn't a mean man, just sort of thoughtless at times. Right now he was mostly being thoughtless about Dad.

This wasn't supposed to be a two-night stay. Paw Paw was happy to spend time with Eden, but he liked getting his quiet house back after a day with an energetic and extremely vocal eight-year-old. However, when he'd called his son to arrange drop-off, Dad had barely been able to talk. Paw Paw was just able to keep the disgust out of his voice as he said Eden could stay another night, but that Mom would have to come get her in the morning. When he hung up, that's when Paw Paw asked her if she'd like to see some fireworks.

The last sparkler was starting to go out, and Eden came to sit next to Paw Paw. His iced tea smelled sour, and Eden wondered if it was A Grown-Up Drink. In his mood, Paw Paw would probably let her taste it if it was, but she didn't like iced tea. She let the silence go on as long as any child would consider reasonable, then confided to her grandfather that Dad's Bad Time was really strong this year.

Paw Paw silently nodded, wiping his mouth. "Ain't been this bad since he was 'round sixteen," he said. "That was right after your G.G. Clara died. Chase took it pretty hard. They were close, and he kept crying in school. Some girl he liked made fun of him over it, and he had been forgetting his pills for months. Your Dad always was kind of fragile."

"Why is he a Tree sometimes?" asked Eden.

"I dunno, sweetheart," he said. "Something in his brain, they say. When he was about your age, it came on during the winter while I was stationed over in England fixing helis. He went to bed with a rash and woke up planted in the hall and halfway hanging out the window. I tried to pull him up out of the floor, but all I ended up doing was breaking his ankle a bit."

Eden had traced her hand over Dad's ankle once after he told her it had been broken and fixed with screws long ago. It was weird to feel the metal inserts hidden beneath the skin.

"Anyway," Paw Paw continued, "we got the base doc to come out, and I remember they gave him some kind of muscle relaxer or something that put him asleep for nearly three days. He missed Christmas that year. Missed a few since then, too, whenever he lets it get away from him. Always in the winter. Gets to be a real pain in the ass, sometimes."

16 December 2016 – Friday

Merriam-Webster Word of the Day: impetuous

Eden's dream-house, like most dream-houses, was far larger than her real house because otherwise how would the monsters fit? This explanation made perfect sense to her as she lay sleeping in the guest room at her grandfather's house, tossing and turning. In her dream-house, she was smaller, which was good because she had to hide underneath tables and couches. She was also slower, which was bad because there was something trying to find her. She would see it lurching through the halls, in and out of rooms. It was tall and dark, but that was all she could see because the rooms were only lit by television screens showing what Dad called snow. It didn't look like snow to her. It looked like an angry carpet of ants.

The tall and dark thing was also slow, but its legs were long. It would catch her if it saw her, but all she had to do was get to the window. That, too, made perfect sense. Not the door. The door would be crazy. She had to get to the window without being seen.

She heard the tall and dark thing in the kitchen, slamming cabinet doors and leaving behind the sound of broken glass. It was no doubt looking for her, but she was smart and hiding under the coffee table. The window was very close, and she decided now was the time to go for it. Fast as she could, she crawled out from the table and tried to run quietly, a skill no child possesses but all think they do. Turning her back on the tall and dark thing was hard, but it was the only way to the window.

With a mighty shove, she pushed the window up and open. It was hard because now she was so small that she could easily stand on the window sill. The dream-house had grown, and most certainly the tall and dark thing had as well. Not that it mattered, because she had made it.

Outside there wasn't the comforting suburban neighborhood she saw every day when she walked to school. Instead, it was an ocean of trees. Tall and dark trees with no leaves being whipped by a furious wind. They stretched up far into the sky, hiding the moon. She could see stars, though. Bright stars shone through gaps in the branches like baleful eyes, winking and blinking as the wind blew the branches toward Eden standing at the window.

The dream-world was dark trees and nothing more. It came to her that her house would soon also be a tree. Eventually, she slipped from the nightmare into a more pleasant dream of sunlight over the dread forest. In the morning, she remembered none of it.

17 December 2016 – Saturday

Merriam-Webster Word of the Day: lave

Some days, even in bad times, cavort and mimic as normalcy. The sun rises, the dog gets walked, there are impromptu trips for ice cream, and sometimes, after a long, hot shower, twisted tree monsters emerge from the steamy bathroom as warm parents full of hugs. Dad smelled of vanilla bean shower gel, though in his hair remained a hint of Douglas fir. Nothing of note or import happened in Eden's life on this particular Saturday in December, and that is precisely why it was so important.

18 December 2016 – Sunday

Merriam-Webster Word of the Day: gallimaufry

Other days, especially in bad times, are best described in list form.

*An argument

*An unexpected expense

*A broken window

*A very old teddy bear with many more hugs left in it

*Crying

*A Tree

*More crying

*A disturbing silence

*A frantic trip in the car

*The smell of rubbing alcohol, vomit, and blood

*Fruit snacks from a vending machine

*The feel of Mom's hands in Eden's hair

*Rhythmic machine beeping

*Seeing midnight pass

*Forms in English on one side and Spanish on the other

*Falling asleep in the car

*Creaking and being carried

*A mutter that sounded like "when the bough breaks"

*Mom in bed with Eden, holding her

*The distant sound of their cat, Daisy, clawing a scratching post in the living room

*The memory that they did not own a scratching post

19 December 2016 – Monday

Merriam-Webster Word of the Day: nosocomial

There was a new wall in the apartment. It was made of soft pastels, safety pins, string, and My Little Pony. It stretched awkwardly from one wall in the living room to another, a barrier of sheets pinned together and hung on hastily pounded-in finishing nails.

Every hour or so, Mom would put on a painter's mask and gloves and slip behind the wall to check on dad. The doctors said that Dad had caught a particularly nasty case of the flu, which in conjunction with his condition had sent him into a dormant stage. The danger was that he might spore and get the rest of the family sick. Already the other side of the sheets was dusted with thick yellow pollen. Mom said they would probably have to throw them all out and buy new ones, apologizing to Eden for having to raid her closet for old linens to help build the wall.

Eden wasn't allowed behind the sheets at all. Mom told her it was to keep her from getting sick, but Eden suspected it was also to keep Dad from scaring her. When she had woken up, he no longer looked even vaguely human. The only thing that gave any indication that the Tree in the living room had ever been a man were the tattered remnants of Dad's *Star Wars* pajamas. Daisy had to be pried out of Dad's upper branches and sequestered in the bedroom. Skittle soon had to join her, as the dog took to nervously gnawing at Dad's roots. Mom left the television on a low volume and tuned to a channel that showed comforting old black and white movies. Neither of them knew if Dad could see or hear, but just in case, they wanted to make sure he had something. Eden resigned herself to watching her tablet in her room.

Occasionally, Eden would press her ear to her bedroom wall. She could hear Dad creaking, softly and gently, over the sounds of Old Hollywood. Sometimes, she could also hear Mom talking to him. She had called in her sick leave, since Dad couldn't watch Eden as a Tree. Also, he needed to be watered.

"Chase, please," she heard Mom say. "I need you here."

The Tree didn't answer.

20 December 2016 – Tuesday

Merriam-Webster Word of the Day: eternize

Chase Pannell was not asleep.

Inside the Tree, he could hear everything around him. Though branches covered his eyes, if he opened them, he could dimly see the world through the twigs. Occasionally, he did so. The television was hard to make out. At one point, he was pretty sure the movie was

Roman Holiday. Another time, Peter Cushing was on screen playing some sort of scientist with a spaceship. All of it was just static to him, though. Even the pleading of his wife brushed against him no more meaningfully than the breeze from the air conditioner.

There was enough of his mind working perfectly inside the tree to hate himself for this. Every second, he felt shame wash over him for not being there for his family. He knew that he was making everyone around him miserable and stressed, ruining the holiday, and being a burden. That was the good part of him. The part that wasn't sick.

But that part was small and weak right now, and it made his retreat back into the Tree all the easier so that he could avoid facing the aftermath of this episode. It felt safe under the bark, a delicious kind of nowhere that blasted all feeling away from him and spun time faster and faster until he was every second at once.

There was pain. The human body doesn't take kindly to being transformed into wood, and Chase could feel splinters puncturing organs all over. Down in his kidneys and liver, up through the nerves of his legs, and into his brain, the Tree consumed flesh and replaced it with lumber. As it did so, the pain retreated to a dull ache that eventually faded to a sense of pressure, and then nothing.

All of it was awful. All of it was sick and wrong, and yet, he stayed there. A part of his mind that was large and growing larger fantasized about never coming out. No one would notice another tree, he thought. And the girls would be better off. They wouldn't ever have to deal with me and this again. They could move on.

There's an armor to complete capitulation to mental illness, a calmness. Chase was at his absolute bottom, and as such there was no need to worry about going any further down. Even his shame belonged to some other version of himself far above who had not given up. Let that man deal with it. Here, there was nothing but an old Tree dreaming.

At some point, he felt Eden's tiny hands on what used to be his waist. She was trying to hug him. The Dad part of him roused and fought through the mist of the Tree. He strained to open his mouth and speak to her, to will his branches back into arms and comfort her. The Tree was strong, though, and thickened the bark where his daughter touched him. Soon, he wasn't even sure if she was there any longer. The effort to become Dad again exhausted what little was left as human, and he faded into the green.

21 December 2016 – Wednesday

Merriam-Webster Word of the Day: purlieu

Eden's favorite place in the apartment was the small concrete balcony off of the kitchen. There wasn't much of interest out there really, just a couple of lawn chairs and the family's collection of dead plants. In the tree that blocked out most of the view from the balcony, caught high in the branches, was a gently rotting plastic skeleton from Halloween that had blown off its hook in a bad storm. The wear and tear of the elements made him look comical as he beamed down at Eden.

Here it was quiet. She had her own room, but Mom and Dad, when he was himself, simply couldn't let five straight minutes pass without checking on her there, and the rest of the house was a constant battle for volume and territory. Out here, people seemed to forget about her. Occasionally, Tessa or another friend would come over and Eden would share the space with them for tea parties or board games, but doing so always felt like an intrusion. This was her place, decorated with her chalk murals and surrounded by the comforting sound of songbirds.

She sat in the raggedy lawn chair with her legs tucked up under her. It was cold enough that she should have been wearing leggings under her dress, but Mom hadn't felt like fighting with her over it today. So instead, Eden sat there, enjoying the wonderful sin that is being a child who has briefly escaped parental overreach regarding the weather.

"I don't think Dad is going to be better by Christmas," she told the skeleton, who nodded its assent thanks to an opportune breeze.

Or maybe the tree is another person like my dad and knows, she thought.

"I feel really bad for him," she said. "He loves Christmas, even though it makes him a sad Tree sometimes."

The wind (or tree) shook the skeleton again, violently this time. For a brief second Eden wondered if it was finally going to fall down. It would be the first thing she told Dad when he was back.

But it stayed there, just hanging. It wasn't going to do anything, and it couldn't hear her. It was a stupid decoration...

Decoration, she thought, and a plan formed in her mind.

22 December 2016 – Thursday

Merriam-Webster Word of the Day: crepuscular

"Are you sure you're going to be alright?" asked Mom.

"Yes, Mom, God," said Eden.

"Don't say 'God,' say 'gosh,'" said Mom. "I don't like leaving you home by yourself, even for just an hour."

"Look, Dad is here, okay?" reasoned Eden. "Someone needs to watch HIM, right? What if there's a fire? Mr. Justason is right downstairs in the other apartment, and he already told you he was going to be home all evening. I can call or go see him if I need anything. And even if he has to leave for some reason, there's ArShauna next door. I will be fine."

Mom sighed and gave in. Her firm had called, and a very important sale had come through at the last minute from Dubai. It was the sort of thing that needed the whole team to get right, and they wanted to do it before holiday. She had to go in. She was the only one who knew the entire file. The lawyers couldn't even sign off on it if she wasn't present. Her boss was very apologetic to the point of offering her own daughter as a babysitter to cover, but everything was on a deadline, and she needed to hurry.

"Okay, I need you to be a big girl," said Mom, holding Eden's shoulders. "Please, stay out of the kitchen unless you need a snack, and then only touch the pantry or the fridge. Do not go outside unless it's to get some help from Mr. Justason or ArShauna. Please keep your iPad on you, and text me in half an hour to let me know you and Dad are okay, and I will text you when I am leaving. Please, please, PLEASE be careful. Amadi says this shouldn't take more than an hour, tops. I will be back by bedtime. You can stay up until I am."

"Okay, Mom," said Eden, and received one of those hugs parents give when the mundane seems like it's inviting devastating tragedy.

Eden walked Mom down to the garage so she could wave goodbye to her as she pulled out in their Nissan. The red car was exactly the color of the sunset behind her as Mom beeped her horn in farewell. Eden waved at her as the garage door closed, and then she got to work.

Packed along the garage wall was a pile of boxes that had no real home inside the house: old CDs that her parents refused to get rid of; a small box of dog costumes that belonged to Skittle's predecessor, Maybelle, which served as a kind of shrine to a beloved pup; plugs to machines long thrown away; and, of course, holiday decorations.

The Christmas ones were right on top. Dad always said that people made the mistake of putting their Christmas stuff in the hardest to reach place, thinking that they would only use it once a year. The smart thing was to put it in an easy place, because there was always stuff in storage people use way less than once a year. Eden was grateful for his foresight now.

Most of the boxes were empty after their house decorating session nearly two weeks ago (Eden sighed in imitation of Mom thinking of the happy time), but the two she wanted were easy to grab. One contained three strands of lights, the other colorful balls and ornaments. In the garage, which was darkening rapidly as the sun went down, she plugged in each strand. All of them came on perfectly. With meticulous patience that Dad would have seen as a mirror of himself, she wrapped each one neatly back up, and replaced them in the box. She took it upstairs and then returned for the ornaments. These she carried like they were a live bomb, afraid to drop them. The box was big, but they were light, and eventually she was safe in her room.

Both boxes went under her bed, away from Mom's prying eyes. By the time she was finished, it had been a half hour, and she dutifully texted mom that she was fine. She watched Nickelodeon teen dramas in the living room, propped up against Dad with a pillow, until Mom came home from her work. Occasionally, she would look up into Dad's branches, and smile at him.

23 December 2016 – Friday

Merriam-Webster Word of the Day: ruminate

Hi.

I'm the author. I generally don't go for dropping in like this. It's kind of a cheap gimmick, I know. Technically, this is all me, of course, but I'm getting distracted.

You know who is not getting nearly enough credit in this story? Mom. Her name is Mei, did I mention that? It means beautiful, and Mom certainly is. I didn't conceive her with any sort of specific look. Her hair is blonde and it's red and it's black. Her skin is perfect, but pick whatever color you like. Almond eyes? Sure, dude, you do you. She's just that acme of womanhood all children see, with a slightly more realistic version of a person filtered through the eyes of an adult. All children think their mother is beautiful, and all children are correct.

This was a day when not a lot happened, but also not in an important way like I mentioned back on December 17. Mom was around, and Eden got sleepy very early so she couldn't pull her grand plan off. Dad was a Tree, still, the bastard. A bunch of cartoons got watched. Dinner was soup from cans with store-bought snack cakes for dessert. It was cold outside. Skittle threw up something that looked like it had once been an eraser. It was just life.

After Eden went to bed, Mom watered Dad. Then she stood there for a time and thought a lot of thoughts. Some were of love and some were of leaving and all were ultimately about how much she cared about somebody. Eventually, she took herself to the bedroom, got the fuck out of her bra and put on some warm jammies. She propped herself up in bed reading a pulp novel about werewolves until she got sleepy, and when she was, she turned off the light.

Through the open door, she could hear the creak of her husband, the Tree, and she missed him beside her.

See her in focus for a bit. I should have done it earlier. Spare a thought, though, won't you? Mei is a wonderful person dealing with the inexplicably awful and the mundanely terrible. She's there, and she's trying very hard. She cares so much about her daughter and her husband that she never questions the madness of the world I dropped her into. She just keeps on keeping on.

I guess I just wanted to say Moms are soul, and that the people who live through these troubled existences as caregivers and helpmates are heroes, too. Even if shitty authors don't take the time to make it a point in the narrative. This is the story of how Eden dealt with her Dad, the Tree, but Mom, who is sleeping, was there too.

I...wanted you to know that. I'll go away now.

24 December 2016 – Saturday

Merriam-Webster Word of the Day: dreidel

A certain amount of banging noises is to be expected when you have children, and they aren't very old before a parent who doesn't have to get up can sort through the noise in their sleep. That is what they sound like when they run to the bathroom or to fetch something from their room they must absolutely have right this second. And that is the sound of them opening the dishwasher for a bowl, to be immediately followed by the sound of the pantry door and the tinkle of cereal being poured. And that, there? That is the sound of whatever inexplicable thing a person's particular child does that makes noise (Eden's was tipping her tiny pink easy chair over to sit on it upside down, then righting it a few seconds later). To a tired parent, these sounds register no more than a wind chime outside or the hum of a ceiling fan.

Mom slept hard, barely aware of the normal cacophony Eden was creating before seven in the morning. She allowed herself to drift in and out of a dream, but a new sound drew her up slowly from the realm of sleep.

It was the rustle of branches, and it made her hope that Dad was perhaps waking from his state. The idea made her smile, and she burrowed into her covers happily. But there was also a strange, glassy noise that sounded out of place. Her sleeping brain cataloged it against the lesser of Eden's symphony of the childhood domestic, rejecting each as not-quite right. Was she trying to wash her dishes to help? Was she working with her beaded necklaces?

It was all just an idle game for someone not ready to wake up until there was a crash, and the unmistakable sound of a child who starts to cry before they realize the sound will get them caught. Mom stumbled out of bed in the dark, nearly tripping on Daisy. The light outside her bedroom door was bright with cold morning sun, and she called Eden's name as she groggily hurried to the living room.

Eden was standing on a fallen dining room chair upright when she froze. Her hands were clenched in front of her, holding a string of lights. She had apparently been wrapping them around her father, gotten roughly halfway up, and had fallen out of the chair. There was a scrape preparing to seep blood on her elbow, and the look on her face was one of pure misery for having woken Mom before she was finished. Colored balls of glass hung haphazardly on Dad, arrayed with a child's sense of reach but not proper spacing.

Mom wanted to be mad. There were so many infractions here that listing them would be pointless. Eden started to cry softly, though, in the way kids do when they can't help it.

"I thought- I thought- so we could- so Dad would be- it's Christmas- It was going to be a surpr-prise," she said, barely able to form sentences.

Mom took her daughter by the hand and led her into the bathroom to attend her scrape. Her head hurt, her child was dangerously willful, her husband was a Tree, and she was sad and scared. It would be so easy to take that out on Eden.

Instead, they went back to the living room where Eden's master plan lay half-finished. Mom set her coffee pot to warm and then walked to the strand. Eden picked up the far end, and Mom began the final process of wrapping her husband in a suit of lights for the holiday. Behind her, Eden spun in a circle to unravel the string for her, at first solemn, and then with the joy children know when they whirl. The job done, Mom sipped coffee while Eden decorated the lower branches of her father. Mom attended the upper ones, topping her husband with an angel.

Something about the lights made Dad seem more there. It was easy to picture that it was him, not the electricity, which shined out for his family.

Later that night, after the presents were under him, and his family was asleep, Dad slowly opened his eyes. He was dazzled by light, and the warmth of electric bulbs. He felt packages and bags around his feet, and as the heat kicked on, he heard the tinkle of the bells. A hole opened in his bark where his mouth should be, and he inhaled the scent of his home. Softly, and low, he began to hum an old Latin carol, and sap, fighting every step of the way and note of the song, gradually became blood once again.

25 December 2016 – Sunday

Merriam-Webster Word of the Day: wassail

The first thought Eden had when she was shaken gently awake was, the tall and dark thing! Her dream-memory immediately retreated, though, and she realized it was just Dad, still Tree-like, but undoubtedly moving above her in the dark. In the dim light through the window, she could see his wooden smile. He was still covered in lights, though they had all gone out when he pulled the plug.

"It's Christmas morning, little heart," he said in a slow, warm voice. "Come and see what Santa brought you."

Eden leapt out of bed into her father's branches. Needles brushed against her face and poked through her pajamas, but she didn't care. Dad hugged her tight and then gently set her down. Eden ran down the hall screaming for Mom, and Dad trudged slowly behind her.

Out in the living room was a proper tree, meaning a plastic one.

Dad had descended in the middle of the night to fetch it, setting it up slowly and methodically. It was a cheap affair, one they kept meaning to throw away and never did. It already had lights attached, and Dad had transferred all the ornaments he could reach on himself to it. A few small balls and other decorations still clung to his back, and he was careful when he sat down not to crush them.

Eden dove for her presents as Mom and Dad watched. It was an unremarkable pile of gifts; nothing like you see on television but everything like what most of us see in real life. Eden catalogued her dolls and costumes, her video game and her telescope, her playsets and puzzles. She deigned to fetch Mom and Dad their presents to each other, and she wasn't looking when they opened them.

Mei Pannell tried very hard to hold back tears. Dad had found an autographed first edition of *The Last Unicorn* by Peter S. Beagle. It had been her favorite book growing up. Just holding it transported her back to carefree childhood days. She planned to curl up with it at the absolute first opportunity.

Her gift to Chase was more bittersweet. It was a pendant necklace with an amber jewel. Inside the jewel was a mosquito, perfectly preserved and trapped for all time. Chase looked at it approvingly, but then at her questioningly.

"I know you're always inside there," she said very quietly. "I thought it would be a good reminder. That there is always you inside there, no matter how trapped you might feel."

Dad's eyes watered and his twiggish fingers grasped the silver chain very tight. He could only mouth, "thank you," as no sound would come out. With his other he reached for his wife's hand and held it until their daughter demanded they now loot the stockings.

Throughout the day, Dad shed his bark, bit by bit. Leaves and hard nodules dropped onto the Monopoly board to be brushed aside without a word. A circle of pine needles fell around him as he raced his daughter on snowboards down a virtual mountain. He excused himself to cough up a wad of sap before returning to his turkey dinner. By the time night had fallen, and the promise to use her telescope was ready to be fulfilled, he was mostly himself, with only the faint smell of trees and small scabs of rough wood on his elbows.

After Eden was asleep, cuddling the massive stuffed lemur that had been the gift of her grandmother, Mei and Chase sat together on the couch drinking warm apple cider and watching Christmas movies. *Toys* made Dad sad, but it was a pleasure to feel anything once again. That was followed by the comforting joy of *A Christmas Story*, which they never finished. The heat of the cider and the lost passions of the week did their work, and the Pannells made halting, but sweet love on their couch before retiring to bed. The last thing Dad did was pull the plug on the tree, and it faded to a shape in the darkness, easily ignored.

Across the apartment, Eden dreamed of the tall and dark thing again, but this time it was covered in bright lights, and birds sang songs in its branches. Eden began to climb it, its limbs like a staircase. She kissed its face as she passed, but moved higher and higher into the clouds. There in the sun were angels, and though down below the tall and dark thing would always be waiting, there would also, always, be angels somewhere within the reach of its upper boughs. There would be darkness and light. Joy and sorrow, in Eden's garden.

THE LAST BOOK

BY AJ MARTIN

When he'd been a boy, long before the soldiers took his life apart with joy reserved for light-hearted games, Damien would ask the same question each S'neich, the first day of the season of the shadow sun.

"Mutera, why do we tell the story if no one will listen?"

"Because, my son, we have to remember who we are in order to understand who we will become."

Fifteen years later, and he was spending his S'neich searching for shelter. It was night as he approached the inn nestled deep in the marshes of the woodlands. He opened his ears but only heard creatures of the bog. No birds flew overhead, especially the long-awaited hawk.

He walked in, approaching the innkeeper's desk. "One room, please."

The innkeeper nodded and turned to grab one of the keys lining the rotting wall behind him. Damien observed them, each key different from the next.

Something new, something he'd seen on and off throughout his travels north, mounted the wall next to it. A wreath of golden leaves with white jewels embedded in threes throughout the woven material.

The innkeeper handed him the key. His eyes were narrow as he said, "Have you had a good holiday, then?"

Damien frowned. "I don't know what you mean."

"It's Glory's Day, the day of the Queen's return to power," the innkeeper frowned.

Damien pursed his lips but did not speak. Despite his best efforts, his glare did nothing to stop the innkeeper.

The innkeeper shook his head in disappointment. "I find it strange that you've forgotten Glory's Day. No one ever has." A rueful smile appeared on his large face, his eyes glittering with happiness. "I was in that battle myself, you know."

Damien curled his fist, his fingernails digging into his palms until he drew blood.

"And we finally rid our land of those wanderers—"

Damien slammed the last of his coin on the counter. "Thanks for the room."

The innkeeper raised an eyebrow as he slid the key towards him, the metal scraping against the wood.

Damien grabbed the key and then walked towards the stairs, monitoring his speed, his breathing. He needed to be calm. He had to be calm.

When he reached his room for the night, he opened the door. A cot with straw poking from the mat lined the far wall. A porcelain basin sat on the table next to the cot with a pitcher.

He closed the door, releasing a deep breath into the darkness. The only light shone from the moon overhead and through the open space carved out of the stone wall serving as the window.

It was not Glory's Day for him. For others, Glory's Day was to celebrate the final battles of the war that had been raging for generations. Centuries of bloodshed devoted to a singular purpose: to destroy those who practiced magic outside of the royal clans. The Queen's army scoured the earth to steal the knowledge made for the people to treat symptoms of magic, leaving the commoners with magic to suffer without their tools and without help.

Glory's Day marked one of the final days of this long-waged war, when all knowledge had been stolen and all people practicing magic outside of royalty were erased.

Damien gritted his teeth.

No, it was not Glory's Day for him.

It was the eve of S'neich, the first day of the season of the shadow sun. As he looked up through the window, he searched for the faint outline of a black mass just behind the moon, the second orb that signaled a change in the seasons.

Instead, the moon shone back, clear in the indigo sky above.

For fifteen years, he searched for the shadow sun. Each S'neich, he would wake just before the moon reached his highest point. He would open the windows and light three black candles, calling on the shadow moon. He would place the three gifts of the Goddesses in three points surrounding the candles: a jar of water, a stone, and a broken arrow. He would sit and pray to the Goddesses Three, and when the night ended he would bow his head and listen for the hawk's call.

He sighed as he dropped his knapsack on the cot. He pulled out three small, black candles and a match. He lined them up at the windowsill and lit them. He kneeled and started to pray.

He was meant to listen, to wait for the sound of the hawk in the sky, which could only appear in the season of the shadow sun. The hawk carried the key to his people's salvation, and they waited to hear.

If they heard the hawk's call, the hawk would deliver the key and they would finally return home.

The hours passed, and he waited. Long after dusk had died and the night turned black, he waited.

He heard the wind blow through the grasses below. He heard the laughter of the other guests, the crackling of a fire lit in celebration. He heard the joyous songs celebrating Glory's Day, and he heard the bugs of the marsh buzzing through the window.

There was no hawk.

Frustrated, he blew out the candles. With his traveling clothes still on, he lay flat on the itchy, rough lining of the inn bed and drifted into sleep.

Sometime later, he heard a great cawing through the wind in the open window. Damien jolted awake, turning his lamp on.

A familiar face in a white shift smiled at him from the end of his bed, the flesh surrounding her mouth gaping open, exposing her small teeth and charred gums.

"Rhania?" His hands shook as he reached towards the figure. "Rhania? What are you doing here?"

"You never told me the story," she said. "You promised me that you would tell me one day, but you never did."

"How...how can you be here?"

"I followed you," Rhania pouted, but her teeth came together instead, her lips burnt off of her flesh. "I was worried! You said you would come right back, but that's been ages ago."

Damien opened his mouth and closed it again. He tried to speak, but the image of his sister, her eyes clouded over and her mouth missing, crossed her thin legs and clutched her straw woven doll against her small frame.

"Please, Grumpy, please, please, please tell me the story! I'm the only one who hasn't heard it." Rhania bounced up and down on the cot, shaking her straw doll with great emphasis.

"That's not true at all," Damien swallowed, sitting up and leaning back against the wall. "All of our little sisters haven't heard it either, Rainy. Brianne was the only one old enough to hear it before me."

"Well...still," Rhania pouted. "Please, Grumpy! Tell me the story."

There was a long pause as Damien observed his sister, taking in the signs of death on her body. He reached over in the darkness, and rested his hand on her shoulder.

Her skin was ice, but her body was solid.

Is this a sign from the Goddesses?

"Are you okay, Grumpy?" Rhania's neck clicked, bending enough to show where the bone had broken.

He swallowed. He glanced at the windowsill where the black candles remained unlit from the night before.

This is penance, he decided. It was his penance for not completing the ritual.

"Alright. Follow me."

He stood up from the cot, and Rhania followed. He sat next to the window and lit the black candles. The light from the candles flickered on the opposite wall, and Damien pointed to it.

"Remember," he began, "you need to watch the shadows, because as we tell the story of our people, the shadows tell another story, a story which matches our own." He held his fists in the candlelight, and two circles appeared on the wall behind them.

Rhania watched in fascination, leaning forward to stare at the wall.

Damien cleared his throat. Despite many years of practice, it was his first telling of his people's story. "It is the season when the sun and moon share the sky, and because they share the sky, we know that the hawk carrying our namesake and birthright will discover us. We tell this story each S'neich, to remember why we continue to tell our story, and why we search until we hear the call of the hawk.

"Long ago, we lived amongst our ancestors in Iribuin Claithe, a castle built high on the mountain where the Peninsula and the Mainland meet. The castle was so tall that the highest towers touched the sun, and there was no need for candles or lamplight because the sun would shine through the marble floors long after it had set. Our ancestors made knowledge of how to treat our magic, and we shared it with the world, translating into many languages so that anyone could read them. This is our legacy, to write and share the knowledge that would let our magic thrive in safety."

Damien changed his hands to reflect a tall tower on a mountain against the flame's light. Rhania's smile grew wider as she scooted closer to the wall, lightly tracing the shape of the shadow.

He then adjusted his other arm into a giant, snake-like creature. "When we were our happiest, there came a creature. A creature unlike any before—a creature which dwelt in the darkest depths of the ice seas—descended onto our home, wrapping the towers in its body and strangling our home into dust." Damien wrapped his other arm around the hand that made the tower in the shadows. He then brought his hands to his sides, and the shadows on the wall disappeared.

He stared at the wall for a moment when Rhania whispered, "Keep telling the story, Grumpy."

Damien sighed heavily and then said, "The creature cast our people out to the Peninsula. Our archives destroyed, we could not share the knowledge like we once did. Because of this, those that used to be our friends cast us out and we began to wander, to seek a new place to rebuild our home.

"However," Damien continued, "after centuries of wandering, trying to preserve our legacy with whatever tools we had, one of our own would emerge in order to complete the work that had been left unfinished.

"Our sister Vonna, daughter of Pirine and Jesynn, had been born with incredible magic, magic that hadn't been amongst our people in centuries. As Vonna grew, she began to hear messages from the Three Goddesses. Just a fortnight before the season of the shadow sun, Vonna heard her first message from the Healer Thresnia—"

"She told her," Rhania grinned, her gums swollen from the burns, "that she needed to write the last book!"

"Don't jump ahead." Damien reached up to grab the sacred objects from the window, moving one of the candles in between them.

He cleared his throat and resumed: "The Healer Thresnia said that, on S'neich, the first day of the season of the shadow sun, Vonna would return to the ruins of our home in the Mountain. The First Goddess told her that the journey would be dangerous, and that there was a gate, a wall of glittering stone, that stood just as the valley met the Mountain pass.

"As our archives had been destroyed, the sweet water, the water used to aid magic users in practicing their craft safely, had run dry, and so Vonna's magic could not be managed. Knowing this, she asked the Goddess, 'but I cannot control my magic, how will I protect myself while on this journey?'"

Damien set down the first object, the vial filled with spring water, and said, "At this, the Healer cast a spell, and a glass vial appeared at her feet. Then, the Healer's image was surrounded by a soft, blue light. In the light, her form broke apart, her body turning to vapor, and what remained of her poured into the vial. When the spell was complete, the gift Vonna had been given was the rarest of things outside of the royal clans; sweet water to protect her from—"

"The Signs!" Rhania shouted in glee, clapping her hands together.

"What did I say about jumping ahead?"

"I know, but," Rhania frowned. "Grumpy, do you remember what the Signs are like? I know what they are, but...I just don't remember what they feel like."

"Well," Damien took a deep breath and said, "You know that the Signs are the symptoms of magic. Remember, magic takes a toll on the user's body. They can lose control, forget where they are, and start seeing things that aren't there—"

"I know that, but...no one's ever told me how they feel."

"Rainy, you know that S'neich happens once a year, right? If you ask too many questions, we'll run out of time to tell the story."

Rhania looked at the floor, twisting her pale thumbs together.

Damien swiped his hand over his face in frustration. He took a deep breath and said, "The truth is I don't know exactly. What makes Vonna's case so special, though, is that she remembered how it felt."

Rhania perked up instantly, "What did she say?"

"Well, she said it was like living inside of the place between the moon and the shadow sun. Instead of watching it from below, seeing two images far away, she could feel it. The symptoms of magic are a result of walking through two different planes of time at once."

"What do you mean?" Rhania asked.

"The moon and the shadow sun are both real, and they both share the sky, but one is a copy. The sun shines during the day, and the moon shines at night. They're not meant to share the same sky because time has to pass for them to switch. But," Damien leaned closer, whispering to give the story some mystery, "each S'neich, a sun that isn't meant to be there appears just behind the moon, things of two different times colliding into one. To use magic, to have the Signs, is to carry the shadow sun and the moon with you always."

Rhania eyes went wide. She folded her charred hands tightly in her lap, her folded knuckle exposing the bone. She gazed at Damien, her white eyes shining as she gave her most serious look.

"Satisfied?" Damien asked. Rhania nodded, glee returning to her cloudy eyes.

"So, we drink the sweet water in honor of the First Goddess's gift." Damien picked up his faux sweet water and poured out a bit in the two cups he'd found. He gave one to his sister and then drank his. He muttered a prayer, and Rhania drank hers, her head bowed in silence.

"So," Damien continued. "Many days passed, but a week before S'neich, Vonna received her second message from the Goddesses. The Great Lnai, the Second Goddess, appeared in the form of a raven made of rock. She extended her large wings, filling the space of Vonna's sleeping tent, and spoke in a low, vicious voice.

"'My child,' the creature spoke, 'you have received word of your task ahead. When the time comes, you must travel far from your home in the Mountain. You are to make this journey alone, as the others do not speak with us as you do.'

"Vonna asked the Goddess how she was to make the journey alone. Yes, now she could control the signs, but she was still afraid. What if the sweet water ran dry once more? What if she lost her way? She had never learned to use her magic, and so she feared that she would lose direction without the others who'd cared for her. The Great Lnai then folded her wings together and from the stone emerged a small rock spun with white and gold light.

"Lnai presented it to our sister and said, 'This will glow when you have found your way. Use this tool as your guide, and you will never be lost.'" Damien then picked up the gray rock he'd found by a river many years ago and clasped it in his hand. He spoke the usual prayer and then presented it to Rhania.

She took it, her hand cold when it brushed his.

Rhania held the stone in reverence. Regardless that he knew she shouldn't be here, alive and speaking with him, Damien quickly grabbed the blanket spread across the cot behind him. He draped it over her shoulders and then returned to his place across from her.

Damien took the rock when Rhania was done and then set it next to the vial in the center, surrounding the black candle.

"Finally, on the eve of the season of the shadow sun, the Wise M'niruene visited Vonna with the third and most important message: 'Once you've opened the gate, you must go to the temple in the Castle Tower and complete the last book.'

"'I don't understand,' Vonna had said. 'There are no books left.' But the Wise M'niruene refused this answer, saying, 'The work of your people is incomplete, and you must create the book that will end the war and return your people home.' The Goddess then presented her with the third and final tool: a broken timepiece, a sundial without an arrow."

Damien turned to the final object, a broken arrow. He sighed, "I'm sorry, Rhania, I...someone stole my timepiece, and I couldn't find a way to replace it. I've been using this arrow and the light in the sky to tell the time, so I figured—"

"Don't worry, Grumpy," Rhania gave her toothy smile. "You thought of it, and you made it important. That's all that matters."

Damien nodded, agreeing with her assessment as he gently placed the pieces of the broken arrow at the third point equidistant from the other sacred objects.

"Vonna questioned the wisdom of the Goddess, asking why she was presented with a broken object. The Wise M'niruene, however, said that it would transform when the time was right, and that she had the tools she needed to complete the journey alone.

"Armed with her sacred gifts, Vonna left her encampment and made the treacherous journey north to the Mountain Pass. As she walked through the swamps of the Northern Forest, she came across a group of soldiers who had escaped, trembling and sick from their journey. As she approached them, one soldier held up his hand."

Damien cleared his throat and in a low, poor imitation of a soldier, he said: "'Halt, who are you and what do you want?'"

Rhania giggled, and Damien flashed a grin before continuing, "Vonna replied, 'I am a traveler on my way to the Mountain Pass. What is wrong with your company?'

"'They are sick, and we have nothing to give them. They will surely die,' and upon hearing of their struggle, Vonna presented them with the sweet water. She gave it to the ailing soldiers, only leaving a drop for herself. Grateful for her efforts, the soldiers quickly healed and then agreed to give her safe passage to the Valley of Thorns.

"Once she parted ways with the soldiers, she climbed down into the Valley and made her way through it, the earth gray and hard where the spindles grew. As she made her way through the dry, dangerous valley floor, she heard a young girl crying. She followed the sound until she reached a cavern of thorns—"

"Can she have my name, please?" Rhania sat on her heels, begging as she pouted.

"She already has a name, Rainy," Damien said. "Remember, her name was Grasha."

"But I like my name better!" Rhania leaned closer, her arms stretched out to poke Damien on the hand, something she would do to get her way. Her sleeve nearly brushed the flame of the candle.

"Okay, okay, her name was Rhania." Damien clasped her arms and guided her farther from the candle. "But be careful, or you're going to set yourself on fire."

Damien sucked in a breath, realizing what he'd said too late. He paused and waited, but Rhania tilted her head and said, "Keep telling the story, Grumpy."

Damien nodded, and said, "Anyway, Vonna found Rhania huddled underneath the thorns, crying. 'What is wrong, little one?' Vonna asked, and the little girl said, ``I cannot find my mother. I don't remember where I am, and I lost them long ago.' Vonna knelt beside the girl, clearing the thorns as she held out her hand. She guided the girl out from underneath the darkness of the thorns and then presented the second gift she'd received from Lnai. She told Rhania, 'Hold on to this and then think of your mother. It will guide you back to them, so long as you listen when it glows.'

"Rhania held onto the stone, the gift from Lnai, and walked with Vonna towards the end of the valley. They helped one another climb the valley wall up onto the grassy plains at the base of the Mountain. Rhania thanked Vonna and they parted ways. Vonna only had one task left to complete: she needed to access the gate at the Mountain Pass."

Damien opened his mouth to speak, but he stopped. Blood pounded in his ears, his heartbeat growing louder.

"She...she met a man at the gate..."

A woman's voice whispered in his ears: "Run. Run from here."

Sweat beaded on his brow. "The gatekeeper had a golden cane—"

The woman's voice grew louder, and then a scream erupted, the base of his skull vibrating. He groaned, holding his head in his hands. The screaming quickly ebbed, and he massaged his temples.

When the silence returned, Damien swallowed. "Um, Rhania, do you want to tell this part?"

"That's not how it's told, Damien," Rhania whispered.

Damien nodded and grabbed the broken arrow pieces. "She... Vonna walked and met the giant wall of rock at the base of the Mountain Path. There, an old man with a gold cane...he—"

Rhania's jaw snapped open, and she screamed, her pearly white eyes rolling back in her head. Her back bent, cracking, and then her body went limp, her arm hitting one of the black candles, knocking it to the side. Damien rushed to stamp out the flame, and he rushed back to Rhania.

He picked her up and held her. Her head whirled on her neck, the screaming blurring into sounds of exploding earth, shouting and crying.

"Rha—Rhania, what—?"

The flames erupted around him. Damien jumped, but held Rhania tighter. He looked down, and Rhania lay lifeless in his hands. The screaming came from the others running past, the flames swallowing the encampment whole. The grasses surrounding his encampment were burning, the flames blue and gold, and they traveled higher, licking the dark sky overhead.

He coughed, the air thick with smoke. The flames grew and wrapped tendrils of fire around Rhania's arms. Damien cried, letting her go and stumbling back.

When he looked back, Rhania was gone.

"Damien!"

He turned to see his mother, blood pouring from her temple, holding two of his sisters in her arms, followed by Brianne holding the twins. They ran towards him.

Three of his sisters were missing.

"Where...where is Rhania?"

The boom from deep within the burning earth reverberated through his body. He flew back, his breath rushing from his lungs as his back slammed into the floor of the forest clearing. He scrambled up, coughing. He crawled towards his mother lying flat on her back, blood pooling beneath her body. Brianne and the babies were strewn across the earth, the flames crawling across their still bodies.

The screams melted into the air with the explosions. Rhythmic sounds of chains, swords, and stomping feet followed him. Soldiers with black plumes on their silver helmets slashed through his people.

He cried, his voice young to his ears, "Momma...Mutera! Brianne!"

The others disappeared around him. She trembled, holding his face with her dirty hand. "Run from here...run now!"

Damien tried to say something, but a force pulled him up from her. A faceless soldier held him by his collar, choking him.

Damien thrashed around and fell to the ground again. He ran towards the river, the wind carrying the smoke and the smell of burning meat. Tears streamed down his face as he ran.

He could hear the water rushing. He ran harder, his lungs burning. Soldiers shouted from behind, and his foot caught a rock just outside the encampment. The soldiers screamed in their language as they came closer.

The stars dotted the purple sky, the flames of the fire stretching wide over the encampment.

His eyes started to close as he searched for the moon in the sky. The shouts of the soldiers and screams of those dying in the fire blended together, and they turned into a buzzing noise. The wind brushed across his face.

His heartbeat slowed.

Up above, high in the sky, a hawk flew overhead, swooping down and resting itself next to him. Made of silver and blue rock, it touched its beak to his hand.

Damien tried to speak, to tell his people that the hawk had finally returned, but the words were stuck in his throat.

He turned. The fire had died, and nothing remained.

All that remained of the encampment was skeletons and ash.

Damien screamed, sitting straight up in his cot. Instead of fires and smells of blood, he was met with the must and mildew trapped in the wooden beams above his head.

He was in the inn.

He searched the mat, looking for signs of Rhania. He scanned the room, but nothing other than his meager belongings and the light in the window surrounded him.

He stood on shaking legs and found the scarred looking-glass on the wall. He stared at himself and examined his face and hair.

He was grown. The river bank and the fire long behind him.

He caught himself against the wall, breathing raggedly. A song drifted into his room from the open window:

"On the glory of Our Queen, the land has been restored, and we seek the power of the magic once more..."

It was morning of Glory's Day. They were celebrating, the other guests and staff of the ill-kept inn.

Damien waited for his heart to resume a steady rhythm. He straightened his back against the wood, catching a splinter in his hand. He pushed himself up, and standing straight, he walked towards his knapsack lying next to the bed. He hauled it onto the cot and unrolled it, revealing ten smoothed colored stones, arranged neatly in the order he preferred.

A cerulean stone glittered in the moonlight, and he held it, the corners of the stone digging into his palm.

Rubbing his thumb on the smooth surface, he whispered, "I promise, Rhania, I will finish the story. One day, I will."

He sat at the end of his cot, staring down at the stone. Wet drops landed on his hand, and in the middle of the singing and laughter surrounding him from the celebration outside, he heard a long, low whine like an animal had been wounded.

After several moments, he realized that sound had come from him.

He held onto the stone until his palms bled. The tears drying on his face, he breathed in and then grabbed a clean tunic and wiped the blood from the stone. He set it down in its place, between the second and third stone. The souls of his family shone in a rainbow of color as the daylight grew stronger.

As he gently tied the knapsack to protect his mourning stones, a trumpet blared outside. The festivities of Glory's Day had begun, honoring the Queen's troops.

He prepared to leave, to move on to another journey and another inn. As he shut the door to the room, preparing to return the key to the innkeeper, the lyrics of joy and victory blurred together, a background to be forgotten.

He could only hear the screams.

SECUNDUM

BY FELIX FLYNN

"Will it hurt?"

The nurse looked up from the digital slate in her hand. Through the clear glass, Lacy could see words scrolling past a static picture of herself. She didn't need to be able to read them to know what it said. She'd submitted all of the paperwork for this procedure herself. With the steely prompting of her mother of course.

It listed her medical history, recommendations from family that she does this and their testimonies. Funny how she hadn't been asked to submit her own, but then they didn't really care about what she thought of her own defects.

"You'll be sore for a few days where the implant is put in and, as we told your family, there will be some disorientation at first as it learns how your brain works. After the initial adjustment period, you'll be right as rain. Breath deep now and relax, alright?" The nurse offered a calm smile.

Lacy nodded, looking up at the tiled ceiling and trying to ignore the too-loud buzz of the fluorescent lights above her. The static sound grated on her nerves and was physically painful to the point that, as scared as she was, she wished the anesthesia would put her to sleep faster. The plastic face mask covering her mouth and nose had fogged up and with each breath she took, it was beginning to feel uncomfortably hot. She was sweating. She realized it when she tried to get more comfortable, but the plasticy cushion beneath her stuck to her arms. The sensation made her skin crawl.

She didn't want to be there, wanted to go home, didn't want this. Her mind was going fuzzy and the corners of her vision began to blur.

"I changed my mind," she said.

Or had she said it? The nurse had gone back to looking at the slate and didn't acknowledge her. Lacy tried to turn her head to look at the woman, to try and repeat herself. She couldn't.

"I changed my mind! I don't want to do this!"

She was sure her lips moved, but they felt so heavy. Frustration built in her chest, pushed up, and got trapped in her throat.

Stop, stop, stop.

Her vision swam from the drugs and the tears that had been building in her eyes escaped down the sides of her face.

The sterile white minimalist room began to melt away, the scent of the anesthesia mixing with the room's stomach-turning scent of bleach and disinfectant. Her surroundings bled away and blurred.

And then there was nothing.

She'd always loved horses.

The obsession had been cute when she was a kid, in the sort of way other kids liked to play with dinosaur toys or made believe that they were part of the Orbital Force, taking a ship to space and exploring the galaxy.

Only she hadn't grown out of her love.

Instead, her parents had exchanged annoyed and frustrated glances when they caught her watching another docu-holo about the species and how human encroachment had led to wild ones disappearing. Even the horses in captivity had died out with time. The robotic ones were so much cheaper to maintain and needed far less attention.

Her love of horses led her to an interest in robotics. Not because she cared very much for the subject, but because there was an old-style farm on the outskirts of the city that her father had taken her to once. The horses there were able to roam wide expanses of grass, their tails flicking, noses lipping at the grass in a faux natural movement, though they never ate.

Her father had looked disappointed when he saw the frown on her face and she commented on how there was a hint of jerkiness to their movement that made them seem less real.

"Do you wanna stay?" He was already glancing back to the car, sure that the trip was a bust.

"Yeah," she said with a nod.

She'd loved exploring the grounds, but had said, in a child's way, how unimpressed she was with the lack of careful detail in the buildings and even the horses themselves.

The robotic movements were a bit jerky. Perhaps from being poorly maintained as there were only a handful of young volunteers working and one maintenance man who hadn't been spotted at all that day.

The stables were built wrong. The stalls should have a door leading out to the pasture and one leading to the interior of the barn. Where were the tools? She couldn't spot a hoof pick, no grooming brushes, nothing for cleaning the stalls out. Not to mention that the tack hanging on the walls was a bit dusty but nearly new and clearly untouched.

At mentioning the lack of gear, her father had given a huff.

"They don't need all of that, Lace. They aren't real. We drove for an hour to get here. For you." He looked exasperated.

"Don't you like seeing the horses?" He gestured towards the nearby fence. There a Palomino appeared to be lazing against the old wood. It eyed them, shaking its big head, a slight tick in the motion pulling her out of immersion and reminding her of what this place was.

"They don't act right," she stated.

He couldn't see the way her mind was racing excitedly, how already she was thinking of ways the place could be improved, the ways that she could make the horses better. She had a few books at home about the mechanics and maybe if she could get a closer look, perhaps talk to whoever was in charge and ask if they could open one up so she could see—

"Why can't you just act grateful for once?" He grabbed her wrist and pulled her back to the car, slamming the doors hard enough that it made her jump.

She had liked the visit, though. She didn't understand why he was angry, but she kept quiet and when they reached the house she murmured a quiet, "Thank you, daddy," before hurrying up to her room.

Her bedroom walls after that had been plastered with pictures of the grounds and scribbled with notes of possible improvements. The farm had been an inspiration, a stepping stone leading to years of schooling in applied robotics, in tinkering of her own as she built life-like equine miniatures in her downtime. All leading her to her dream job at that farm. Whoever had built it had done all right, but she could make it better.

And she had. On her eighteenth birthday, she'd made a trip back to the farm and asked for a job. She began with menial cleaning jobs while she went to school, then, after she graduated, worked her way up to Head Equine Roboticist.

Her family hated her job, often nagging at her; with her knowledge and her degree, she could be doing something more important, something with better pay and benefits. But she loved this.

She loved seeing a broken horse come to life again as she tinkered around in the seamless hatch on its side. She loved designing them, loved making improvements. She loved making them more and more like the live horses she'd watched in her docu-holos.

Her coworkers were alright, but there was only one person who she got along well with. Braxton was his last name. She didn't know his first, which was fine. The others often wanted to make small talk, to go into detail about their personal lives and families. She hated it. Not because she didn't care, but because she didn't understand what she was supposed to say or when. She was odd, she'd heard them say, and, after a while, they stopped trying to interact with her. Not that she minded much. Braxton had been different. When they met, their talk was all work. There was a natural rhythm to their back and forth that became comfortable, slowly letting her get used to his behavior and conversational patterns.

She'd learned, over time, that he had a wife and two kids. That sometimes he and his wife bickered about his spending his weekends at the farm instead of focusing on his real job or their family. But he loved this, he'd told her, and in him she saw a reflection of her own obsession.

He worked during the week at some office that handled advancements in cybernetics. This was his passion, though, he'd confided in her.

Braxton didn't seem bothered when their conversations lapsed into silence or when her responses were sometimes abrupt, too honest, or what others would consider off-putting. She liked that he seemed to understand her.

Which is why he'd been the first she'd told about the procedure. Her mother had stopped by her tiny apartment, complained about the mess, and then dropped a pile of booklets onto her kitchen table. They called it the Aut-Implant.

"It'll help you not be so—" her mother frowned, searching for the right words. When she came up empty-handed, she changed her tactic.

"Just read it over. I worry about you. All you do is this...horse stuff. You don't have friends. You don't have hobbies. I want you to be happy."

"I am happy," she stated, ignoring the stack, "and I have a friend. Braxton and I talk every week."

"He isn't a friend. He's a coworker. Girls your age go out and have fun. You spend all of your time with your holos and...books, for

Maker's sake. If you aren't working, you're here. Alone. When are you going to start dating again?"

Lacy frowned, ignoring the question and instead retorting with her own.

"What does dad think of...this?" She waved vaguely in the direction of the table.

"He wants you to be happy."

They kept saying that. Her whole life they'd talked about how they wanted her to be happy. She was. She'd said so time and time again, but they never listened. Because her pleasure didn't mimic their own.

She'd intended to throw the pamphlets in the trash once her mother had left, but made the mistake of looking them over.

The pictures printed on them were all laughing happy people her age, surrounded by friends, out in the sunshine. In big text things like, "This could be you!" were plastered across the pages followed by information about the implant underneath.

She could be normal, they said. She could be just like the people in the pictures.

No more nasty looks when she flapped her dirty hands excitedly after fixing a horse. No more laughter when she failed at following social norms. No more meltdowns when lights or sounds were too intense. No more getting overwhelmed, no more biting comments from her family. She could fit in with everyone else.

Braxton had frowned and lowered his gaze when she'd told him, well, everything. They had a glitched stallion between them and she was pointedly avoiding Braxton's gaze by staring at the intricate metal in the open hatch on its side. Not that lack of eye contact was out of the ordinary; they didn't look at each other much anyway.

"Nothing wrong with you, ya know. Just cause you're different doesn't mean you're wrong."

"Then why do they act like I am? Like I need to be cured or fixed or," she paused and recalled what she'd read in the pamphlets themselves, "augmented to make my brain work right." She grumbled back, focusing on the delicate screw she twisted into place after reinserting the animal's power core. "It's no different than the hundreds of other cybernetics that people get every day."

"People just," Braxton frowned, worried his bottom lip with his teeth, then continued, "they don't like things they don't know. They can't help themselves. Doesn't mean you have to change cause they won't."

They lapsed into silence, the uncomfortable sort that they hadn't shared before. She finished her work, tossed the screwdriver aside, then delicately clicked the side of the robot closed. She didn't answer right away. Instead, she ran her fingers through the stubbly short and reddish-brown synthetic fur below the horse's mane.

She tried to ignore the way her stomach twisted at the thought of the implant and her defect. She liked her life, liked the routine that came with it and the comfortable friendship she had with Braxton. Not to mention the horses. But being told day in and day out she was broken weighed on her. It hurt more than she'd like to admit. Better to brush them off and not give it another thought, better to pretend the people who hated her didn't exist and that their words fell on deaf ears.

Only they didn't. She heard the nasty things they gave voice to, whether it was whispered behind her back or said outright. It made her heart heavy. She didn't understand why people couldn't leave her alone, why she was seen as an oddity simply because she wasn't the same as them.

"I'm tired." She finally said as tears welled up in her eyes. "I'm tired of being told I'm wrong."

He'd hugged her while she cried, a hand rubbing her back while she let it all out, his gruff voice telling her that it'd be okay, that he understood.

It'd taken weeks for Lacy to build up the courage to schedule an appointment and get a consultation for the implant. They'd assured her that her life would improve and that with their help she'd be like every other girl her age. That she'd be happy like they were. They told her not to worry. Given her condition and that the implant was still in the trial stages, she'd be able to get it with only a small down payment. A down payment that her family was more than happy to cover.

Everyone was thrilled about this first step she was taking to get better. Everyone but Braxton.

~

The nurse had been right. The days following the procedure, she was sore. And not just where the implant had been put at the base of her skull, but all over. She was in a fog. Her aversion to touch and sound had been intensified for a period, added with overwhelming headaches that made her sick.

She was miserable, but her family had told her this rough patch was worth it. They'd kept her at their house, in her childhood bedroom, where they could keep a close eye on her until the worst of it passed and she could go home.

More than anything, she wanted to get back to work, especially since now her apartment felt off. The whole world felt off, honestly. Foreign. Her own body was a stranger. Her emotions muted. She didn't have the depressive lows she was used to, but she didn't have her highs either, those times when she'd be giddy with excitement and had to move.

Her family loved it.

During her time off, they'd helped her clean up her place and had invited over friends of friends that were Lacy's age, to test how well she could socialize.

They were ecstatic. Lacy didn't have any more of her long-winded horse talks, no stilted silences.

"Dear, you made eye contact the whole time," her mother praised.

The implant was a success, she and dad crowed at the end of the night.

Lacy, on the other hand, didn't think so.

They hadn't been able to feel what she did. When her job came up and her excitement at the subject began to soar, the elation was cut off like flipping a switch. They didn't feel how words that she wanted to say died in her mouth as if an invisible hand reached up her throat, grabbed them, and pulled them back down. She found herself talking about things she had no knowledge of or interest in. Words, in her voice, with intonation she didn't use. Her face moved, her golden-brown eyes meeting other eyes with that same discomfort she always felt, but she couldn't lower her own.

She was a prisoner in her own body, possessed by someone she didn't know. She could see the world as if she were watching a holo, could feel her own wants, but something else was using her as a puppet.

Success? This was hell. She was swallowing down who she was, changed into someone else, and no one seemed to notice. Worse, they seemed to like her better this way, as a stranger that blended in. How could they not see she was ready to crawl out of her own skin, that she felt trapped?

She was in a prison of flesh and bone, her natural urges stunted, her wants regulated, and her thoughts processed through the thing they'd put in her.

Still, her parents had smiled before they left, told her how much they loved her and how proud they were.

She was the daughter they'd always wanted.

Braxton hadn't been pleased, she could tell, and when she asked him about it, he'd said, "You just don't seem like you, is all. Are you alright?" he asked, a concerned look crossing his features.

No.

"Yes," she smiled and gave a little nod, "Plus, Mom and Dad are really happy. And I met a girl I think I like. I've got plans with her this weekend. We've known each other since grade school, but, well, she said I'm different now. That I've changed so much and she always thought I was cute."

"Where are you two going to go?"

"The theatre, then dinner."

Braxton scoffed, paused, realizing Lacy was serious.

"Last time you went to the theatre you said it was awful, that you could hear the grinding of the mechanics in the performers and it drove you nuts. You had a meltdown in the bathroom," he reminded.

"That's not a problem for me now," Lacy said.

"Huh," was Braxton's reply. He rocked back on his heels and cleared his throat.

"Buck has been limping a bit. Think he's got something caught in his hind leg. I was waiting for you to take a look at it."

"219." Lacy gave a nod. "Silly to give them names, isn't it? They're not real."

Braxton gave a grunt, his brows furrowing.

She wanted to cringe. She didn't know why she'd said that or where the thought had come from. Like most of the things she said these days.

The rest of the day was awkward.

Where she and Braxton chatted easily in the past, things were tense and quiet. She found herself missing his easy companionship. She missed the animals too. Each day brought with it a new joy in touching their short coats or feeling their chests expand with each simulated breath. She no longer felt delight in having them nudge her face with their big, soft noses or lip at her hands. She liked how when she'd pop them open, they'd stand there, lazily shifting their weight from one foot to the other or snorting loudly at her. Now, she just saw delicate wires, flickering lights, and strong metal covered in synthetic skin that could be bought in bulk like bolts of cloth. She remembered loving them, knew she held a fondness for them. Only that love was muted now. Wrapped up in a numbness that she couldn't shake.

As the days wore on, she didn't just miss them. She missed herself. She missed all of the pieces of her that the implant ripped away.

Calling Aut-Inc. about the issue was a bust.

Unless there was a malfunction with the piece, they wouldn't remove it. She told them what had been happening, how she'd changed, how different she was, and the man on the phone had laughed and said that it sounded like the implant was working as it should. He told her that if she had concerns, she should have her family call in her stead, that it wasn't unusual for there to be an adjustment period where the defective wanted to go back to the way they were. She needed patience, he said.

She hung up before he could finish his spiel.

Patience.

She didn't want this. She didn't want others to want this for her. And now she couldn't even get rid of the thing.

Lacy reached up, her fingertips blindly delving into her long chestnut hair, searching for traces of the implant. She felt a still-healing scar against her scalp and a lump just under where the implant was. Fear pumped through her veins at the sudden thought that if they wouldn't take it out, could she?

She didn't know exactly what the implant looked like or what it was attached to. Really, she'd been given minimal information about the whole procedure. Most of the discussion had been with her parents, who the doctor said knew more about her defect than she did.

But she couldn't keep living like this.

Determination and frustration won out over what fear still lingered. Whatever happened, she wanted that implant gone.

She searched her kitchen, sifting through various knives until she settled on one that was small and sharp enough to do the job. The bathroom was her next stop. She hastily set up a few mirrors, the reflections bouncing off of each other so she could see the back of her head. She should have grabbed a first aid kit or something, anything to take care of the wound she was about to inflict on herself, but she couldn't think of anything beyond the need to get that implant out.

She parted her shaggy hair, pressed the tip of the knife above her skin, where the implant bulged and her surgery scar still ran pink, showing her just where she needed to cut.

She froze. She wasn't sure if it was out of lingering uncertainty or something else. The same something that talked out of her mouth and used her face, but wasn't her at all.

"They're happy with you like this. Are you really going to take that away from them?" Her mouth moved, her own voice reaching her ears. She wanted to believe that it was the implant talking.

Her arm was immovable, despite how she tried to press the blade forward.

Why shouldn't I? They want to take everything from me.

She pushed hard, fighting against the invisible chains that were keeping her still. Sweat broke out across her brow and her arm began to ache, but, inch by inch, she forced her hand to move.

Pain hit her hard as the blade pressed into tender flesh and she watched as crimson welled up around the knifepoint, spilling down into her hair and down the back of her neck. Skin puckered and parted, the wound opening for her, revealing the part of her skull that had been replaced with glinting blood-coated metal. She blinked away fresh tears, trying her best to focus on the task at hand despite the way her nerves screamed for her to stop. Her skin had gone unbearably hot, the cut throbbing in protest, but she wouldn't stop. Not now. Not when she was this close to being herself again.

The knife clattered to the floor a moment before she dug her fingers into the gash, her fingers becoming slick and wet as she sought the edge of the metal to dig it out. Her stomach turned, her mind going foggy. Maker, she was going to pass out.

Not yet. Almost there.

She found the seam where metal met bone, dug her nails under the lip, and pulled as hard as she could seconds before her world went black.

TAPESTRY OF SENTIMENT AND SUNSET

BY SUMIKO SAULSON

Chloe was a natural witch. The rocks called out to her, and the rivers. Tiny trickles of water burbling soothing sounds over smooth earthbound rocks sang to her as she strode past brilliant estuaries and warm grassy knolls redolent with fresh loam and newly cut grass. Chloe had a way of dancing around campus, her short floral print summer dresses dancing mid-calf against legs as long, thin and brown as cinnamon sticks. Her hair and clothes were constantly fragrant with spices and herbs from cooking, growing tea leaves in her garden, and doing kitchen magic. She had been speaking to the trees and stones since early childhood, but she was not a child any longer.

In her second year at Berkeley City College, she looked forward to graduating in a year and hoped to transfer to UC Berkeley, where her girlfriend Bethany attended. To Chloe, Bethany was made of magic... the way she glided across the green in her baggy camouflage army pants and black tank tee with a beret cocked askew atop her russet dreadlocks. Her magic was musky and bone-deep, from her creaky dark laughter to the way her round steel glasses like John Lennon's or Harry Potter's sat carelessly above her pert brown nose. Bethany's round plum mouth tasted like her hip clove-oil vape, late-night snacks of cheesy puffs. She was encased in the aroma of forbidden delights from hot nights spent entangled in her arms (and between her thighs) in her purple-silk-scarf- and incense-adorned dorm room all Spring long.

One day Chloe might have a dorm of her own, but Bethany would have graduated by then. For now, she lived with her parents. And her mother insisted that she go to the school psychologist about the way she kept talking to the plants and animals. Her father, African and a practitioner of the Igbo religion Odinani, found her mother's concerns unwarranted, but her mother was an atheist and didn't believe in magic. Chloe shrugged and went obediently to the school psychologist's office. The voices of nature spirits were the cause of some consternation for the nineteen-year-old city college sophomore's school psychologist, Dr. Maya Robbins, as was the impulsive nature of the young woman.

Before Chloe Anna Mayfield could get enough credits for an A.A. in Psychology, the spirits of her ancestors interfered. They told her to take his text *Totem and Taboo* and set it to burn. Closing her eyes, she leaned back into the plush green lounge chair in her therapist's office, relishing the memory. In her mind's eye, she recalled tossing the hateful racist tome *Totem and Taboo: Resemblances between the Mental Lives of Savages and Neurotics* into the flames as they licked the sides of the stainless steel ash can in front of the blue and white fiberglass bleachers. The book hit the hot coals and disintegrated, tiny bits of paper alit on the summer heat like fireflies. Tiny fire spirits spread upwards in hot tendrils of smoke and flame, dancing in synchronicity as they rose into the sky. These were not theelementals known as salamanders to Paracelsus, but animist spirits known before the birth of the world in Africa, the place of our ancestral mother. Mmo, the spirits of her Igbo ancestors, manically giggled as the pages of the oppressor's tome withered in the heat.

"How long have you been hearing voices?" Dr. Robbins asked somberly, her dour face elongated with a look of deep sadness she fabricated for communication with the most depressed of her therapy clients.

Chloe giggled and put her hands over her mouth, increasing Dr. Robbin's impression that she'd lost her mind. "I don't hear voices," Chloe responded, refusing to make eye contact. "The nature spirits communicate with me. They aren't voices in my head, they are spirits. I told you, it's a religion."

There was a way the rich cocoa-brown skin over Maya Robbin's high cheekbones drained to a sallow, corpse-like ash gray when she thought you were saying something crazy. It was happening right now. A concerned, dark shadow settled over her deep-set umber eyes. The school psychologist usually appeared a youthful age of thirty-seven. All of her anti-aging creams melted away in an instant, leaving her furrow-browed and stewing in an authoritarian haze of maternal consternation. She looked her full fifty-five years and then some in its wake.

Was this lady seriously using *the look* on her? Chloe's grandmother used *the look*. All black women over fifty seemed to have *the look*, an incredulous glare that made most young folks shut up the minute they saw it. It was like side-eye, only straight at you, letting you know the lady in question thought you were ignorant, insane, and all kinds of imbecile.

Chloe pressed a palm against her aching forehead as a blood vessel began to tick angrily on her temple. "I am not crazy, Dr. Robbins. Animism is a religious practice, not a mental illness," she explained patiently for the fifth time. "I am an animist. Magic is a part of my religion. My spiritual practices are valid. You and my mom are interfering with my Fifth Amendment rights!"

Annoyed, Chloe began calling to the wind to blow open the office window. It was stuffy in here anyway. Dr. Robbins huffed when one of her bay windows flew open, but didn't get up to close it. Chloe giggled into her hand as she playfully suggested the African violets on the psychologist's desk begin to release an aroma enticing to honeybees.

"I am concerned about you," Dr. Robbins prattled on. "Let's talk about your decision to change your major. Don't you think it's rather impulsive?"

"Impulsive...hrmmm..." Chloe chewed her bottom lip and nervously kicked a leather sandal against Dr. Robbin's imposing wooden desk. Just that morning, she'd changed her major from psychology to English. She didn't know if Dr. Robbins needed to know too many details about her selection process. The truth was, the ancestral spirits had told her to ditch Freud and his colonial oppression.

"I've taken most of my general education course load. I have only taken two psychology classes. I knew I could easily transfer those credits to an English major, so I did. What is so impulsive about that?"

"You tossed your entire psychology textbook collection into the bonfire after the homecoming game," Dr. Robbins said sourly. "They were worth about three hundred and fifty dollars. Didn't you need the money?"

"As I told my mother," Chloe explained, rolling her eyes, "the ancestor spirits told me it was patriarchal, colonialist garbage that would only poison my thinking. If I had sold it, it would have only brainwashed other unsuspecting souls. Kill it with fire, they said. And so I did..." She grinned as she saw the first of the bees slip into the room and quietly saunter over to the flower on the desk.

"How did that feel?" Dr. Robbins asked. Unaware of the insect, she had her head down, scribbling frantically into her notebook.

"It felt like liberation magic. Liberation magic is invigorating, like a pot of hot lemon tea with honey in it on a cold winter's day," Chloe stated serenely.

In her mind's eye, she saw the front page of Chapter Three, "Animism, Magic and the Omnipotence of Thought," part from the book *Totem and Taboo* and rise in rebellion as it began to singe and furl. It floated up in the air in slow, cinematic sequence and languidly spun in the smog. Her forehead furrowed, she stared at the wicked text, muttered an incantation under her breath, and watched as it exploded. It was a protection spell against Sigmund Freud, the long-dead colonial oppressor. Her spell was proof against Freud's further attempts to infiltrate her mind and soul with internalized loathing.

"You certainly have a way with words," Dr. Robbins admitted. Stunned, Chloe wondered if Dr. Robbins had read her mind. Then, she realized, the school counselor was referring to her line about liberation magic.

"In order to rise from its own ashes, a Phoenix first must burn..." Chloe quoted enigmatically.

Dr. Robbins nodded and smiled. "Octavia Butler."

Chloe smiled. "Indeed."

"So you think of the burning of those texts as symbolic, then?" Dr. Robbins asked.

"Yes!" Chloe shouted. "Bethany and I held hands, smiled triumphantly into the flames. On Monday, I went in first thing, changed my major to English. You know, those old psychology books aren't too far from the scientific racism of Georges Cuvier and Henri Marie Ducrotay de Blainville, the monsters that labeled Sara Baartman the missing link and encouraged her to drink herself to death so they could dissect her—"

"I already know how you feel about psychology," Dr. Robbins sighed.

"You read books by old dead white racists and worship a dead white man on a cross, yet you think I am the crazy one?" Chloe groused.

Dr. Robbins shook her head. "My religion has nothing to do with this. This isn't about me at all. You were diagnosed with bipolar disorder. I think you should be on your medication. Don't you agree?"

"Sure. I'll take it," Chloe lied. "Write me a prescription." A second bee entered the office window, accompanied by a fly. They buzzed around the flower, annoying Dr. Robbins, who wasn't allergic or anything. Chloe snickered when the fly landed on the psychologist's eyelid, making her blink in irritation. Always professional, she refused to swat it away until the prescription was written.

Petty, she knew.

Chloe danced on out of the door, prescription in hand. As soon as she was a safe distance away from the campus resplendent with

Berkeley's non-smoking zone signs, she rolled it into a Swisher Sweet with some marijuana and watched it burn as she self-medicated.

Totem

The honey drip of the sun setting upon the shore serenaded the start of summer. Rustling trees at the edge of the beach spoke soliloquies to the waning days of May. Chloe ran sandaled feet through the river, arms spread wide as eagle's wings to embrace its magic. Skipping through the narrow creek under the wooden bridge at UC Berkeley, she felt sandy water sliding between her toes and the leather thong of her sandals. The school year was coming to an end. Spring, with its season of birth and new life was giving way to lazy days of sun and intellectual shallows absent of reflection. It was a time for sudden change.

"It is religious oppression," Chloe's girlfriend Bethany Sue Brooks said, bare feet dangling over the wooden bridge, toes dipping into the pond below.

A series of brooks, streams, and ponds filled with colorful frogs, koi, and lily pads covered this part of the campus. Bethany was two years older than Chloe—already attending university and old enough to get a drink in the local bars. Chloe's mother was African American, her father Nigerian. Both of Bethany's parents were African American. She was a third-generation Oaklander, the granddaughter of a local minister. An out and proud lesbian, Bethany parted ways with her parents' congregation three years ago. She went to a queer non-denominational Christian church called the Rainbow Congregation. Practitioners of other religions were welcomed.

"Yeah..." Chloe mumbled. "Yeah, it is..."

Bethany's continued interest in Christianity bothered Chloe. Why worship a white God, the God of the white colonizers? It was best not to mention it, lest they fight again. Bethany didn't believe in magic and spirits and unseen worlds, which was strange, given how much her religion spoke of them.

"How is your mom taking it?" Bethany asked.

"Mom?" Chloe laughed. "She named me after Toni Morrison. She always wanted to be an author herself. Mom is over the moon about my major change."

Bethany laughed. "Screw psychology, then."

"Agreed," Chloe grinned, slipping her sandals off before she slid off the bridge into the water with a plop. Koi scattered away from her immersed toes, and she felt the water spirits calling to her as they slipped in and out of her soles. Souls to soles, soles to soul...Bethany leapt feet first into the water and grabbed both of her hands, and the two girls laughed as they splashed in the water.

Hands held, they spun in circles, and Chloe uttered another incantation under her breath. Bethany opened her eyes and mouth, the words spilling out unbidden as she fell in synch with her beloved. She said she wasn't a believer, but she spoke the incantation anyway. Her religion forbade the worship of other gods, and the thought of the broken taboo sent a shiver over Bethany's spine. Water was moving upwards in synchronicity with their bodies as they swayed in rhythmic dance, in a magical, mystical movement. It was like a shower in reverse, or a series of lawn sprinklers. Then the water dropped down over their heads in the summer heat and poured down their warm cheeks and bare arms in steamy rivulets.

Were these magic things simply invisible to nonbelievers like Dr. Robbins? Chloe wondered, leaning in to drink up Bethany's tender kisses. Plum lips, sweet and sticky with flavored lip gloss. Body heat and promises of future nights in Bethany's dorm, where their bodies lay intertwined. There were memories of popcorn and late night movies and chilling with a cold beer and a slice of lime.

All of that magic was broken like shattered glass when the brittle voice of the angry man broke into their reverie. "What you are doing is an abomination unto God!" he screamed, fists balled in anger. Chloe remembered seeing this guy standing on the corner with his signs and his bullhorn, preaching bigotry and hate. The homophobic zealot grabbed a pile of rocks from the side of the bridge and tossed them at the young lovers. One hit Bethany on the side of her nose, and it began to trickle streams of blood. Her temper rose hot and fiery behind Chloe's eyes and she turned to swing at him.

Her open-palmed hand was a good twenty feet from him, but a gush of wind hit him hard enough to knock him over the side of the bridge. He fell into the water, hard on his ass, brown hiking boots up in the air. Blood pooled around his skinned elbow and the torn sleeve of his seersucker suit jacket flapped in the stream. A hungry orange koi fish sucked at his nicotine-stained fingers.

"Witches!" the bearded man screamed, blood rushing up to his ruddy cheeks. Sweat poured down his forehead, plastering dirty, blond hair against sunburned skin. "Burn, witches! You are an abomination to the Lord!"

"Let's go!" Bethany shouted, grabbing Chloe's hand and pulling her up the side of the incline at the bank leading up from the pond. Snatching up her sandals, Chloe ran barefoot as the big, angry man chased them.

"That's the guy we saw protesting at Fanime," Chloe said angrily.

"Are you sure?" Bethany asked, looking over her shoulder as they scurried away. "I'm pretty sure the protesters at Fanime were less homeless-looking."

Chloe snickered. "That's so classist! Anyway I don't think he's homeless, just a wingnut."

"That's so ableist," Bethany shot back, giving Chloe side-eye.

"Yes, it is..." Chloe admitted. Both girls laughed. They skittered away down the pathway, leaving the bearded man climbing up the muddy slope behind them. They had a good two-block lead on him by the time he stood on the sidewalk, looking like he'd peed his pants.

Taboo

The loom in her attic, where she worked on a tapestry depicting a warm honey sunset at Berkeley Shoreline Beach, had struts as thick as her fingers. The tabloid-sized wooden box in her hands was a traveling loom. Chloe used it to weave long, whimsical scarves and compact, sturdy potholders. It kept her hands busy when her mind was full. Hands winding yarn around twine, or yarn around yarn, weaving soft textures in and out of the rough, were hands engrossed in the simpler magic of sentimental tokens of love.

They were hands safe from unleashing the loamier, needier magic that arced outward from her temples, or her chest, or her loins, and that inhaled particles of sunlight only to expel them in a subatomic particle explosion into the corporeal world. The power plant hidden inside of the deep, wide, and ravenous canyons of emotion that rested between her collarbone and breastbone, pumping blood. The fierce hunger of her system was enclosed within a ribcage sturdier than any loom she owned. That, the core of her power, would unleash itself into the world, leveling buildings of concrete and steel, if she didn't restrain it.

May was coming to an end. The scent of cherry blossoms filled the warm spring air. Finals this week, and soon the semester would be over. Jo Chan swung around the side of the wooden ramp on her old-fashioned wide wooden skateboard. She skated with a dozen other punk-rock kids in various combinations of flannel shirts, oversized band tees, Vans, Converse, cargo shorts, board shorts or faded jeans shredded around the knees in the courtyard. They'd all be out of school for summer when next weekend rolled around.

Watching from the bleachers above, Chloe was leaning into Bethany's shoulder. Bethany's thick dreadlocks were dark brown at the root and russet where the sun bleached them at the tips. They spilled out of her black, red, green, and yellow tam over one shoulder in a simple braid, where they were bound by a leather thong. Setting her loom down, Chloe leaned in to give her a kiss...fingers entwined, lacing in and out of one another like woven lattice, mouth softly tasting rosebud lips, bare knee pressed to warm thigh. Bethany's free hand ran through Chloe's soft black curls, eliciting fragrant notes of shea and cocoa butters under the dancing sunlight.

Chloe looked over her shoulder to see Jo staring up at them, a smirk twisting one corner of her purple-glossed lips, and laughed. Busted, the skater girl quickly looked away, and casually brought a steel bottle of cool ice water to her lips in the parching near-summer sun.

"Yo! Wassup, Joey?" Chloe called out, breaking away from her girl, a knowing look in her eye. Jo had been crushing on Bethany since before she started dating Chloe, but sometimes when you snooze you lose. Bethany, seemingly unaware of the infatuation, still counted Jo as her best friend of the platonic kind. As a result, the cute girl with the flamingo pink pixie cut had become their favorite third wheel. She was hot, and if they weren't monogamous, who knows what would happen?

"We saw Jesus Dude on Campus!" Bethany shouted down, finally spotting Jo. "You know, Jesus Jerk from Fanime?" Fanime was a big Japanese animation convention in San Jose all their friends went to over Memorial Day weekend. Almost everyone had finals the week before Fanime, but some were doing last minute extra credit work to catch up—like Chloe. Classes rarely ran past the holiday weekend. Spring football games and graduation ceremonies kept the kids on campus the last week and a half of May.

"His beard is extra gnarly!" Chloe squealed, making a face. "It's like a single filthy, matted, white-boy dread. I guess he really wants to represent the great, unwashed masses?"

"His horrible body odor represented the grotesque stench of the downtrodden masses..." Bethany cackled, waving a hand in front of her wrinkled nose.

Joey Chan, a skate punk and zine maker, was a familiar face at the Alternative Press Expo (APE) and every comic book and zine festival under the sun. There were several in the Bay Area. She was an aspiring comic book artist, who dreamed of having a table in the Fanime dealer's room...although so far, she could only afford the SF Zine Fest, East Bay Zine Fest, pop-ups during First Fridays in Oakland, and one tenth of a table at APE shared with nine other artists.

She was down at Fanime with Chloe and Bethany last weekend when three Fundamentalist Christians, carrying signs, started shouting them down. The Fundies said that cross-play, the practice of gender-swapping animation character costumes, was causing homosexuality, lesbianism, transgender people, and all kinds of other things they hated. Joey Chan, being nonbinary and transfemme, had lots to say to them. If they'd seen the boy/boy comic illustrations Jo did for YaoiCon, they would have keeled over of a heart attack on the spot. One of them was that crazy guy they'd just seen at UC Berkeley.

"Was it the tall one with the jaundiced eyes?" Chloe asked.

"You mean the one who looked super high with a greasy beard? He looks sort of a young Tommy Chong from Cheech and Chong?"

"Who else would she be calling Jesus Guy?" Chloe snorted.

"Well they all seemed stuck on Jesus," Jo snickered. Jo being an atheist, Bethany was the sole Christian among them, but didn't consider dissing the guy to be blasphemy of any sort.

"He looked more like an artisan-bread-eating, microbrewery-loving, lumberjack neck-bearded hipster when we saw him in San Jose," Bethany sighed. "Just now, he looked like maybe he'd been packing crack or meth in his vape. And, like, it recently exploded on his face and got stuck in his beard."

"Dude is freaking scary," Jo nodded, "dirty or clean. He has scary shit going on in his mind."

"You and Chloe with the spooky mind-reading witchy shit," Bethany hissed, wriggling her fingers in mockery of their alleged spells. "There is no such thing as magic!"

"His mind is filthy, like the trash can behind that roach coach in the parking lot of the laundry over on 45th by my house," Chloe concurred.

"He has a roach-ridden mind," Joey agreed, "If hateful, bigoted thoughts were roaches and flies, his mind would be riddled with vermin and in need of pest control."

"We should cast a binding spell on him," Chloe suggested, "and prevent him from harming himself or others."

"I'll pray for him," Bethany sighed uncomfortably.

"We should get a 5150 emergency psychiatric lockdown to prevent him from harming himself or others," Joey laughed.

. . .

Anima/Animus

"How can someone who sees magic as much as you do deny its existence?" Joey said, leaning over a skateboard, one gray-camo, ankle-high skate shoe perched next to the Power Puff Girls logo on its center, the other on the floor.

"I don't deny the existence of magic," Bethany said carefully. "Magic runs in my family. My mother told me these stories as a child, of Lacey Evans, Niecey Evans, Brynn Evans, and Dewlyn Evans. The Evans clan were Welsh and among them, witches. Powerful witches with hereditary gifts, which if not managed, would make you go mad."

"Your Christianity makes you deny your gifts," Chloe argued. "If you were an animist, you would just accept them. But instead, you cling to the old patriarchy. Free yourself, witch! Join me and your ancestors and embrace your African roots. Embrace the ancient folks who wandered with the fae in your Welsh ancestors' past. Be one with the heath-people, and set aside the chains ofRome."

Behind her, the wind whispered haunting tunes, and among the eucalyptus trees, faeries played. They giggled in pretty bell-like tones, and chattered among themselves that some of them were Christian too, having converted back when Chaucer was a mere literary babe in arms.

"King Solomon was cursed with insanity for being disobedient," Bethany said. "He worshipped other gods, when Jehovah said, 'Place none o'er me.' And He is a jealous God. But he protects his children with madness before letting them become accursed due to the Sight."

"Maybe your God got to that nutcase back there and put a Judeo-Christian binding spell on his bigoted ass," Joey snickered.

"Cursing homophobic and transphobic idiots must be a full-time job for Jehovah, then, considering how many of them have gone mad in his houses of worship and those of his prophets Jesus and Mohammed," Chloe hissed.

"Solomon was cursed for practicing demonology!" Bethany screeched.

Not demons! We are not demons! Is good is good! the tiny house sprites buzzing around Bethany's hair, unknown to her, cried out. The small magical hitchhikers looked like Tinker Bell from *Peter Pan*.

"Not demons?" Chloe laughed, spinning in fanciful circles as her voice rose in musical chorus with the fae. "Girl, it is a good thing you aren't more psychically sensitive. You have travelers all around you, Bethany."

"Hitchhikers?" Bethany shrieked, first applying the sign of the cross over her chest while chanting under her breath and then spraying frankincense all around her.

The protective sprites, confused, crossed themselves in unison and started looking in and around Bethany to make sure she wasn't affected by any pesky demons. How strange it must be to be a house faerie in service to Christian households? Chloe thought. Bethany was constantly surrounded by protective Celtic fae creatures, the kind faerie princesses attracted. They were mischievous at times and good at both losing and finding your house keys. Hers were Christian faeries, who protected her from unauthorized travelers in their naïve and innocent subservience.

"They're harmless," Chloe assured her, as the sprites quietly incanted the Lord's Prayer in shrill, childish Latin like manic schoolchildren.

Joey shook her head. "Afraid of common household and garden variety fae? Wow! You're totally brainwashed, girl."

"Half of that crap you believe comes from the Roman religion anyway," Chloe huffed, waving her arms angrily. "They invented new religious practices that made gods of Julius and Augustus Caesar, and then polluted the newest of the Abrahamic religions with them so they could perpetuate your enslavement by the white male forces of cishet patriarchy!"

"Down with the patriarchy!" Bethany called out...an inside joke.

"Down with the patriarchy!" Joey and Chloe added.

"Speaking of the patriarchy," Joey said, "and not to change the subject, but to change the subject, I am thinking I should change my pronouns to he/him pronouns..."

Bethany laughed. "You owe me $50, Chloe!"

"You aren't supposed to tell him we bet on it," Chloe hissed. "Besides, you said Joey would be using they/them pronouns soon, not he/him!"

Joey laughed and popped his skateboard up with one foot into his hand. "I think you owe her $50," he said.

"Tell you what," Bethany teased, "you can pay me $25, since I was only half right."

"Fine," her girlfriend replied, quietly pulling a twenty and a five dollar bill from her wallet. "But we can still say 'Down with the patriarchy!', right?"

Joey nodded, a warm grin overcoming his face. "Of course you can, sister."

HOW PACE WILKENS DIED

BY GRAHAM SWANSON

Deputy Burke waited all night long for the phone to ring, dressed in his uniform. At four a.m., only flashes of passing headlights disturbed his dark home, red and platinum beams casting long hurdles onto his ceiling that wound to the wall. The phone sat still. He ran out of coffee, eggs, bacon. He sat in the dark of his home watching the night slip away. An hour and a half after he gave up trying to sleep, he received a call from the Wilkens residence. At first he sighed, recalled all the domestic turbulence he'd been summoned to address in the past. This time, he dropped the phone and bolted out the door. He drove past the coffee shack and the fast food parlor, despite his urging hunger and shaking headaches.

Morning rose over the Wilkens farm. The frost of late February stiffened the dirt. Curtains of mist swirled around the house. The deputy came into the Wilkens' kitchen. The dog chewed on a human mandible. Lilith Wilkens held her robe shut. The deputy didn't ask about Pace's absence. Lilith didn't need to say a word. He began his search. No chickens occupied the coop. No machines idled in the barn. The windmill stood tall, rusted in place. He thought for a moment that he saw a caped figure watching him from between the blades. When he shined a light towards the dilapidated rotors, a flock of dark birds lifted away. The deputy zipped up his coat and made his way to the field. He walked along the barbed wire. Far-off cattle bleated. A school bus droned down the highway at the end of the property. The deputy turned and walked along the drainage ditch. He shined his light within. The sun rose and burned away the clouds and mist, but the trench still stunk of dark mire. His foot kicked a glass capsule. He looked down, sucked on his teeth and put his light back into his belt. Several broken bottles lay scattered among a few intact. In the middle of the broken glass rested half a pelvic bone, the lower segment of a spinal cord, and some ribs peeking from the dirt. The deputy nudged the bottle from its nest in the dirt.

He called off the search on his radio, and went inside. He watched Lilith sip steaming coffee, and his lymph nodes stiffened. He swallowed dry spit, and told her he found her husband.

"I was worried it would end this way," she sighed to him as he took a seat before her.

The dog devoured the mandible. A few teeth lay under his foaming tongue.

"This harvest, I finally kicked him out. I boxed up his whiskey and wine, and I sent him away."

"I just want you to know, that whatever happened, I don't blame you. The report is going to say exactly what you told me. He went out there, drank himself to death. Animals got to his body. Not much is left now."

The deputy stood up and walked to the door. In his car, he called for a coroner. In the middle of the driveway, under the shadow of dark clouds, stood the hooded figure from the windmill. The deputy got out, and walked with rapid strides, calling for the faceless stranger to reveal himself.

When he came to the figure, he pulled away the hood, revealing canvas stitching with worms squirming out of crude eye holes. Hay and fur fell out from under its torso. The cape and straw blew away in the wind. The deputy shielded his eyes from the hail of dust and hay. When he opened his eyes, a heap of maggots devoured a heart at his boots.

Lilith Wilkens went to check on her daughter. She carefully tapped on the door. "Gwynth...please get up," she whispered, then tapped again and repeated herself louder than before. Lilith ripped knots from her hair, and dropped blonde tangles to the floor. She worried—perhaps Gwynth might fail to recognize her own mother. So much had changed since she killed Pace.

He lived up to his tyrannical reputation before she married him, and it grew worse with every year. He started fights with strangers as much as her. He broke into an old woman's home and urinated on her couch after her dog scratched his truck. Every bar in the county banned him. No farmers lent him any supply or equipment. Most intolerable to Lilith, he swerved to hit animals in the road, living or dead. Each hunting season, he hung up and gutted deer on the front lawn to rot for everyone driving by to see.

After ten years of mayhem, he crashed his car into the creek, and, after spending weeks in the hospital, swore never to touch a substance again. Lilith watched him transition into the nicest man she ever met. He went to town meetings. Volunteered to clean up litter. He even made her a stained glass window from his old liqueur bottles and placed it in the barn.

One night he received a phone call and left without explaining where he was going or why. When he returned, he didn't say a word to anyone, and over the following nights, developed curious habits. He ate with his hands, and threw up anything he ate. Lilith gave him stomach medicine, but he tossed it out, telling her he didn't want any pills.

His behavior only grew more outlandish. Words of books and manuals no longer made sense to him. He worked short hours, let the crops die, and watched as pieces of the house crumbled. At last, a strange derangement tormented his behavior.

Lilith awoke every night in sweat and shivers. Pace stopped sleeping and lived the night breathing in the moonlight, glaring out the window into dark leagues. After a week of silently observing, Lilith bothered to ask him, "What's out there?"

"Can't you hear them?" he trembled to whisper. When he saw his wife's confusion he snapped back to the window, smacking both hands onto the pane. "They're coming, they're closer..."

She climbed out from the sheets and pulled him towards bed. He growled and shoved her to the floor. She covered her head with her fists. The nightstand corner caught her by the eyebrow and both slid against the side of the bed. Lilith rocked on the floor, the socket of her eye crunched like a can. Blood dripped from between her fingers. She looked up at Pace opening the window and sticking his head out. Only when the blood tapped the floorboards did she take her quivering eyes from her husband to see the blood on the nightstand, and the drops on her bare legs. Vision faded and floated back. No pain alarmed her. She touched the bleeding gash, ran her finger over the edge of a broken plate above loose flakes, and scraped the red flap of flesh in the corner of her eye with her fingernail before she realized what happened. Pace's breath escaped in white clouds. When he stepped away, Lilith tried to crawl in his way, but he stepped over her. Glass broke, and he returned bearing a bolt-action Remington. His attention remained on the window; his nostrils flaring, he stomped from the doorway. Lilith covered her wound as he planted a heel between her forearm bones. Blinding flashes stripped the dark away with each steaming round fired into the darkness. Pace slammed the window shut, stepped into Lilith's blood and tracked it down the hall back to the cabinet. His daughter came from her bedroom, sleep-stolen eyes near closed, walking in the dark with short, shackled steps, until she saw the blood print reflecting in the moonlight. Her mother crawled from the bedroom, her eyes shining under unfurled fringes of hair, moans tickling the back of her throat.

Gwynth pulled her mother into the passenger seat of her car. Lilith spent time waiting in the doctor's office wondering what happened. The doctor took his glasses off and asked about her husband.

"No, he quit drinking years ago."

They gave her pain pills and sent her home with the top half of her head wrapped up.

She awoke at five a.m. with a love note and a flower from the garden. She robed herself and went down the stairs. As she cracked open eggs, she wiped the fog from the window. Blue sun-rays peeked over the distant bluffs. Treeline shadows sharpened against the wet lawn. Another shadow stood at the chicken coop stabbing hay bales with a pitchfork. The roosters called.

Pace Wilkens impaled the hay bale. Wind blew lost strands against the wire fence. He gasped at the paw print in the dirt. He got down to brush away the loose hay, uncovering a trail leading to the chicken coop. He stole the pitchfork. The scrap-wood door ground against the frame, bending the screws as it pulled against the hinges. The hens bocked in their nests like quivering warts. He stalked the aisle, looking to the corners, stabbing piles of hay, but finding nothing. Scratching noises rained down from the rafters above. Pace listened, and through cracks in the ceiling, he saw short fur. He left, came around the back, and climbed up the stack of hay bales to the roof where he sighed in relief. A fox curled up and looked at him with evolving concern. Its nails clicked on the roof as it bolted to its feet and darted into the retreating fog over the harvested fields. As he climbed down, the re-emergence of cold wind reminded him of the coyote howls. The barks and yips strained the fabric of his neurons. He still remembered the attack in the recesses of his earliest memories—when he awoke from his father's screams, and rushed to the window to watch a pack of coyotes pull him apart on the front lawn.

Pace came inside, wiped his boots on the rug, peeled his gloves off, and shoved them into a corner of his coat pockets. Dark fluid soaked into his facial hair. Lilith asked nothing of it. Her stomach closed when she thought of the days when Pace started fights with teenage boys and crashed cars into ATM machines.

"I have something to tell you—" but the dog barked from the porch. He let the animal inside the house. The dog's nails clacked on the tiles. It braced itself before the clock shaped like a lighthouse, with the dial replacing the bulb. Pace had made it himself and given it as a gift to Lilith after quitting alcohol and painkillers. The dog growled, and persecuted the clock with a chain of unleashed howls and barks.

Lilith stopped scraping the pan with a spatula to pull the dog away.

"Leave the dog be," he shut the stove off, "and come to the basement with me."

He led her down the steps. He pulled the chain and light flooded the basement. He took her to the drain in the floor. He removed the cover, reached inside, and pulled out a heavy bottle of dark fluid. Red lather filled the neck.

"Where does this come from?" he asked. "Who is placing this around the house?"

Lilith shook her head. Pace ripped out the cork and drank from the bottle. The bittersweet reek of nightshade permeated from the fluid. He assembled his tool box and left to fix the holes in the chicken coop.

Their daughter sat down for breakfast. Pace repaired loose boards. Lilith took the bottle, sniffed the fluid, and her guts heaved. She took the opened bottle outside and hurled it against the pavement once used to bath cows. Whispers escaped. The fluid ran down cracks and steamed until it all soaked into the earth. While inside, the dog still barked at the clock. She opened the bottom and retrieved a hidden bottle. She poured its contents out into the grass. The grass turned yellow, curled up, and blew away in the wind. She put her ear to the bottle. In the droning waves within, she heard coyote snarls and paws beating nearer, the patter of bare feet fleeing —and the ripping of flesh.

Pace drove to town. When he returned, he found another bottle under his brake. He spent the daylight scratching at shadows on the wall and boarding up windows.

Prowling steps awoke Lilith from dreams. She felt around and found her husband not in bed. She panicked and put on slippers; rummaging through the house, she found cold mist blowing in from the open back door. Outside she heard a storm in the chicken coop. She recoiled when she saw her husband emerging shirtless, on all fours, with a hen bleeding over his collarbones and down his chest, his teeth deep within its neck. He sat before the musk of feathers and dust, tearing the chicken into strips, swallowing its guts, and sucking the marrow from its bones. Lilith ran barefoot through the mud. The hen still kicked and fluttered its wings. Pace growled at her with red teeth, his eyes darker, pupils dense with bronze.

She ran back to the house with his pouncing heels digging through the mud towards her. Lilith slammed the door behind her, waited in the bedroom with the Remington, and watched the windows for Pace.

He stayed in the chicken coop, devouring chickens until he vomited up a stomach full of splintered bones and vermilion slush. He sat in the corner, his sweatpants moist and coated in feathers. The sun rose, and he simmered in a stew of sweat, blood, and goo leaking from his ears. Putrid tubes and bladders rested on his shoulders. The cold wind swept through and the fluids frosted on his body. An unfamiliar engine revved. Pace rose to look out the window.

Headlights appeared down the driveway and stopped at the tree line. His daughter waltzed from a gleaming Pontiac Firebird—he recognized the 1983 model, with no license plate. She walked through the morning dark to the back door where she slipped into the house like a sock behind a dryer. The tail lights glowed in the morning mist and with a brief rev of the engine, it crunched gravel and disappeared down the far road.

Pace looked around at the carnage he caused. He tore his hair out, trotted across the yard. He had stored all the bottles he found in a hole under the porch. He dug them up, and drank them until his pupils returned to normal.

He walked upright into the house, showered, clogged the drain with the flayed remains of fowl. Unable to drain, the shower filled up with a pink, steaming soup. Pace wandered around the house. The dog slept on the marital bed. Lilith's car still idled in the garage. He went to his daughter's room, and found her sleeping. Lilith stood over her with the gun leveled towards him. Bags of name-brand clothing peeked from under her mattress.

"You need to leave," she demanded of him.

"Lilith, it isn't what it seems." He stepped forward. The board creaked. His daughter rolled her head, and from the window glare she saw a black bar materialize into the weapon. Lilith's shadow cut across the room.

"Leave now. Take all your possessions with you."

"The gun isn't loaded. I spent all the bullets."

Lilith noticed his pupils had returned to their natural shade.

"It's all a bad dream. One that I can't wake from," he pleaded.

Cold air flushed through the screen and brushed the dust from the floor. Pace kicked dirty clothes out of the way. His daughter held her breath at the sight of her mother aiming the rifle.

"Come, let us be a family once more..."

The daughter lifted, and backed towards the screen.

"Gywnth," her mother pleaded. "Stay there."

The girl listened to nothing; she reached to unhook the latches. With a shove, the screen popped out. She stuck her head out, but her mother caught hold of her foot with one hand. The muzzle dipped floorward. Pace pounced for the gun. Lilith pulled the trigger, and Pace collapsed to the floor, pressing his ankle. Blood flowed to the floor. His howls echoed down the hall, stairs, and out the door. Gwynth's silence shattered and she screeched like a falling missile. Lilith released her, and rushed to her husband rolling into the vanity table. The mirror on top swayed. Pace watched his eyes widen, his face tipping nearer to him. Lilith tried to catch the mirror, but she saw daughter slip out the window so she reached back, catching the end of her gown as glass crashed.

Gywnth climbed down the trellis, and jumped into the bushes. Once out, she fled towards the rusted windmill. Squawking crows watched from the blades. She climbed up the ladder to the small seat, weary and fatigued, even hungover from all the substance her suitor had provided to her. She held his invitation close to her chest—he promised her everything bedreamt, if she came with him to the city. The barn door scraped. She looked towards it. A hooded figure strolled out and approached the windmill.

Lilith walked over the broken glass to lift the mirror from Pace. Shards protruded from his cheeks and neck. She quivered, hiding her teeth behind her hand, dropping the weapon, and pulled out the glass. With each fragment her husband moaned a little more, until his fingers reanimated and grasped her windpipe. His grasp constricted. Lilith's tongue swelled from her mouth as her lungs shriveled up. She reached for a long piece of glass in his cheek. Holding it firmly, she guided it across Pace's neck.

Finally his last breath escaped in a white puff. The open window chilled the room with late autumn shivers. Lilith's flesh felt like marble. The dog barked from outside, and jumped at the door.

Lilith rolled his body onto a sheet and dragged him to the stairs where she slipped and the body tumbled down. Dust fell from the ceiling. She dragged a wagon from the barn, hoisted her husband inside limb by limb and plowed the wagon through the harvested field to the drainage ditch where she rolled the body down. She took his clothes off and burned them in a barrel.

Gwynth remained on the windmill. The hooded man walked with two crutches and braces on his legs and spine. He stood beneath the windmill, filled his cheeks with air, and when he expelled the breath, purple clouds gathered and sunk. A cyclone of dust speared the harvested fields. Sediment mist filled the air as windstreams deafened the sounds of distant highway travel and the grating of wagon wheels. Gwynth held on, her hands slipping, her legs fell from the seat, and she grabbed onto the windmill blade. The crows lifted and fled. Her weight shifted the blades. As she slid they sliced into her palms. She held on tighter, but the blade bent, and broke away and fell down with her.

Lilith dropped her wagon when she saw her daughter fall. She ran through the mud, through the uncut thistles, to a sight that sucked the life from her. The blade fell against her neck. Gwynth's head rolled to the boots of the hooded man.

"You did this," Lilith accused. "You're behind all of it."

"Yes. This may be..." The dog ran and heeled at his side. The wind died and bursts of light burned through the clouds behind the hooded stranger. He staggered on his crutches, shifting his body like an adjusting track. A grin stretched across the lightened half of his face. "...the proudest moment in my life."

He wiped away a tear.

"I will offer you what I offered Pace—" He produced a bottle of pulpy wine from his sleeve. "I'll leave this for you. Keep it. Don't let anyone else drink from it. And I will make this scene appear like suicide. As for your daughter..."

The dog brought him her head and dropped it at his feet. "...she can return to life yet."

"You're a liar."

"No, no. To show my good faith, I will give her back to you. All I ask is that you keep this bottle. Go ahead, take it."

Lilith reached, her eyes latched onto the hallow horror like a person sinking in quicksand expressed on the drooping flesh of her daughters face. She took the bottle.

"Good. This recipe is all that's left of my family. You don't remember, because it was so long ago. Your husband threw me across the room, fractured my skull and nearly tore my lumbar in half. While in the hospital my father burned all his assets. My mother drove my Firebird into the river. And I inherited nothing but this degenerative disease. So please, take care of it. Go inside. Now. Hide it. And I will bring your daughter to life. Then, I will see to it that Pace Wilkens' body is never found."

Lilith took the bottle from him. The dog followed the stranger into the barn. The door closed behind them.

Lilith spent the remaining daylight scrubbing blood and sweeping broken glass. The clocks stopped. The dog lay on the bed. The front door ground open. Footsteps went up the stairs. Lilith found something she missed before. The bags of clothes from a store in the city—one she never dared spend money in. The tags on the clothes, the lowest price—fifty dollar stockings. Nylon, lingerie—straps and belts, and a love note at the bottom. The hallway planks moaned. Lilith tossed everything back inside the bags.

"Oh my god, mom—what are you doing in my room?"

Lilith hugged her daughter. Her neck felt soft like warm cheese, but the rest of her felt as animate as the day she escaped from the womb.

Harvest season cooled to winter, froze and frosted, then upon the thawing period, Lilith cleaned the chicken coop and sold Pace's tools and belongings.

Even as the frozen pastures melted to slush, she awoke before sunrise reaching over to find spare room where she had expected to find warm flesh. The dog barked outside. Short, muffled, slobbering barks. She lit a cigarette and watched the sunrise over the windmill. As the sun's rays reached over the distant bluffs, the windmill shadows stretched towards the house, standing between the blades she thought she saw the hooded stranger's cape flutter in the screeching wind. The dog tore the screen with his claws. Lilith idled down the stairs. She let her daughter sleep in, and no longer made breakfast for her. She tried to remember the last time she saw Gwynth, but her mind always swept to the red bottle on the shelf of her fridge door. Every morning she poured it out. Every morning, another bottle returned.

She let the dog in as she poured the new bottle down the drain and tossed it in the bin with the others. The dog growled at her. She turned to him to see what at first looked like a piece of riveted lumber. She took hold of it, but the dog tightened its grip. It broke in half, and only then did Lilith see the teeth. She held a human jaw bone.

When Lilith entered her daughters room to tell her what happened, she met a cold gust of wind. The window wide open, the closet empty, the sheets and blankets on the floor. The expensive clothes gone. A nylon stocking hung from an open drawer. Weeks' worth of dust coated the makeup table, the mantle over her bed, and the floorboards.

Lilith went downstairs. The dog entered the room with the bottle of red elixir. She took the bottle from the dog's panting mouth. She uncorked the mouth, and swallowed hard.

IMAGE MONSTER

BY E.F. SCHRAEDER

Damon pressed the heels of his palms into his eye sockets until a psychedelic burst of Rorschach-esque spots emerged. "I can't believe this is happening to me."

Damon looked up, staring at the dents in the tan carpet fiber from where the furniture used to be. He glanced around the empty living room, then he focused.

The vacant room is my life.

A week ago, Damon's partner was here, making the final arrangements for their anniversary. A Caribbean cruise. They'd spent thousands on it.

Nonrefundable, of course.

Now Damon was going to spend a romantic weekend for one on a couples getaway. Overeating. Drinking too much. Probably watching porn on his phone. Jesus I'm a loser. Why hadn't I just forgotten about it?

It. That was all he could call what happened.

His stomach ached. He hadn't slept. He didn't want to think about anything but Steve. Well, Steve and Gerald, to be accurate.

Gerald! What kind of name was that? Would anyone ever call out that name in the sweaty throes of passion? Damon chuckled.

The stomach ache returned. Damon frowned as scenes from the argument replayed in his head like a bad movie.

"It's about rejecting conventions, Damon. Not adopting them," Steve had said.

Steve with his crew cut and swimmer's build. His pale gray-green eyes. That chiseled chin. The perfect man.

Gone. Not dead. Just gone. Damon felt like he was dying a slow death. Death by humiliation. Death by abandonment. Death by boredom.

Steven and Damon had been together forever. Since they were both in college. Gerald was probably a fling. After what happened outside the bar that night, who could blame either of them for acting out? For needing a break from the night terrors and panic attacks? Not to mention the great depression hanging over him ever since.

But I turned the Gerald incident into a problem. I couldn't overlooked it. Now I've lost the love of my life. For what? A point of pride? Oh shit, PRIDE is next month, too.

It'd be the first PRIDE in years Damon would spend alone. The first PRIDE after surviving the hate crime, too. Plus what happened in Orlando not that long ago.

Maybe I shouldn't go.

"And the nightmare continues." Damon slouched in the plush chair, the only seat left in the living room. "Why'd I give him the furniture? All the furniture?" He let out a loud sigh, glancing around the empty rooms. No part of the house felt safe anymore.

Damon caught himself shivering. He hadn't felt secure since the night of the hate crime when four big, bad white college-aged men attacked them near the parking lot of their favorite club.

Don't go back there. Shut it out. But the memories flooded him.

First the bats. Steven folding over, clutching his stomach. Those howling screams as he collapsed. The crunch of pummeling kicks as he squirmed on the ground.

Their huge hands pressed Damon face down in the asphalt. The wet residue on the ground he hoped was rain stuck small black pebbles to his cheeks. Then knives. Damon stopped fighting back, glimpsed the glint of a blade. They sliced him straight through the back of his shirt into skin, tearing him open like a fish. Shredding material and skin twisting until his back looked like a horrible red tattoo.

After it healed, the scar tissue puffed along his spine. It looked something like a centipede. All the way up to his shoulder blades, thick pink hash marks crossed his vertebrae like one hundred nasty legs. Every single one of them bloated with anguish, a sickening memory like a pus-filled infection that wouldn't go away.

The night that cut through their lives. Through their relationship. The night that led Damon to retreat further into himself and left Steven in the arms of another man.

There was no going back. Damon shuddered as the memories rippled through him, flooding in like scenes from a bad movie. A movie he couldn't turn off because it was a memory, his life.

The phone rang. Damon stared at it for a few moments, deciding whether or not he could answer while looking at his friend Ravi's face on the screen. The picture didn't do him justice. The warm brown eyes didn't twinkle in the picture like they did in person, and the blue cap hid his beautiful wavy black hair. Men our age should be proud of a full head of hair.

Damon sighed and picked up. "Hi, Ravi."

"It's time to reach out, sweetie," Ravi said. His voice was smooth and light.

"Already?"

"How about my place? Brunch?" Ravi said.

"How about, not ready yet?"

"Come on, you've got to get out. See the light of day. There are people who are glad you two called it quits. Steve was a prick for ditching you after what you two went through."

"Thanks for that, but it's just too soon." Damon sighed, looking around the empty room. "I mean, talk about having the rug pulled out from under you. Literally." Damon didn't want to be on the phone anymore, but pushing people away was a symptom of backsliding. At least that's what the therapist said.

Ravi's smile was audible. "I know, baby. But it'll get better soon. Promise."

"I just want to disappear for a while," Damon said.

"Aww, come on. Don't say that. It's time to be seen." Ravi's voice sailed with a dramatic tone.

Damon flinched. The idea of 'being seen' felt more like a threat or a dare than an invitation. He bit down on his tongue, resisting the urge. Damon sighed heavily, considering his options. "You want to go on a cruise next week?"

***

The pit in Damon's stomach grew into a hard, unrelenting knot. He'd packed a single suitcase, and had to drag himself to do it. If it weren't for Ravi he probably would've skipped it altogether. Stayed home. But now here he was. He'd decided to go on the trip. Be seen. Even something for fun felt like a nightmare.

"Now we have to get you out of the cabin, sweetie. Come on," Ravi said, coaxing. He smiled. The tiny room wasn't much to look at, and he was anxious to enjoy the warm sun and all the ship had to offer.

Damon recoiled, plopped back down on the edge of the bed. Single. Recently dumped. Loser. Would everyone on the cruise see that? He felt like his bruised heart was as visible as the ugly scar on his back. Sitting there in his flowered swimsuit, practically naked. How could I leave the room like this? What if someone asks about the scars?

Ravi smirked. "Come on. You've got to get back out there." He motioned his head to the door.

"You go. Maybe I'll be out later." Damon dropped his head.

"You want to hide. I get it. We've all been there." Doo-Doop. Ravi's phone chimed. "Ooh. New message," his face brightened. "What do you think of my new profile picture?"

"Great," Damon said, but he frowned. Ravi definitely didn't

understand the need to be invisible. How could he? His idea of a long relationship was one that lasted through dessert. "I just can't deal with all the couples right now." Damon's face drooped. "Or singles."

"What makes you think they'll know we're not a couple?"

Damon laughed.

Ravi squinted at him, raising an angry, well-groomed black eyebrow. He tapped his foot on the parquet floor, jutting out a hip.

"Oh, you're serious!" Damon smirked. "Well, I guess," he paused, "I don't know."

"That's right. You don't." Ravi scolded. "Look, just keep a certain distance out there," he said, motioning to the hall, "or you'll ruin my image. We're all here for the same thing. Just to be ourselves." He checked himself out in the mirror and flexed. "Fourteen days of sun, swimming, and relaxation." Ravi was going to say 'sex' but thought better of it. That these cruises were notorious for onboard romance was not something he thought would help Damon at the moment.

Damon rolled his eyes. "You're a monster."

"Aren't we all?" Ravi flexed again, winking at himself. "Come on, you're dressed enough for the pool. Let's go," Ravi instructed. He reached for his friend.

Damon pulled away, slipping further back on the bed. The feeling of emotional nudity became acutely painful. Between the hate crime, subsequent breakup, and PTSD, Damon couldn't shake the sense of being exposed, too vulnerable. He felt it lodged deep beneath the surface of his dark skin like an invading presence. The scars only made it worse, drew attention to the middle-aged spectacle in bright swim trunks. He wished he would've just given Ravi the tickets to use with someone else.

"No you don't," Ravi said, pulling him up from the bed. "You're getting out there. You're coming with me. And we're going to have fun."

Damon reluctantly stood up, and followed behind his friend like a stray puppy, head down. The infectious vulnerability still gnawed at him like a parasite.

"There we go. Drinks are our first priority," Ravi clapped. He let the door slam as they left.

Drinks sounded good. Lots of drinks.

Damon kept his eyes low as they headed for the bar, but his legs wobbled with every step he took. The world felt upside down without his Steven. He'd been in a committed relationship for so long that he feared eye contact. Besides, that was the first window for flirtation.

Unacceptable.

Even without glancing up at anyone, by the time they'd reached the bar Damon was coated in a glistening sheen of sweat. His posture sagged as he slumped at a stool next to Ravi. Before ordering, Damon felt someone looking at him. The centipede on his back began to tingle and burn until his whole back went stinging hot. Like people could see it and know what happened. He felt marked.

"Baby, you're getting scoped." Ravi poked Damon's ribs.

Damon wiggled away. "Stop it." He sat up straight and tightened his stomach muscles. "Can we just order and go to the pool?" His scar itched.

A well-muscled twenty-something man with tanned skin and beach-blond highlights wearing aviator sunglasses appeared from the other side of the bar. "What would you two like?"

Ravi winked at Damon. "I have an idea." He glanced at the young man and nodded. "I'd like a long island iced tea. Light on the tea."

"Same," Damon said, doing his best to avoid looking at the bartender's reflective shades.

The bartender smiled, flashing his perfect white teeth at the older men, just like he'd been trained to do to maximize bar returns. And tips.

Damon waited for his drink and planned an escape route. When the drink came, he'd slink behind Ravi, B-line for a chaise lounge under an umbrella on the outside of the pool. He'd take in the sea air, and hoped the sway of the boat would relax him. The bartender finally handed over the drink. He took a big swallow, then pushed, "Come on." He felt the legs on his back pinching as people stared at them. Can't they just not look? He wished he'd brought out a T-shirt to the deck, regardless of what Ravi would've said.

Ravi led the way, making time for friendly smiles and hellos as he went. He left Damon trailing just far enough behind to indicate he was open to offers.

Damon felt Ravi's energy searing through the crowd, searching for a landing point. Someone to fuck. Damon felt ill at the thought of being left alone poolside. He decided to sneak back to the room at the first sign that Ravi's socializing had succeeded.

Ravi stopped to enjoy the view of a particularly fabric-light bikini. Damon ran into him, spilling the drink.

"What is wrong with you?" Ravi snapped. "Oh, sugar, I'm sorry. I know what it is and what it isn't. I think my eyes got carried away." He shrugged.

Damon took another sip, glancing around. Monsters. All of them. Staring. Laughing. Flirting. The scar still seared on his back. Maybe I should've tried to use cover up? Applied more sunscreen? Something felt very wrong. Like it had a mind of its own. Trauma was like that.

"Aren't you even going to notice anyone?" Ravi asked.

"I just want to chill, Ravi. I'm sorry to be such a drag." Twenty more feet. I forgot how it felt to be on the market. On display. "I'm not ready to feel so naked." He couldn't wait to lean his back against a chair and hide the scar from sight.

"Damon, you were never much into that gym rat scene, but come on. You've got to admit. I know we're past a certain age, but for Baby Boomers we're still looking good," Ravi spun on his feet like a dancer.

Damon laughed. "That you are, my friend." He sighed. He couldn't help wishing he was here with Steve. Even if marriage wasn't for everyone, or for Steve, he thought they had something special. Worth hanging onto...Damon slid into an empty chair.

"You're thinking about Steven," Ravi said, his finger wagging.

"Busted." Damon sunk deep into the lounger, looking dejected. "Is the word, 'jilted' hovering above me?" He slung one hand toward his back, scratching.

"Like a halo."

Damon scowled. He wanted to disappear. He probably shouldn't have come.

Ravi glanced down at his phone. "There are 2,401 guys within—"

Damon laughed, "Would you get off Grindr for a minute?"

Ravi shrugged.

"At least while we're onboard? I mean, we're all gay." Damon couldn't imagine using his phone to meet men. He started seeing Steven before internet dating, let alone apps to meet people. He shivered, mildly terrified to imagine that kind of constant availability.

"Your loss." Ravi took one more selfie then powered down his phone.

For a second, Damon's body reacted, warmed to the attention. Little ripples of excitement shot through his nerves. He felt a rush of enthusiasm beneath the hot sun. Maybe the glances were a little gratifying. Being exposed still felt unnerving, but he was glad he'd joined his friend on deck. It was time to get out there again. Maybe being noticed wasn't all bad. But the warmth didn't last.

Damon noticed the ship-wide surveillance cameras, hovering from hallway ceilings and in doorways. He knew it was for security, maybe to discourage public sex. Yet once he saw the little black orb and glowing red light, he suddenly noticed the villainous eyes everywhere, all over the boat. He shifted in his chaise lounge to avoid them.

Then the sensation worsened. His skin went from tingling to burning as he looked around. All around him, men pointed their phones, taking videos and selfies. The sound of candid snapshots, howling laughter, and escalating flirtation surrounded him until it reverberated in his head. Everyone on board the ship clamored for the spotlight, their moments clicked into memorialized view, stored up in the cloud for all to see. Forever.

Damon knew the photos were the tip of the iceberg, and he imagined them being uploaded, sent around the world instantaneously. Damon cringed to picture the internet alive with images from this so-called private getaway.

How long before Steven sees me online?

What am I doing here? I'm not ready for this.

The sensation of being watched burrowed into Damon's warm flesh, fierce as a gnawing insect. He'd forgotten the intense pressure of being on display. He wanted to go home. Pull the covers over his head and vanish.

Was it one set of eyes? Four? How many were recording? Watching?

Damon felt like he'd die of exposure, and his body ached in every crevice of exposed skin. The scar got hotter with every pair of eyes that landed on him and the centipede.

Damon pushed himself upright, running back to his room.

Snap.

Click.

The sounds of cameras, extended exposures capturing every step scalded him more than the hot beating sun. Digital beeps pinged. Damon covered his ears, picked up speed.

Damon's head spun around to see someone standing beside him, face hidden behind a large black lens. The shutter ticked opened, closed, and repeated. His feet slipped on the wet deck. He grasped the rail, but his legs slid, splaying him facedown.

"Not safe anywhere," he said, gripping the rail from below. He tried pulling himself up but slipped, tumbling overboard.

Splash.

The centipede sank.

***

"The security feed clearly shows this was not my client's negligence," a lawyer pressed play, starting the video on a large screen at the hearing. "Damon's tragic story is the stuff of legend, starting with a horrible hate crime, ending in heartbreak and trauma. But no matter how terrible the accident, this death is not a matter of operator's negligence."

The lawyer did not villify Damon's need for escape or retreat to a gay cruise with his friend. The jurors would make those leaps on their own if they had the inclination. Instead, he took the high road, speaking of Damon's personal life. He thumped on the table, explaining Damon's ache for privacy. Then he rattled off statistics about how the injuries of that night impaired his motor skills, his nerves, and his mental health.

Jurors gasped, watching the footage. A few looked away, covering their eyes just before the splash.

The centipede did not swim.

Whether Damon slipped or flung himself overboard wasn't news anymore. Surely everyone at the hearing had seen the loop, witnessed the death of someone who wanted to be left alone. His agonized face and scar were familiar. For weeks, the world watched the plunge a hundred thousand times, dissecting the faults that drove him overboard.

Even with a million views, no one really saw the centipede, how its legs pushed.

HER EYES WERE BLUE IN LEBANON

BY SARA THE BLACK

We never expected that morning. The new century was born in the rage and fire of human frustration. Civil War overwhelmed already fragile political situations, the fallout of a moment of failure in government ended the web of lies Society had told Herself.

It became a decade where private contract mercenary companies made a fortune on the greed and suffering of unstable regimes. Black projects ran unfettered, regulations on human genome editing were tossed out with hope in a desperate race to create a new generation of Winter Soldiers.

War isn't pretty. It's not glamorous. The price we paid in mind, body and soul was exponential compared to the miserable Judas pieces that were tossed at us.

I

"Actions prove who someone is; words just prove who they want to be." — Unknown

Undisclosed Safe House
DMZ/Disputed Israel Border
0530
October 13, 2101

My ears knew that my eyes were closed. I could hear him breathing steadily, I could smell him taking one last puff of that cigarette before letting it drop to the floor and stomping it out. It burned my nostrils, an acrid aroma that assaulted my hyperactive senses in a flauntingly obscene manner. I hate smokers, but worse than that, I hate rogue Contractors. The striking reality of that last statement was emphasized by the sudden shock of the cold steel pressed against the base of my skull. My eyes remained closed, my breathing was stilled for the moment but in my chest beat into red line the soul I had always forsaken as being a foolish notion.

I breathed in sharply as I heard him cock the hammer. I waited and seconds seemed like eons.

Do it, just bloody fucking do it.

Quit making me wait, just do it! I gulped involuntarily, ashamed of my own fear, ashamed at the pointless existence I had led.

I waited, prayed even, that this salvation in the guise of an a-hole would deliver me from the Hell I had created for myself.

I said my goodbyes as I instinctively felt him pull the trigger.

Click.

Time stood still for the longest moment of my life.

Nothing.

I took a deep breath.

There would be no martyred redemption for me on this day, the reality made achingly clear by the laughter that filled my ears next. I opened my eyes and, for the first time since this ordeal began, looked up at my would-be executioner.

He pulled up a chair, sat down seemingly quite amused with himself, and lit up another cigarette. He offered me a puff but shrugged at the scowl on my face before sticking it back into his mouth and leaning forward in his seat. He was eye level with me now, I stared intently into his eyes for a moment before looking away and struggling against the ropes that held me securely to that uncomfortable wooden chair.

"Stop." It was not a request or a command but a simple statement.

I flinched in disgust as he gently stroked the side of my face and drew my face up to look at him again. I started coughing against the dirty strip of t-shirt material he had fashioned into a makeshift gag earlier. He put the cigarette into an ashtray on the table next to him and leaned forward again, pulling the gag off in one fluid motion from back to front. I coughed a few more times, my eyes tearing up with the effort. He reached towards my face again, tentatively at first, then with more confidence as he used the cleaner corner of the makeshift gag in a vain effort to wipe the tears away from my face. He stroked the hair away from my face but withdrew his hand immediately when I finally jerked away, still struggling to breathe.

"Why are you so damn eager to meet your own end, brown-eyed goddess of mine?" he asked in an almost whisper, his dark eyes searching mine for an answer that was unspoken.

"All of them...dead. You bastard! It wasn't supposed to go down like that, and you damn well know it!"

"Hey, it's the matter of business we deal in, love." He matter-of-factly shrugged and scratched his balls before letting out an impressive combo belch and fart that made my eyes water. God this disgusting fuck needed to lay off the Armenian daily special. It was cheap because the bulk of the slop was near-rotting onions. I shook my head, trying to get my head to focus again. He was trying his best to distract me.

"I want out."

"I want you to love me, we can't always have what we want." He boldly brushed the barest whisper of a kiss on my forehead before reaching down and undoing the ropes that had begun to cut into the tender skin of my wrists and ankles. He walked back to his chair and quietly watched me as I stood and stretched. He chuckled softly at the unexpected moan of pleasure that escaped my lips from being free at last. I turned to him and searched his face in return for an answer. Not finding one, I finally raised my head in a moment of defiance.

"Why?"

"Why not? Exit is that way, Mia...See you around." He stood up and glanced over my slender form once approvingly before leaving out the door he had just pointed to. I stood for a while letting the events of the past hours sink in before I walked over to the table and grabbed my .44 Ruger Redhawk off the table. I opened the cylinder and counted the rounds before returning my big-bore friend to its trusty holster on my thigh.

There was a pack of cigarettes still on the table along with a battered brass Zippo lighter.

"Oh, what the hell..." I grabbed up both on impulse and stepped out the door and into the bright light of a new day. I popped a cig into my mouth, flicked open the lighter and lit the accursed thing. The smoke filled my lungs briefly before I exhaled.

When dealing with zealot Anarchists, there is definitely no shortage of interesting moments.

2

"My past is an armor I cannot take off, no matter how many times you tell me the war is over." — Unknown

Company Safe House

Beirut, Lebanon Liberated United Caliphate 0730

Morning

February 12, 2106

. . .

Dodged two shots, and now I'm cornered behind a pallet of random building supplies, a random piece of oxidized rebar jabbing uncomfortably into my shoulder padding. I'm breathing deep, trying to stay focused. A rough hand suddenly grabbed me from behind, and I immediately spring into action—

"Aaaaaargh!" I sat up in bed drenched in a stale cold sweat, heart racing.

Click

It takes me a long moment to reorient myself back into the moment.

I'm in a lumpy safe house bed with a gorgeous woman caught up in a choke hold with a Russian .44 flat against the shaved side of her head.

"Good Morning!" she replied cheerfully, her unbelievably blue eyes full of a rare emotion in our line of work—trust.

I took a deep breath and released her immediately, holding my hands up in our default-range safe mode. She nodded at me with a huge pearly white grin and an eye-roll. I flopped back in bed still trying to catch my breath. The room is damp and the air overwhelmingly stale. I rolled over and laid the hand cannon on the scarred surface of a repurposed crate.

The pain hit me soon after. The ache in my joints, the bum knee, and the other ravages of age and a stupid youth full of dumb mistakes in a not-too-distant past.

She lit a hand-rolled cigarette, took a drag, and passed it to me before following suit with a half-empty liter of state-issued vodka.

Breakfast of Burnouts, yo.

I'm propped up with several questionable pillows on my second healthy swig of vodka when I feel the heavy weight of a speed loader on my chest. She followed it up with a feather kiss to my brow and cuddled in, ignoring my feeble attempt at resisting.

"Can't have you shooting me in your sleep, Mia."

"Morning...damn cunt." I groan out in a hoarse voice before leaning over slightly to take another swig. She pouted and grabbed the bottle from me, polishing off the rest in one go. She scooted back over and caught me in a long deep kiss, the metallic taste of an unspent round mixing in with the cheap hooch burn. We broke contact and she rolled the bullet around in her mouth like its a freaking lemon drop.

Crazy gorgeous bitch was going to be the death of me.

3

"You are stronger than you think. You have gotten through every bad day in your life, and you are undefeated." — Unknown

Undisclosed Ops Location

2315

March 2, 2106

I grimaced at the ache in my shoulder and readjusted my shoulder rig. Behind me I heard the crack of a spank on a heavily padded ass followed by a squeal of delight.

"Would you two quit it? Leave the spanky shit for after we seal this fucking objective." My growls were met with a mix of fuck yous and whatevers from the crew behind us.

"Form up! Quit the spanky shit now or I'm docking your premiums and taking me a pooncation on the team's dime!" The captain's voice came in loud and clear on our coms and we immediately changed gears.

. . .

“Mad Dog to Red, confirming objective Quadrant A3 of compound!”

“Red here, confirming Queen move A3. Moving King to B1. I repeat: moving in for the check!”

“B1, Affirm!”

I grinned and hunkered down low, waiting for the team lead to wave us in.

We had the party neatly tied up within 10 minutes, the objective secure and Red back to tongue fucking Tiny. I rolled my eyes and leaned back against a wall, out of breath and feeling every ounce of gear on my rig.

“I'm getting too old for this shit, kids.”

Mad Dog laughed and gave me a bro shoulder punch on his passing-by, loaded down with the comms gear. I centered for a moment before creaking my sorry ass back up and grabbing one of the field gear totes. Sooner we are packed out, the sooner I can get back to my lumpy bed.

Hours later, I staggered into ops base housing and unceremoniously tossed my mismatched rig into a dusty corner before grabbing a cold beer from the unreliable fridge.

A trail of filthy clothes followed me towards the tiny excuse for a bathroom. A family of roaches scattered the moment I pulled on the shoelace attached to a sad naked bulb dangling from the moldy ceiling.

I turned on the water full to hot and waited while the ancient pipes sputtered and protested before spitting out an anemic excuse for water.

I stood under its welcoming escape and just let myself go blissfully numb.

I tuned out long enough for the water to run ice cold. Teeth chattering I stubbornly remained under the blast, still feeling utterly filthy.

I'll never be clean enough.

4

"It's a war within yourself that never goes away." — Unknown

Sleazy Motel

New Republic of Montana

Time and Date Redacted on File

I let him sit in a darkened room every year. He'll sometimes call me in to keep him company, gently rubbing his back and holding him tightly from behind.

Irest my face against his warm skin and sigh, adding my tears to his own. He leaned back slightly and patted my thigh before taking another drag from the beer bottle and tossing it against the wall with a roar that climaxed into wails of sorrow as the satisfying break of glass violently pulled me out of the quiet moment we had shared.

The war was over but the battle within continued raging. The calendar was an old frenemy, a perpetual reminder of all the comrades, friends, and lovers we'd lost over the long struggle to have Truth prevail against unbelievable odds. We were dispensable, obsolete—relics of a now denied and heavily sanitized past that the capitalist consumerist nation was trying to bury under shiny new strip malls, consumer debt and heavily-advertised fantasy on high-definition screens. It was blindingly bright, clean, and distracting to most civilian personnel. We on the other hand, the Company Children—we saw the lies of progress behind the fog of propaganda. We had shed blood for them to be able to have all the conveniences of modern living without any of the struggle for resources that fed the Machine.

Elijah Allen Huutz stank of cigarettes, sour body sweat intermingled with stale alcohol. He blinked, annoyed at the sun streaming into the room through the half-broken blinds.

"Ugh..." he grunted, slowly sitting up on the narrow, hard bed shoved up against the farthest wall of the otherwise sparse apartment. The smell of fresh coffee assaulted his nostrils, nearly turning his stomach.

"Good morning, sunshine!"

"Oh, fuck you. You leave that cheery go-go shit to Red." He reached for the Irish coffee he knew I was bringing over without looking up at me. He took a careful sip, nodded and grunted in approval before taking a long healthy gulp, drinking most of the cup at a go. He sat on the edge of the bed staring at his boot-hardened feet and scarred toes, twirling the last bit of coffee before finishing it off and holding the cup out in a silent request for more.

"Love you too!" I kissed him gently on the forehead and patted his hands before carefully taking the cup from his trusting, calloused hands and fulfilling his unspoken request.

"Eli...are you going to leave this dump soon?" I asked, tucking the refilled mug into his grasp. He cooperated, sitting still, refusing to make eye contact with me.

"Yeah. I'll snap out of it soon, Lieutenant. Worst case of deployment drop ever, I swear." He took a drink, frowned, and held out the cup. I grabbed the bottle of whiskey and poured into the cup until he gave me a nod to stop.

"Thanks. You know me better than my own wife, Mia. Pity the bitch hates you; make one hell of a triad." His voice cracked into a dry chuckle, the first hint of any hope out of him in weeks.

"You shameless pervert!" I snort, taking a long pull from the whiskey bottle with a wince as the heady hooch burned its way south.

"You know its against Company regs and you aren't my type anyways. Besides, we're from the same genome batch—we're damn near relations, Captain. Your wife is an angel for putting up with your shit, you stop badmouthing her before I smack you one."

I gave him a playful punch on the shoulder before sitting next to him on the bed and resting my head on his shoulder. We sat in silence for a while, passing back and forth the bottle of rotgut after he had finished his idea of morning caffeine.

"She wants a divorce." He finally worked up the nerve to tell me what had pushed him over the edge this time. I knew there was more than just anniversaries of recent tragic events and losses that were on his mind.

"Yeah, she called me last night and told me you were holed up in this shit-hole. You think my intel network is so good I can magically find you every time you drop out of link? Wrong, boss; she ratted you out. Still cares enough to send someone to come find your old battered carcass."

"Fucking bitches, both of you. I'll make sure your cut of the last deployment is docked for insubordination." He grabbed the bottle out of my hand and, taking a long drag, finished it off.

"You do what you have to do, Captain, but make sure you get the paperwork right this time." He half-struggled against my attempt to give him a hug before sighing and relaxing against me.

"We didn't ask for this, Lieutenant. We didn't sign up for a retirement plan, Mia. What the hell did the Company do to us?"

"Used us like a dollar store condom."

He chuckled at that and patted me on the head.

The sun outside filled a good portion of the efficiency housing and the birds chirped loudly in dueling songs and territorial tantrums.

I slowly stood up and held a hand out.

"Come on, let's get you cleaned up. I brought a change of Civies and a new pair of boots, not Company-issue. I've got enough creds on my ration card for a decent meal out for once."

He reluctantly allowed me to lead him into the spartan shower and numbly cooperated with me as I undressed him out of the filthy black BDUs we had all been wearing on the day we'd been recalled. I pulled off my own minimal clothes and pulled him into the shower. He said nothing as I washed him, starting with soaping up his hair and working my way down. I turned off the water and toweled him carefully, tucking it around his slim waist and coaxing him out.

"Thank you. You always have my back on this shit." He finally had the strength to look me straight in the face with clear blue eyes. The man had a striking gaze that could make a normal woman's panties go instantly moist. I was immune to that reaction fortunately, too much water under that particular dilapidated bridge.

"Just watching out for my captain." I shrugged before handing him his clothes bundle and turning my back to towel off before putting my own garments back on.

"You'll be a hell of a wife for one lucky fucker someday, kid. Don't waste that loyalty on the first asshole that comes along."

"There isn't anyone suicidal enough to claim my ass, Captain. Come on, gear up and let's get the hell out of here. You can't avoid paperwork and debriefing forever. I'll be there with you."

He snorted and shook his head before pulling the shirt over his head.

"You are still getting a dock in pay, Lieutenant!"

"Whatever keeps you motivated, boss!" I called in from the main room as I was lacing up my boots. He joined me shortly after, grabbing his rucksack out of a corner and giving the room a final sweep. He nodded at me to take point and with a sigh we stepped into the day and back to our familiar way of survival.

5

"Strength doesn't come from what you can do. It comes from overcoming the things you once thought you couldn't" — Anonymous

Undisclosed Ops Location, Unsanctioned Action

Time and Date Redacted on File

. . .

I knew I was going to get a good shagging by fate.

The kind of fuck that changes your entire life, goals, and perspectives.

I didn't have time to double the knot tying the rigging harness to the anchor. I slapped the stake into the cliff side and the spike deployed on contact, burying in deep. I set the detonation charges to 2 minutes, said a silent prayer to whatever Elder Deity laughed from above, and jumped down. I immediately encountered rough crags and sharp edges that tore through my flimsy tac-gloves within minutes. I cursed and glanced up briefly in the quickly fading light. I couldn't risk popping on my infrared goggles right now; I'd be spotted by whatever drones were trying to hone in on my ass even faster.

Wristwatch: 1:20 remaining

Fuck!

I grabbed the rigging line and kept rappelling down, crashing through more foliage and uncertain terrain. The charges above my head were going to take down the entire ridge, and me with it if I didn't hit the solid ground a few feet still underneath me.

"Bitch is down there!" I heard shouting faintly from above.

Damn it!

"I'll give you really good fuck you, assholes!!" I tapped the panic button on my wrist coms without hesitation, growled, and released the half knot on my harness.

There was a deafening explosion from above followed by a shower of incredibly painful debris as I braced into a free fall. Objective was strapped secure against my chest; I wasn't going to fail this one.

It was only a few seconds, but time for me went in total slow motion.

The last thing I remember was hitting the ground with a jarring thud, a sharp pain shooting up my right leg.

I found out later—when the retrieval team dug up my sorry carcass—that I ended up with a compound fracture on the leg, blown kneecap, and several broken ribs. Even with the advanced orthotic devices that were covered in our nifty health premium, I wasn't going to dance again. I'd be lucky if I ever walked again without a limp.

I completed the objective. That's all that mattered.

6

"The world is full of nice people. If you can't find one, be one." — Unknown

New York, New York
Founder's Territory
845
April 20, 2106

It was an absolutely gorgeous morning and there was still a bite in the air before the morning fog totally burned off. The city was vibrant and fiercely alive around me.

I didn't really exist, lost in my deployment playlist and memories. I stopped briefly on auto-pilot to knock out a long list of errands before making a contact drop at one of the most amazing Jewish delis in the area.

I stopped at the door and take a deep breath. A fake smile immediately came on as I greeted a civilian in the process of opening the door for me. I pulled off the headphones out of common courtesy and utter a courtesy in a raspy voice barely audible.

"Shabbat shalom, friend."

The old man gifts me with a resplendent gap-toothed smile, the crinkles of his eyes deepening. He nodded once and goes on his way, disappearing into the morning madness.

The smell of indulgence hit me.

Greasy, hot-peppered, orgasmic pastrami.

Fuck this contact.

I'm going to take a personal moment and reacquaint my waistline with the true meaning of retired.

"You are getting soft, Mia."

I looked up from my mustard/pickle/meatgasm and growled before reluctantly putting the indulgence down and wiping off my hands.

"I'm allowed to. What the hell do you want?" I groaned out with my still raspy voice while unconsciously adjusting my scarf. The bruising was still a sickly faded yellow around my neck and upper chest. Every word I spat out was achingly painful. So was eating but this dickhead across the table didn't come with a promise of a toe-curling good time.

"There's a POTUS detail in Qatar..." he said in a lowered tone leaning in closer and making eye contact.

Ugh. His breath stank of cheap booze and pussy.

"Mr. 'You Girl on Girl, Then Shoot'??" I snorted out painfully.

"Shhh! No...his business rival, Khalid." Bear breathed out heavily before leaning back in the chair. Greasy hipster hair flopped halfway over his face. He looked around briefly for a moment before grabbing my sandwich and taking a huge bite.

"Mmmm, fuck that's good!"

I sat dumbfounded.

"Um, you owe me a sandwich skank breath. Also, your client won't like me. I sorta shagged his wife...and the daughter."

Bear's eyes went wide before almost choking on the bite he took from laughing so hard. True to his namesake, he broke into a full-blown belly laugh complete with a stream of tears rolling down his cheeks and disappearing into the thick red manscaped beard.

"Only you, Mia...man...those were some good times, bro."

"Yeah. Were. I'm done."

Bear sat looking pensive for a moment, running a big meaty hand through his mop of hair.

"Cool. Just message me the bank details for your comp package."

"Send it to some Syrian freedom fighters or Somalian orphans. I don't want that blood money, Bear."

"...A'ight."

He got up to leave.

He turned around once at the door and made eye contact. His eyes were the bright green of fresh grass on safe civilian lawns.

He nodded once, pulled up his hoodie, and faded into the crowd.

I opened up my phone and flipped through some images, stopping at a particular one of Red, Tiny, and myself partying at the night market in Tel Aviv.

Those blue eyes.

I'll never forget you.

I got up and left soon after, forgetting the sandwich and hopefully in time—

Everything else.

I survived.

It was time to start living.

I turned off my phone, pulled out the battery and sim and destroyed it. I stopped to adjust my knee brace before hailing a cab out of this freezing-ass place and back home to the sunny West Territories.

An old womanizing pervert like me still had a few tricks left.

"Out of suffering have emerged the strongest souls; the most massive characters are seared with scars."

Kahlil Gibran

BLOOD LOSS

BY OMEWENNE

Alongside the lake, lay Gisela and Edward, side by side on their backs looking up into the vast collage of stars. Next to them, set on a flat stone, was a jar of leeches in water. Edward was grateful to Gisela for joining him on this venture. To his mind, she had been following him around like a stray waif in search of guidance. He had reciprocated in his downward spiral towards suicide-like experiments to see how far he could get towards entering a new tableau of reality, psychotropics.

Gisela was not a stray waif in the sense that she wanted guidance. Yes, Edward was beautiful with his pale skin and long, curly mane of black hair, but what she wanted was to get lost in herself, to get answers about who she was. Edward was a means to an end; whether this became more than a simply sexual relationship or not. She could get lost in herself with him as a vessel. They did have a bond not unlike brother and sister in a kind of incestuous disarray. Still in their early twenties, they had met in a college philosophy class and had noticed each other from across the lecture hall. He in a black Edwardian (a pun?) suit, she in her 1920s gray flapper dress with an amber silk slip beneath, her long, wild, amber-colored hair done in finger waves, her face heavily made up in ivory with dark eyelids and maroon lips. They found they had a mutual apathy for life. Believing in some of the death cults popular to pick and sift from in modern times, but unwilling to go as far as seeking death as an escape from the mundane ways of everyday life.

Gisela had all but thrown away her phone, sick of being a part of social media and its parasitical trappings with people feeding off of each other even if she denied that was what was going on between her and Edward. No, they had more mutual benefits from each other. Edward, too, had stopped with all the social media—so much so that a few of his ex-girlfriends had left copious messages on his accounts and phone, hoping and weeping that he had not gone off the deep end.

The idea was that they strip down to their undergarments and apply the leeches. This would lead to opening a portal to another light-headed nothingness. As Edward had (poorly) planned, a release from the heaviness of everyday life and their problems with their families, friends, and society.

Gisela had recently been thinking of pouring drain cleaner into her father's morning coffee. His presence in her life was crushing her. His vice-grip over her, her mother, her two little brothers, was disturbing. Still in the military, he was coming up for a promotion, a higher standing of rank, and his control over the family was tightening more, his rage more intent and focused. Yet somehow he went about like a gregarious hero to everyone else, laughing loudly, Mr. Popularity, while picking apart each person as he went along, trying to be in charge while still the everyman. Everyone was to laugh when he laughed. Gisela's mother had diverted herself with her job in department store sales, snorting lines of cocaine in the ladies room to keep her personality bright and perky, always smiling even when she was putting sleeping pills into her husband's double whiskey at six o' clock sharp every night before dinner. Hell, she took them herself. Gisela's brothers were much younger than she. The youngest, Eric, was disappearing into himself as she did long ago. What would become of him? Her other brother, Darrin, was following in her father's footsteps, playing war games, mimicking his father in all ways: the gregariousness, the power plays. Unpleasant and monstrous. Darrin was shooting at squirrels and rabbits in the backwoods with the small gun given to him by his adoring father.

Edward came from a single-parent situation. His mother showered him with attention, much of it highly inappropriate. Anita was still a very attractive woman and dressed seductively to attract men but her true love was her son. Fighting off his train of never-ending, obsessive girlfriends, Anita would often surprise her son by climbing into his bed with him in the mornings wearing nothing more than a see-through negligee and running her hands through his long, curly, lovely locks to awaken him. Edward felt trapped but never spoke a word of this to anyone, not even Gisela. His mother knew nothing of Gisela but was more than often very upset with Edward for not coming home by eleven every night. "I'm twenty-two, Mom..."

Edward had tried to get a job, as had Gisela, but both of them seemed too hazy in the mind to hold onto anything, so employers took one glance at them and decided—NO.

Gisela lifted one of the leeches and placed it on her ankle. She felt nothing. No teeth biting into her, nothing. After a short time, the both of them had covered their bodies with the leeches. Even to their jugulars. Some time passed before they became dizzy. On their backs, holding hands, a flood of stars blurring out of sight.

Blackness like a stone in water.

Then, the sound of gentle waves rushing in on a shoreline. Gisela began to feel her legs walking over something uncomfortable, jutting up at her feet. Looking down she saw bones, human bones she was certain, skulls. Up and down the place were nothing but human bones, dismembered skeletons replacing sand and shingle. And the water. The water was deep red blood, or so it looked. Gisela could smell it. It was blood. Her arms moved to close around her torso, naked pale arms, pale green fingernails. Dressed in a champagne-hued 1930s slip which fluttered in the wind as she strode, a pale shadow, toward what suddenly came into view as sea caves. A storm crackled like bronchitis in the gray sky, whirled in circles, spitting out rain, lightning, and thunder. Gisela stumbled her way over the bones, her bare feet bludgeoned by the hardness of them but uncut, strangely. On and on she climbed over the skeletons until she reached the mouth of one of the sea caves. Once inside, she found Edward sitting on moist, cold earth in his black Edwardian garb. Had he been crying? Gisela found that she too was silently weeping in symbiosis. The inside of the cave was earthen, with roots and pieces of bone straggling out of the roof and sides of it. Further down, the cave separated into three different passages and into darkness. This did not look very inviting. Gisela plopped herself down next to Edward, resting her head against his.

"Where are we?" he asked, his voice quivering with fear.

"This must be the other world you spoke of."

"Not very nice is it?"

"It's kind of beautiful in its way...No."

"Do you think our bodies are safe back by the lake?"

"Edward, we really ought to have thought this through."

"Perhaps one of us should have stood as sentry."

"Too late for that now."

"Sorry, I should have thought on this more."

"Don't worry. I knew I was letting myself in for some danger."

The two sat back in the sea cave, listening in their own silence while the sound of waves of blood washing up on the strand and the storm's thrashing about outside rose up in their ears.

"Where did the leeches disappear to?"

"I expect they're still on us but we can't see them because we're here in this place."

"I was hoping for one of those parallel universes where my father was dead, or different, or something—not something that looks like the aftermath of some great war."

"Do you regret it?"

"No, I don't."

A great ball of light came rushing down the strand of bones and blood toward them. The two rose from their places, standing, and saw that it appeared to be a small sun. Within it, as it drew closer, was the form of a baby with a dangerous expression on its face. As the sun hadn't seen Gisela or Edward as yet, the two both thought it best if they were to move further into the cave as quickly as possible.

The earth was both soil and blood, making it mucky which they could both smell and feel through their toes. At least it's better than bones, thought Gisela. But suddenly the child in the sun saw them and its fury was intense. Into the cave the sun whirled, its eyes fixed upon the two. Gisela and Edward stumbled and slipped their way down the cave's passage at as quick a pace as they could, into one of the adjoining passages once a choice came of three different ways. They went to the right.

The sun chased them, shedding some light in the cave. Edward looked over his shoulder and saw the sun-child gaining on them and shooting rays from its eyes which lit up the passage even more but burned where it searched in the dark. The danger in this was evident but the benefits were that the two could now see ahead of them in the darkness.

A blow to Gisela's head as a ray hit her, a blow to Edward's back as another ray struck him. They both fell. The sun was hovering over them, silent, but the raging baby's face eyed them with ferocity.

Edward, able to move, reached over to Gisela who seemed uncoordinated.

"Are you alright?"

"Not really. What in the hell does that thing want?"

"Seems to be angry with us."

"Yes, I figured that! What is this, its own private beach?"

"Don't be angry with me."

"I'm not angry with you Edward. My head hurts, can't think straight."

A blow hit Gisela in the side. Another to Edward's jaw.

"PLEASE STOP!" pleaded Gisela to the glowing baby's face.

It laughed mischievously then sent two more rays to Gisela and Edward; her in the leg, him in the chest.

Gisela cried out, then she said to Edward, “We've got to get away from this thing!”

“How when it can clearly move faster than we can?”

“Just get up and keep moving.” They crawled up the walls, earth and blood in their fingernails, till they were upright.

The sun child squinted angrily at them and sent more rays from its eyes, pummeling the two until they fell once more to the ground of the cave, unconscious. Blackness.

On the lakeside, Gisela opened her eyes and saw the ancient stars above her, not a sun baby in a glowing orb. Sighing, she tried to feel for Edward's hand but found she couldn't even feel her own hand. Looking down over her body she saw that the leeches had grown to immense size, engorged with blood; they were monstrous!

“Edward?” she croaked weakly, unable to move her head towards him.

“I cannot move!” he croaked in turn.

“Neither can I.”

The two were breathing very heavily and soon their breathing slowed down even more. The huge leeches were not moving but growing. In the night, no one could come move them off. No one knew where they were but Gisela and Edward. A plan not very well thought through. Thought through in haste, in desperation. Now, a different dimension enclosing.

THE SECRET LIFE OF RANDOLPH JAMES

BY CAROLYN SAULSON

(An Excerpt from 'Living a Lie.")

R**andolph**

His hair was short-cropped and brown; he managed to look like an upwardly mobile thirty-to-thirty-five-year-old Anglo-Saxon Protestant, but who was he really? Not who he was pretending to be. He had been in jail and he'd come from the wrong side of the tracks in a town in Northern California so small and of such ill repute that it seemed ridiculous to have a bad side of town.

What did she say?

Let's meet at which restaurant tonight?

Things were getting too serious.

"Oh well," he thought, "It's another Monday. I need to be at work on time."

So he uncurled his long, thin, pale body from around a pillow and sat up abruptly. He looked over at his old-fashioned alarm clock, noticed that it was about to go off, and sighed. Time to get into gear.

He went to his closet, and took out a very conservative gray three-piece suit, after which he selected an also-conservative tie to match. After gathering his necessities for faking the image he was trying to perpetrate, he took a bath.

His eyesight was nearly perfect, but he preferred the way he looked in glasses, and he wore some sharp, expensive brand that he thought made him look more subtle or intelligent.

Lately, he'd been going by the name Randolph James, of course this wasn't his real name, but he made it work. Looking into the full-length mirror in his bedroom, he forced his body to stand erect, checked his stance.

He wasn't who he was pretending to be.

He was neither white, upwardly mobile, nor Randolph James.

Love

Why had he allowed himself to be seduced into this emotion that threatened to unravel his whole world? Love. If that's what one should call it.

Long ago, he had decided that love was a delusional state necessitated by the overwhelming reality that death was the only outcome to existence. The joke was death. No measures could be taken to prepare for it; after all, who could predict the accident, or murder, even. Too much randomness to process.

So in the back of everyone's mind, he imagined, was the fact that any moment on any day could be their last. How could a self-aware being stay sane? He imagined this all-encompassing simple solution to dark thoughts was the distraction of love and romance—to keep these thoughts at bay, and to continue the human race through families and procreation.

As he daydreamed the improbable, he put in a little discipline and effort and it all made sense; not a bad life, either, unless you had so badly run awry of morality and the law that your fantasy or distraction could never quite be realized. A pinprick to his euphoric bubble.

Oh God, his mind was slipping away again, toward her, even toward marriage. He knew better. What was wrong with him?

Maybe it was because he was almost thirty now. Yes, his age. His body was betraying him, making him give way and yearn for what was dangerous to even think.

"Well, how dangerous," he thought. "I'm not a felon, petty crimes; embarrassment, if I tell the truth. If I must, what is the worst I'd be facing? Rejection?"

Somehow he'd lost track of his beliefs and what was once a convenience had become intrinsic. What was two individuals coming together for fun and sex became a fusion of weakness and incompleteness, and some symbiotic wholeness.

False, thought it may be, his need and his hunger for this illusion of completeness was getting out of control. He could no longer tell reality from illusion. How could he live without her?

He told himself that he was a survivor, and somehow he'd break it off. He'd make an excuse for a fight. She was getting too close. It was that. Or tell her everything.

Impossible! His whole life was a lie! It seemed every lie necessitated another, even more elaborate lie. So far, so good.

But once more, maybe?

No...not even he could manage it.

Or could he?

Mother

When he was thirteen, living in his seventh foster-care situation because of his "moods" or "fits", as his foster parents liked to call them, things weren't going well. In those times he often thought about his mother, Amelia. He wondered where she was and what she might be thinking at any given moment.

At this moment, things weren't going well for her either. His mother was having a more intense version of the same problem. She was having trouble focusing on her daily tasks because she heard voices and was hallucinating. His mother believed that she inherited these genetic "gifts" from her father Jimmy Dee. Being homeless did not help; she often was unable to get a good night's sleep and sometimes her medication got stolen along with her other belongings. She had tried sleeping in local shelters, but she got hassled for being unruly; the men working there seemed to expect deference and sexual favors; it wasn't safe; and nobody seemed to believe her when she complained to social workers, or homeless clinics. Their favorite response was to ask her if she drank or used drugs; she was regularly drug tested then ignored.

Her only sanctuary was found in an alcoholic friend or perhaps boyfriend who sometimes slept in People's Park. He brought her cigarettes and coffee, and watched over her physically at night—when he wasn't too drunk—so that other men didn't bother her or her things. She called him Ben; she knew that wasn't his name, but it was better than calling him has-been, as others tend to do. Ben wasn't always around—he was a party animal and drank profusely. When he ran into some good old boys with enough spirits to get him good and drunk, he would spend the night and part of the next day in a gutter sleeping it off. His drunken unruliness often led to incarceration.

Randolph's mother's life was never without challenge of one type or another, it seemed no matter what measures she took. Could she get off the street and find a way to get him back?

Today she was meeting Ben at a free food program near People's Park, at 8:30 if he remembered. He had promised several days ago, but he hadn't showed up for 2 nights; today they were going to the free clinic to see a doctor.

Amelia watched and waited for Ben. She got into line with the rest of the homeless people thirsty enough and hungry enough to drink bitter coffee without milk or sugar and eat oatmeal overcooked with no margarine, butter, sugar, or milk, and cold to top it off. In walked Ben, and her heart leapt with relief.

The Girlfriend

Randolph could remember the days he dreamt of being included in a meal such as the one he would have with his "girlfriend" and her family. Back then, he was busing tables, always aware of his status, his clothing, his assumed political affiliations, his haircut, and what they insinuated about him and his past or current life. He already had the feeling that there was no way out. The pretentious friends that he had were always looking for weaknesses and had placed him at the bottom of their pecking order; he was already feeling trapped.

Life was not as simple as he had thought. Nothing like "they" said it would be...if you were a "good nigger," you could always work hard, get a decent job and place to live, find acceptance, and work your way up.

He wondered who really believed all that, or was it just a societal justification—like keeping his mom, or anyone else who ever got overwhelmed in life, on psych drugs and "stable" (under control) for the rest of their lives. When he thought of the effects of drugs like lithium, and the patients he'd seen on dialysis as a result, or dying from kidney failure at an early age after being over-medicated...

He put two and two together and decided it was best to hide his so-called condition the best way he could. From his point of view, he was too intense and maybe a bit too imaginative, kindly put: creative...and on the downside, when he was manic, his inventiveness took on some interesting attributes. He was a few steps in front of himself, and others too if he wanted to be and had the resolve to use enough discipline. But back to the problem at hand.

Did he even want a family? Could he take such a step now, or later? Maybe he could placate them? After all, he was a busy man. Needing to take a trip or travel wasn't inconsistent or unreasonable. That would buy him some time to think about the future he might be getting into, or make it easier to get out of it without too many hurt feelings if that is what he decided to do.

The Memory

The smell of the homeless man on the side of the street brought back a memory, but what was it? Somehow he thought of his mother, Amelia, and, as always, he wondered where she was and how she was doing.

In that moment, his mother was in her office. He didn't know that she had managed to graduate school and to finish a partially-accredited law school; he was completely unaware that her heart had been broken because, no matter how she approached it, as a single parent she was unable to get him back.

Things had always been difficult for his mom.

The harshness of homelessness gave no quarter for a young, pregnant girl who couldn't go home.

She had been beaten up more than once. She tried getting involved with teenage runaway organizations but they inevitably asked about her background or tried to get her to put her child up for adoption.

As bad as it was, it was better than what she had run away from: the repeated beatings and sexual assaults from her mother's boyfriend with the threat of death hanging over her head like the sword of Damocles if she told anyone what was going on.

The guys in the park were no better; it is true that they always started off being friendly enough, but when it got cold or food was scarce, the façade ended; they took what they wanted or needed and left her to deal with the pain and fear she felt on her own.

Birthright

Randolph wasn't his name, but he'd been using it for so long now that it made little sense to tell his fiancée, Marjorie, that his real name was James. Named after his grandfather, Jimmy Dee. It didn't make much sense, but that was what he was going to have to do, and soon.

He'd been writing to his birth mother once again, and there had been a lot of talk about reconciliation as of late. How ironic—two things he wanted, seemingly in conflict with one another. How he had yearned for an ordinary life all of these years...and now, two opportunities. An outwardly-normal relationship with Marjorie, or the biological family that had been stolen from him when he was less than a year old?

Perhaps he could have both? Maybe he could start a new family with Marjorie, even have children? But if he did, and also renewed his relationship with his mother, Amelia, he'd have to come clean about a number of things.

Although Randolph himself was white passing, he knew damned well that the man he was named after was a black man. James Rodney Daniels, or Jimmy D. And while he had been given Amelia's last name, Ferguson, at birth, he knew his middle name was Daniel. James Daniel Ferguson. Jimmy Dee Ferguson. Jimmy D Junior.

That's what Amelia and her grandmother, Jimmy Dee's mother, Sally Mae Daniels, used to call him as an infant. Jimmy Dee Junior.

Maybe if Sally Mae had lived to see his first birthday, Amelia could have stayed in housing and Randolph wouldn't have ended up in foster care. Maybe if she had severed her parental rights voluntarily instead of trying to get him back for a few years, some nice couple who wanted a white baby would have adopted him as a toddler, pretended he was white—the way the Johnson family did when he was in their foster care as a teenager and they didn't want to get any shit from their neighbors.

Then, he'd still be Jimmy Dee Junior.

Not Randolph Cavanaugh, the latest in a long series of pseudonyms he used for convincing nice young ladies and sometimes not-so-young ladies like Marjorie Brentwood that he was an up and coming lawyer with a high-heeled lifestyle at an obscure law firm and larger pay grade than they. These ladies were free with the spending, and their wallets might dry up if they knew he was a thirty-year-old former waiter whose closest relationship to law school was performing as a lawyer in a Berkeley Repertory Theater production of *Merchant of Venice*.

A quarter blood quantum of African genetic heritage, a.k.a. quadroon, wasn't the only birthright Randolph inherited from his maternal grandfather. Neither was his name. Like his mother, Amelia, he'd inherited Jimmy's bipolar disorder and his mood swings.

He'd also inherited his psychic powers.

Not everyone understood properly his mental abilities. Like his mother, he had a smooth way with people, an ability to talk them into almost anything. One might easily conflate these with the simple manipulations any con man was capable of, but it was more.

A form of telepathy he could use to influence minds.

Jedi mind tricks.

But his doctor assured him this was untrue. He was basically insane.

The Andersons

As for Marjorie Anderson—she could never know who he really was. Poor. Uneducated. A quarter black. Out of foster care. While not exactly a person who swindled women, Randolph was known for befriending those who were economically generous and more than often a bit lonely—older women, widows looking for a second chance with open pocket books they used to fuel his playboy lifestyle.

Her parents would surely never allow the marriage if they found out.

Marjorie's parents were never openly bigoted against black people—no one in the Bay Area ever really was—but they made little snide comments whenever they ate fancy meals out at the Ethiopian place that let Randolph know how they really felt. Ethiopians, Indians, and Thai people were great, as long as they stayed in their place, which was usually in the kitchen, or behind the desk at some fancy spa white folks attended, or in a dress or spice store offering things that the upper crust and the upwardly mobile needed to perpetrate an image of superficial liberality.

Although Marjorie herself claimed to be an independent, having lobbied with equal vigor for Ron Paul and Bernie Sanders, both of her parents were Reagan Republicans. Horrified by the nude model First Lady Melania Trump, disgusted by Barrack Obama's progressive reforms such as support of gay marriage, and horrified by his public identification with Travyon Martin.

The Andersons were well to do—a real estate mogul with a chain of local hotels to his name and his charming wife, an optometrist he met while she was working. He babbled on at parties over his usual one-drink-over-the-line champagne glass about how he met her when she fitted him for glasses. Sherry Anderson was UC-educated, charming, and professional. Joe Anderson was self-made, one of those guys who listened to a ton of self-actualization tapes by various inspirational speakers and attended real estate seminars until he flipped property after property and jetted his way out of his boring office job into a stellar career, first as a real estate developer, then a professional rent collector with a string of rental properties and hotels.

In a way, Randolph and Joe were a lot alike: likeable, outgoing, and able to sell swamp water to crocodiles. But Joe had a B.A. in English and had been working as a professional administrative assistant, considering following in his parent's footsteps as an English professor, when he started flipping houses and forging his own path instead.

He hated homeless people even more than he hated Melania Trump. Not that he hadn't voted for her husband while crying into his morning coffee about how great the Bushes had been and how the mighty Republican Party had fallen. He'd been a proud, gun-owning, country-club-joining, deer-shooting member of the GOP for three decades now.

Randolph was beginning to develop a headache.

How much telepathic energy would it take to convince Mr. Anderson that he was a lawyer? Would he have to keep up his Jedi mind tricks indefinitely in order to get past the engagement?

His future father-in-law was insufferable. Randolph began to wonder if he had enough mind-power to change the man's politics. Bored and pensive, he began to quietly fantasize about exerting enough mind control to turn Joe Anderson into the Manchurian Candidate, while the good old boy bragged about shaking hands with Ronald Reagan and playing cards with Tricky Dick Nixon.

ADUALITY {0≠2;1=108}

BY SERUUS UALERIUM TRISTISSIMA LIBER

AN EXCERPT FROM A WORK IN PROGRESS...

She's saved my life dozens of times with it by now, but that Associations-damned giggle of the captain's still grates on me. It's not even the sound of it so much anymore, but the immediate image that flicks its way across my brain, the conditioned response. I'm not even looking at her at the moment, and I can see her wide-blinking pink eyes, devoid of concentrated furrow context, finger twiddling bright blonde hair. At least her great-grandmother had chosen an interesting eye color for her genetic strain to carry.

"You'll just have to refuse the job, Captain Ulysses."

I'm sure that I'm showing the strain of keeping my voice unirritated—in my hands, posture, and fidgeting feet— but it's the tone of my voice that matters.

The lights glare and whine in a slight crescendo, warning me that the effort is costing me. I pull up a diagnostic in my AR; nothing about their current, luminosity, or functioning has changed in the last twenty minutes. It's confirmed, then. I sigh, just to convince my muscles to relax.

"Dove can't power the Electrical Messiah with me in eir condition, and I'm supposed to attend the Union Tent on Franklin Prime to get trained in emergency solo operations a month from now. As in the future, as in I'ven't yet."

I watch the ripple of facial changes spreading from that statement.

Shit. I bet those are looks of disapproval; I must have mouthed off to the captain again. Luckily, she herself is oblivious, as always. I wince as the light becomes distracting, and my back curls seed-like as my abs try to pull me into myself. I need to go, now.

"Your face just went flat," speaks First Officer Grippe, absent-mindedly flipping green-and-purple hair back over zir head while bent over the sewing that kept zem busy during these meetings, "and I see those muscles working, Awiti. Problem is, we think this job comes from the Company."

A hush claims the dining table of our tiny little semi-criminal starship, the entire crew quiet for once. The Company kept plans within plans, and never let even the smallest risk to humanity stand for long. Rumors claimed that they offer their jobs to very specific crews for very specific reasons, and that to refuse them is to be a risk to humanity.

The problem is thinking only moderately. If your crew never thinks deeply about their jobs, where they come from, and what they mean, then the Company's black-jumpsuited agents will have no problem making sure that you would do what they wanted you to do. On the other hand, if the meaning of your jobs is a constant riddle probed by a deep-thinking crew, they'll be able to identify the faint clues that indicate that they have less choice than they think, and will be able to decide to save their lives. It is only those who think enough to question but not enough to notice what they see who are in danger.

My overwhelm building, I can't modulate my volume very well. "But we've only a single Unionist, and I'm useless alone!" Great. Now Ship's Ecologist Brazil is backing away from me, taking refuge in the door frame vacated by its barrier with a soft woosh. He doesn't really do well with loudness; ironic, really, considering the rough-weave-clad man had fled a planet clanging with constant advertisement.

A giggle ~ that giggle ~ answers like an unseasonal summer rain, quiet slipping its way into sleeping dust. "Like, I can totally do it."

Noöpilot Paramhamsa is still new to the crew, and insufferable. Bending slightly from the bottom of his rib cage, he looses his creakily-refined voice: "Christmasing yourself demoted, then, Cap?"

A raspberry blown from a young mouth answers his retort, eliciting an indulgent chuckle from the trench-coated queen of a man. It comes from a small girl whose pink eyes, thin and floating atop impossibly high cheekbones, power-clashed quite nicely with the hummingbird colors of her hair, shock of red bright against rainbow-glinting green.

"You wouldn't have a ship to fly if it wasn't for my mom!"

"That, you're true, Doll." He knelt to look Doll in the eyes, his upper body never changing shape. "That you're for certain true, small friend."

I begin to flex my hand, hard fist to splayed star of fingers trying to escape each other to dawn-smoked umber skin stretched bone over knuckles to as big a circle as my five fingertips could spread and back again, repeating in simple rhythm, rhythm slower than my breath. My brain sunk into the tendons and cartilage of my phalanges, I almost miss First Officer Grippe's comment. "No, wait, that actually could work."

"Jaomai, how?" demands New Mary Desiderry, slick and polished despite the industrial mess that clung to him occupationally, hair agleam with constant brushing. "She's not a Unionist! I love her, but she's a glorified ideal of a slave-wife who managed to wiggle free of her planet's patriarchy despite them trying to kill her for it, not a Unionist trained by the Guild to raise and direct orgone in conversation with the Spirit Association of Benevolence!"

"But that self-same patriarchy had a vested interest in making sure she knew how to fuck well, Seligman—"

"It was, like, the only schooling," Captain Ulysses interrupts her spouse with another of those incessant giggles, "I was, like, allowed."

"Exactly, my sweetly-beloved cunt. And that schooling included techniques derived from those the Guild teaches. I've seen both standard Unionist practices and what Toy does myself, up close and personal, and there is indeed a lot of crossover."

Ome-Mazatli-Miquiztli, Esquire, asks through a mouth of tortilla wrapped around spicy honey-candied cactus (her favorite dessert), "We're talking five days here, though. The Guild spends a lot of money and effort heavily modifying Unionists' bodies for endurance, stamina, ability to produce and maintain high levels of sex hormones and neurotransmitters for extended periods, responsiveness, and many more qualities in order to allow them to do this work."

"Ummmm, like, I don't know what all that means," another giggle, this time with a bounce, "but, like, my ances . . . umm, ansis . . . like, my mom's mom's moms made sure that we would, like, always be ready to serve however we were meant to. My name is, ummmm, Toy, so I was, like, sposeta be used as a toy. For fucking. So it's, ummm, kinda like what they do to Unionists, I guess?"

"Why are you looking at me to confirm?" First Officer Grippe snaps at the crew. "Toy knows her own body as well as you do, genetically engineered brain or no. What do you think, Awiti? Can you make it work with your captain as your partner?"

A diaphragmatic sigh rocks my body. "Do we ever have a choice? I guess I'll have to try."

"Like, yay!" A torrent of giggles glitters poundingly on my ears, complete with bouncing—at least her petite clapping was rhythmic. "You're, like, dismissed. Do what you, like, need to do to, like, calm your body down, okay? And then, like, figure out what we need to do. Meeting, like, totally over."

She stands there, twirling her hair, blinking over-large eyes at the copper and zinc machine which seems stark against the matte persimmon of the brushed metal wall behind it. I know the feeling. I remember with typically-perfect accuracy the first time I met the machine, which sits unfazed across the room from Captain Toy

Ulysses, survivor and instigator of the Lover's Quarrel, doomed to the freedom she desired. Its waist stretches out like the four elegant corners of a large table, the only languorously simple bit of the New Motive Power, the Electric Messiah. The legs beneath angle in with a slight bulging curve and are meticulously scrolled with writhing bodies, gender and even species getting lost somewhere amid their quiet frenzy, giving metal the appearance of warm and salty flesh.

An outline of a rectangle, like a hexagon pulled upwards, formed by two metallic rods rising until they are connected at the top by a revolving steel shaft which supports a crosswise arm of harsh steel, reaches up from the table surface. Two large square-bottomed pyramids of epoxy resin and metal shavings contain magnets and dangle from this arm's two extremes. Under each is that very curiously constructed fixture which so casually fascinates the eye, a sort of shallow oval bowl, formed of a peculiar layering of magnets, wood, and metals, filled with water, and above that a number of zinc and copper plates, alternately arranged; the two serve as orgonic and electric reservoirs, respectively. These are supplied with lofty metallic attractors that reach gracefully upward. As with most ships, various metallic bars, plates, wires, magnets, insulating substances, peculiar chemical compounds, etc., adorn our Electric Messiah according to the doting arcane nuances of our New Mary's incessant tinkering. At certain points around the circumference of these structures, and connected with the center, more pyramids hang alternating with small, steel, magnet-enclosing balls. A balloon structure hanging between the table legs inhales and respires gently, like the chest of a sleeping lover, growing to delicious size and then lazily draining air into the rest of the machine.

I feel myself begin to be aroused, blood rushing to my cheeks and sensitive bits, the invisible shift as my cardigan accommodates tightening breasts and assertive nipples, the muscles of my hips and legs loosening. My dress worries me, as my trinket presses against it, ruining the line of its fall past my hips; I no longer feel the hem along the front of my thigh. I wiggle my toes—a ritual of sensuous anticipation—and a giggle interrupts my enjoyment of the precision with which this ship part was made.

"Ummmm, okay, so how do we start?"

"I usually start with a moment of appreciation of the well-made machine we'll be powering, Captain. Gets me in the mood, as it were. That being said, I suppose it's time to engage with you."

She prances closer, steps too quick for me to track, and suddenly all I can feel is the sticky slipperiness of her latex, pink with her considerable features offered with pale blue outlines, as our closeness presses its bulges against me in ways both random and predictable.

My hand somehow finds itself swimming through her blonde hair, so wavy and full it might be froth. "And then, like, what?" Her breath smells of flowers and the musky, moist dirt from which they grow.

A tightening finds itself in my fingers, gripping her head from the back and dropping, inch by inch. Her knees bend and, upon the slightest caress of the floor, splay. More smells accompany quiet moans as her excitement leaves the psychological behind and exudes from her body. I manage eye contact as I reached over to press the button letting Noöpilot Paramhamsa know that he can start telling his steering story.

Now it is my turn to break the moment, as that notification calls all the usual AR readouts and graphs to crowd the negative space around my captain. I blink them away with a shake of my head, unable to deal with that much information in such an unfamiliar mindspace, and whatever had come over me, that self-same mental state I had hoped to protect, dissipates.

Panic. A racing of the brain neurons that seems too heavy to move, a paradoxical metaphor. The lights hum and the floor flashes. I am aware of each cell of my skin and its unique experience of clothing, and of an oddly comfortable giggling. My muscles want to move but have forgotten the six directions.

Cold air sharp on my trinket is followed by the scratchy softness of a tongue creeping up its length. The point of a chin poking the pillowed organ beneath it. There is no envelopment in this, no gulping or pulling, just a calling forth (giggled vibrato pressed up against my pelvis sending heavy pressure through all my joints) to which I rise. A shuddering breath pushes my eyes open with the feeble strength of the wisps of muscles clinging to my ribs, rather than the force of my lungs.

Captain Ulysses sits back on her heels, steadying me and maybe herself against the backs of my knees with meticulously-maintained nails. My trinket peeks as if from genital curiosity from beneath the soft cloth that once hid it. She waits, patient, permissive, unable to even comprehend that something might be wrong.

Maybe her ancestral gene-tampering wasn't such a cruelty as the rest of us think.

I squat, taking her hands from my knees to my shoulders. Unready for eye contact to resume, I let her lips take my full attention. Plump and shining with gloss, they seem to have more in common with overstuffed vinyl cushions than flesh. She is plastic and she is free.

My own brain turns itself off, my lips tugging the rest of my body forward, mashing against hers with unprecedented fervor, tongue darting out and then hiding back in its toothed pocket. I give myself over to hormone-driven momentum and jackknife my legs open, right hand grabbing my captain by the throat and the left stretching vanguard to catch the wall I was propelling us toward. The length of her body is pressed between the stretch of mine and that persimmon-colored metal that squeaks beneath my fingers as I bury my mouth in hers. Certain of the sustainability of our verticality, I slip my left hand to the bubble of her butt. Just below, actually, to the unclad spot where the muscle of the thigh shrugs off the fat of the ass, but the texture of flesh feels wrong. A couple of inches upward and plastic pleases. I grip and knead and need, and the small husky cords among my vocals begin to plead in words that are not quite gasps and not quite moans.

Captain Ulysses' arm brushes mine as she lifts hers to point, pulling my mouth behind my eyes and off of hers. A slight pulsatory and vibratory motion can be seen in the pendants around the periphery of the Electric Messiah. "That just means it's working, Captain. We're doing a good job."

"We are?"

"Yes. You're a good girl." This is met with a happy giggle that invites me to mentally run through all the sociological information about Kore's Retreat I'd found in the ship's databases. Eager to be a reason for her to feel pleasure, I seek culturally appropriate ways to raise the orgone. "Well, maybe ~ what makes a good girl?" A crinkling of the brow, a slight fear in the eyes resonating with the flutter in my chest. Against all odds, we are syncing, without struggle or awkwardness. My hours of study worked!

"Doing what I'm told?"

I throw her into the pillowed pit in the center of the room, fuchsia and ruby cushions swallowing her like candy still in the shiny wrapper. "Get up." She does, and I am shocked at the grace. "And?"

"Ummmm...Always being on display?"

"Press that blue button on the wall next to you."

She complies, twittering as feet float off the floor.

"And?"

"Like, being dumb?"

The bottom half of my face transmogrifies into an unfamiliar smile. Plush fabric bubbles begin to fall upwards like slow-moving sakura. Captain Ulysses' feet begin to drift apart in the absence of gravity and floor's friction, making a wishbone of her legs and rolling her skirt into a belt. Well, more of one. "Right! That's a good girl, which you most certainly are."

I wish I sounded more like I believed it, but blame it on the queasiness the suddenness of zero-gee always brought on. Once again, she has no idea anything is wrong. Biologically-enforced no-mind is a wonderful thing. Wet glistening provides matching contrast to latex shine as she slowly revolves, her waist an axle. My mouth waters and I dive.

She tastes rich—spiced must and good olive oil, complete with that masochistic burning freshness at the back of the throat. Jammy, silky, and oaked, I drink her like a fine wine. Like an eager dog drinking fine wine, that is—I use my nose as much as my lapping tongue, wagging my head back and forth to flick her clitoris with its tip and distort the words I am writing upon her lower lips in overlapping salivary letters.

We spin slowly, lost in these complexities until she convulses with a gasp, slicing her body folded. My ears become handles as she slathers her body with my skin, squeezing arms and legs around my body to stop my emergence where she wants me. I thrust my pelvis back to change our momentum and then breath explodes from me as we bounce against the ceiling. I hear her moan.

A seed-like curl brings her steaming wetness dragging along the length of my trinket, sending sensory overload blazing through my body. I wonder if she studied like I did or had an AR HUD giving her predictive heuristics like I do—somehow she knows not to fill herself with my trinket, that this would raise my orgone but the resultant gender-freakout would ground the ship as there'd be no way to power the Electric Messiah after that. But she can't even read: her brain never grew the specific neuronal pattern to process visual information that way.

Leaning back, Captain Ulysses uses one hand to plop her large breasts over the top of her neckline, struggling against her dress's tightness to make them all the more available. Her heart-shaped nipples are a vibrant red painted beneath her pale skin. This moment of breath allows me the time to process the fact that my overwhelm has passed by. I bring my HUD back and check where we were in the orgonic generation process, and how that matches up to Noöpilot Paramhamsa's progress in attaching our von Neumann hook to the Casey Jones Effect. Crap. We are about to miss the simultaneity point. This needs to get fixed fast.

I grab Captain Ulysses' ass and hurl up with all my strength, spinning her again, this time quickly, like the flywheel on an engine, carrying myself around as well. Hands on the floor arrest my motion and with as much speed as I can achieve I scuttle backwards to where I know she will be. An oof brings her fingernails scraping across my now-bare belly. Ah, there it is, sweetly aggressive growl lurking in my throat, “Take me, Captain.”

Toy shoves my hips straight down, flapping one arm out to hit that blue button. Gravity empties my breath in one firm pound and my breasts jiggle from the impact of her fingers, firm flutter finding each hidden parcel of nerves, scraping firm nipples. My trinket strains with rhythmic blows that squeeze it between our bodies, growing harder and more tender with each beat. Teeth like panicked butterfly wings nibble my windpipe like she could swallow all my polysyllabic words, make my speech simpler and hers more complex, like this union of bodies could make communication possible between what too often seem like our two separate species.

Like this family of a crew could finally cure each other’s loneliness.

Her ministrations twist my spine into an arch that doesn’t know whether it is going to the left or right and screws my eyes so tightly shut that new landscapes of light burst against the blackness of their constriction. My mouth can only open in a soundless forever gasp, a guppy-shocked inhalation that leaks whimpers across the eggplant-colored floor. It seems to feel too good, like the lightning that flashes across my neurons is going to light my serotonin on fire, ignite my oxytocin, flash-electrolyze all my dopamine in an explosion of thoughts dissolved into flesh.

Suddenly, everything ceases. Cool, dry air caresses my skin rather than moist warmth. Cautiously, I open my eyes after a moment passes, just in time to see that Captain Ulysses has discovered the toy rack in the wall. Finger cutely tapping chin, she gyrates up and down to investigate her options, lingering on each toy that catches her eye while I make a game of running my fingers up and down my trinket in the same exploratory motions as hers.

That is when the shift happens, the moment when the starship and everything in it is transmuted by the noetic drive, twisted from physical space into storyspace. As we’ve both witnessed many times, the other person grows both more individual and self-defined and more iconic, distilled into a unique archetype that feels somehow symbolic of large groups of people. We become two communities fucking in intertwined narrative styles, Freytag's pyramid inserting itself into kishoutenketsu, syuzhet dilating its ring structure so nivolas could enter.

Our journey, always the same five days in length from our perspective, has begun.

DARK DJEMBE: DRUM OF THE DAMNED

BY SUMIKO SAULSON

Ginnie Evans feared the drum. Sure, all of the Evans women used the drum. Each awakened to her powers on the night of her thirteenth birthday. But there was a price to pay for that awakening. Each girl had to learn the day and the manner of her own death! That concession to the gods of fate was sometimes a painful one. It had been for her baby sister, Mary Evans, who upon her thirteenth birthday learned that she would only have four and a half years left to live and that she would die in childbirth. She also foretold other deaths that night.

Mary's first vision struck her with the force of a freight train, rattling the entire house. Everyone knew something was dreadfully wrong. While the young girl pounded on the drum, Mary spoke in tongues of her vision. She incanted, eyes wide and vacant, the irises and pupils rolled back behind her head so only the whites showed. Mary screamed a high keening noise like a wounded animal before collapsing on the hardwood floor, unconscious.

The next morning, Mary wandered around in a zombie-like daze. Ginnie could still smell hot metal on the stove that morning, burning hair as her grandmother Lacey leaned over her with the hot comb. Grandma just kept straightening Ginnie's hair as though nothing were wrong as the mesmerized Mary headed straight for the drum, thumping it.

"Don't touch that cursed thing!" Ginnie cried, snatching Mary's hand by the wrist. But woe unto her! The hand, raised mid-strike, finished its arc coursing toward the drum. It struck, and Ginnie saw her sister's blood-soaked visions telepathically transmitted to her own mind.

A white woman screamed and cried as a bullet pierced her husband's flesh. A crowd screamed. A bearded man of gaunt appearance and unusual height collapsed in a theater. Across the country that night, a train derailed, a bearded black man in a stovepipe hat caught in its wheels dragged bleeding along the rails in a screeching hail of sparks, the stink of hot oil burning against metal when the brakes failed to engage in time to stop from running him over. Another woman screamed in childbirth, a child born inhaling her first breath, her young mother her last. Ginnie's eyes turned to take in the image of the woman—her sister, bleeding to death of hemorrhage in childbirth.

Mary was never the same after the ceremony. A ragged wraith of a girl, she wandered their home wide-eyed and vacuous like a dead spirit. She ate, slept, and did little else but pound on that blasted drum. Touch her, and the visions would come upon you. Leave her untouched and she'd make any number of predictions in a terror-haze, speaking in tongues. Sometimes the preachers came by to pray over her. Other days, witch doctors burned candles and shook gris-gris at the thing that used to be her sister. Often, Ginnie wondered if her sister were some sort of arisen undead creature. Undead or not, she produced life. Her swelling belly reminded everyone that she was destined to die in childbirth. That was why Granny never married her, but she was pregnant anyway. Was it one of these ministers or shaman who made Mary pregnant one day? Was it little Jonny who bought the wood for the fires? Perhaps it was the storekeeper who always seemed to have an extra jar of milk for her. Who knew?

It went on that way until the day President Abraham Lincoln died, a woman named Mary Todd screaming as he collapsed to the floor. These moments happened in sequence, although only Ginnie knew and saw. A train derailed and plowed into a building owned by Grandma Lacey's plantation-owning, white-passing half-brothers… dragging the corpse of a freed black man trapped in its wheels. Then Mary died in a pool of blood while Grandma Lacey gently plucked the infant, Anise, from her mother's arms and smacked it across the rear. The gray baby warmed up and breathed deep, ashy skin rising baked-bread brown. Mary inhaled her last breath as her daughter took in her first. Only when her body fell, cold and lifeless did Mary drop from her hand that which was clutched in her fingers…a leather-headed wooden drum, the djembe.

And so, Ginnie always hated that drum.

Her little sister had died April 15, 1863. Thirteen years ago. So today, April 15, 1876 was her daughter Anise's birthday. Everyone called the child Niecey. With Mary dead, Niecey's aunt Ginnie was left to instruct her on how to wield the djembe—a drum that was both a powerful divination tool and a weapon. If she could have, Ginnie would have avoided passing it on altogether. Her grandmother passed it on to her, and with grandma gone, she'd tried to just dump the drum. Like so many hexed objects, the damned thing just kept popping up. She had no real choice but to pass it on. But such a gift couldn't be passed on without a warning.

"Let me tell you about the night your grandma Lacey died," Ginnie droned on, calmly applying grease to young Niecey's ears to prevent any accidental hot comb burns. "It was a historical night, you know. Juneteenth, they call it. June 19, 1865. That was the day they finally freed the slaves in Texas."

Her eyes darkened appropriately as she gave Niecey a poignant stare. "It was on that very day that they dragged the old witch Lacey Evans from her home and set her to burn at the stake!"

"I already heard that nasty old story," Niecey snapped. "No one wants to hear that nonsense." Annoyed, Ginnie yanked the hot comb she was dragging though niece's thick mane.

"Don't sass me, girl!" The child flinched and tried to wiggle away, but Aunt Ginnie pinned her down by the shoulder and grabbed another handful of pig's lard from the Mason jar on the stove. Hot gray smoke rose up from the steel comb, laden with the stench of old bacon grease and incinerated hair. "Ouch! Be careful now, Auntie!" The heat from the red hot iron straightening comb landed less than an inch away from her previously scalded earlobe.

"All of us who were there to bear witness to it remember it well," Ginnie droned on, her familiar litany filling the hardwood cabin's crusty little kitchen. "As many a freed slave gathered around bonfires to celebrate, your Uncle Charlie's old washboard and jug band started in with the songs he learned out West during the gold rush."

Niecey rolled her eyes, kicking the stove door lightly with her bare toes. Paying no mind, Ginnie continued. "There was a hoop and a holler from Lady Bertha, who always sang so golden in our church choir. She belted out the first few lines of *Go Down Moses*, and everyone from far and wide gathered round to hear her deep-down earth-rumbling tenor."

Niecey stifled a yawn and started fiddling with the tulle underskirt beneath the stiff hem of her formal Easter dress. Easter wasn't the only Spring party these fancy gowns were occasion for around here, and today she wore it as a birthday dress. Aunt Ginnie was in full form now, gesturing wildly with the hot comb like a conductor issuing instructions to an invisible band. "And then the sopranos and altos from the church choir started up!" she belted. "Soapside Sam brought out his fancy new guitar, the sweet silver twelve-string with the steam amplifier. Junkyard Joey lit up the place with that homemade fiddle of his. And that's when we knew it was a party."

"I just love, loooove, Uncle Charlie's band!" Niecey lied as convincingly as possible. "Can you play the stereograph of Uncle Charlie's Jug Band from the Barbary Coast in 'Frisco? I sure would love to hear it just now, for my birthday," she begged, hoping to end the boring old story. To no avail, as Aunt Ginne chattered on, barely stopping long enough to breath.

Niecey was excited as today was her thirteenth birthday. The church would administer the sacrament of Confirmation later tonight in her fancy Easter dress. Before this could occur, her Aunt

Ginnie insisted that she perform some other secret rite with the djembe. It was boring, and didn't involve all of her school friends, a fancy dress, and a party afterward where she was assured there would be yellow cake with lemon frosting.

Her Christian name was Anise Louise Evans. Ginnie's was Virginia Mae Evans. But nobody really used such names here in Freedom River, Texas, except for church folks on Sunday and the mortuary service on your tombstone. A small settlement outside of Austin off the Colorado River, it was established just after the Civil War by Brynn Evans, the unmarried sister of plantation owners Andrew Evans and Delwyn Evans, Junior. Those Christian names would be on her confirmation certificate, though...along with her mother's, Mary Josephine Evans. Ginnie was her adopted mother officially, but she still called her auntie.

"Can we just finish the stories and go to church already?" Niecey whined, dreaming of lemon frosting. "I heard the yellow cake will have buttercream frosting between the layers, and then lemon cream on top, and decorations in buttercream and lemon custard. It will match my dress perfectly, so even if I drop some cake on it, no one will probably see it."

"Why, no, child, no!" Ginnie chided. "It is the day of your awakening, as well you know it. And you shall hear all of the old stories, not just what you think you know, young witchling! The Confirmation ceremony can wait!"

"Fine," Niecey sighed, kicking at the tin bucket near her foot, where Ginnie kept the water to cool the iron if it got too red hot, just hard enough to make an annoying noise—*tack*, *tack*, *tack*. She didn't want to get in trouble for spilling it, but she scowled and daydreamed about kicking it really hard—hard enough to spill the greasy, lukewarm water all over Aunt Ginnie's nice, clean floor. The thought made her smirk.

Ginnie grimaced when she saw that, and kicked the unruly girl on the shin before continuing. "Then good old Luke from Jameson Farms came out with a wheelbarrow full of pork ribs and chicken thighs..."

Blah, blah, blah...so boring! Niecey began to tune most of it out. If thoughts could punch people, Niecey would have slapped the crap out of Aunt Ginnie for forcing her to sit through this boring story.

"Are you paying attention?" Aunt Ginnie asked, catching her by surprise. Fortunately, Niecey already knew it by heart. "Yes, ma'am, yes...you were saying that my great-grandmother Lacey didn't know that her half-brothers Delwyn and Andrew were cooking up a barbecue of their *own*," Niecey intoned portentously, all of the spooky vibrato on the word *own*, just like Aunt Ginnie when she told it. To make sure she knew this wasn't the first time she'd heard the story...or the tenth, or even the twentieth.

"Yes, yes!" Ginnie scowled. "So why don't you tell the story, then... since you know so much. Then you can just start pounding on that magic drum you're inheriting right away. Let the gift run through your fingers, child. You need no training. Thirteen years on the Earth and already, you are a wise woman, with a gift you need no training to use!" Ginnie really didn't want to give her the damned drum at all.

"I'm sorry, auntie," the little girl sighed, sufficiently chastened to lower her head and silence herself for a full fifteen minutes. Finally her auntie finished.

"So, pick up the drum, then, child..." she sighed.

Niecey bent down to pick it up. Then she sat upright in an uncomfortable straight-backed chair by the fireplace, the magical drum, djembe, cradled in her lap. Hardwood brushed against the inside of her bare foot, cocked up on one knee. Her other scrawny nutmeg-colored leg dangled down to the floor, toe scratching nervously at the dust on the cold mud floor of her aunt Ginnie's pinewood cabin. Ginnie's eyes were as bright as the coals on the old iron stove.

"All I have told you so far, you know. Sit and listen, then, child, as I tell you the secret and dark legacy of the killing drum you hold cradled in your lap. Run your finger gently under the hardened leather at its lip. Below it, dug into the wooden kettle, find the carved Welsh incantation left by your great-grand-aunt Brynn Evans for her half sister, your grandmother, Lacey Evans, back in 1814," Ginnie whispered heavily, stoking the coals with the hot iron, her eyes distant and unaware.

Pastor Leon Mathews at Freedom River Baptist Church would have been having conniption fits if he knew what old aunt Ginnie was up to. Good Christians practiced neither African Animism nor did they worship Welsh gods. The magic-imbued djembe wasn't just for the purpose of divination, as her African forebears intended it to be. Thanks to the Welsh inscriptions carved into it by Brynn Evans, it could also call up Mallt-y-Nos, Matilda of the Night, a Welsh demon able to control beasts known as Cŵn Mamau, or the Hounds of Hell.

"Lacey Evans was sixty-five years old by the time freedom came to Texas," Ginnie whispered huskily, shoving the iron comb into the hot burning coals on the stove. A wild arc of sparks lit up the air around her like fireflies. In front of her, Niecey sat, softly tapping the drum in a steady rhythm that soon became a crescendo. Every word the older Evans woman spat out was punctuated by the hard slap of a soft young hand against the hardened leather.

"Freedom for Lacey came at a price," Ginnie pronounced. "She lived free only six hours before her father's heirs Delwyn Junior and James Evans came for her. Grandma Lacey was here in this very kitchen, cooking up a big pot of collard greens for the picnic, when they showed up on their horses. You were just three months old when it happened, but I assure you that you were not born a free woman. Neither did the hate of hundreds of years of slavery magically disappear in a day when that foul and heinous institution came to its bitter end. That end came in a slow and quarrelsome drawn-out death rattle, and the smell of its overripe corpse haunts this town just like your great-grandmother Lacey haunts the drum that you hold."

"Yes..." Niecey whispered huskily, vacant eyes cast far afield in a thousand-mile stare. "The Evans brothers dragged Lacey away and burned her at the stake in the middle of the town. She saw it happen the first time she played the drum, and it were cursed. And like her, I will see the time of my death this very night." The thought should have terrified her, but her mind was far away now. Niecey watched from somewhere overhead as her body, detached from its soul, pounded away at the drum.

"While their older sister Brynn stood and watched," Ginnie hissed, unaware of Niecey's psychic peril. "The two were very close, you see. Brynn Evans was Delwyn's eldest daughter, seventy years old at the time. Some claimed that his sons, Delwyn Junior and Andrew, were born to Brynn's mother Sally Mae Evans and that she died in childbirth with the younger one, Andrew. Everyone living in that home knew it was a lie. Sally was so torn after the birth of her first that she never had another child after Brynn. Brynn was thirteen when Junior was born and sixteen when Andrew followed. They were the product of incest between Delywn and his own daughter. After Junior was born, they say, Sally and her husband got into a screaming match all the slaves heard. 'You have your damned heir!' she cried. 'The blasted son you always wanted. So don't touch my beautiful daughter ever again!'

"And she thought he was done messing with Brynn," Ginnie lectured on. Speaking was easy now that her niece was so taken with the drum. She stopped interjecting, instead sitting wide-eyed with wonder as she caressed the rough skin of the magical djembe between her rough fingers. "Until Andrew was born and she knew right then and there that Brynn wasn't just putting on a little weight. Delywn strangled Sally with his own hands when she found out what he'd done to her daughter. And when her family came out for the funeral, he pretended the child was Sally's.

"They stayed a while to help raise the children and keep an eye on creepy Delwyn. That's why he laid off Brynn and started in on Lacey. And so, the sisters Evan did the old man in. I tell you this because it has been my sworn duty as your guardian to care for you and instruct you in all womanly ways. And now that your thirteenth year is upon you, it is important for you to learn of all womanly things and how to protect yourself in a world that hates and uses women, especially women who are born to slaves.

"Brynn's Uncle David took over the farm and raised the two boys," Niecey relayed, "and he tried to marry poor Brynn off. But then,

Brynn, who was twenty, told him that those were her sons not her mother's, and that she was likely to tell it if she was forced to marry. And so he quietly granted her a plot of land here at Freedom River and signed her own sister and nephew to her as property. Brynn freed Lacey and Jimmy, and the three of them lived here peaceably until that Juneteenth. Until they came for Jimmy and his children, afraid that the abolition of slavery gave their little half-brother some claim to their land.

"Blood..." Ginnie spat at the girl, turning steely eyes on the squirming child until she held herself still. "Blood begets blood, and the hate blood has for blood is the legacy of those of us born to slaves and begot by slave owners. Born into hate and of hate was your mulatto great-grandmother Lacey Evans, who, with her white sister Brynn Evans, cursed the drum in your lap. It was their hate that killed their father Delwyn. But it was love that caused Brynn Evans to strike down her own twin sons Delywn Junior and Andrew on Juneteenth, and leave all their estates to her black nephew James and so establish Freedom River, Texas."

"I thought this drum could tell the future," Niecey sulked, running her fingers over the rawhide head of the djembe. "I thought that it told great-grandma Lacey the day and the very hour freedom would come to Texas. I thought it told the future, but all you ever talk about is the past."

"And they burned her for it!" Ginnie screamed. "They burned your great-grandmother alive while her sister Brynn watched in horror. Only her race kept them from burning her as well for they never knew she was their mother. Not as though Brynn wasn't in danger—even white women can burn for the craft. The world is dangerous for women of the craft. Sweet child, innocent and sheltered child, you must know that with every fiber of your being. I was there when my grandmother burned, holding you in my arms. The smell of her flesh and hair at the stake was as real as this pig fat and the brush singeing the hair on your spoiled little head.

"And Brynn was also the subject of rumors—living alone as she did with her father's inheritance and her black sister Lacey and her black nephew Jimmy. My father, James Evans, was so pale that, upon his birth, it was immediately known to all who mattered that he was the son of his own grandfather, the wicked Delwyn. Delwyn died six months before Jimmy was born. The townsfolk believed that the two girls conspired to murder him. No one could prove it because they used the magic drum, the one that is in your hand.

"Powerful magic. It is that magic which protected this household from the wicked Evans brothers for years, magic that predicted their arrival. That magic which made it so Grandpa Jimmy knew to hide in plain sight, standing in front of his very own brothers, claiming Brynn as his mother!" Niecey swore fiercely, stroking the drum affectionately. "Passing for white while you, his daughter, stood there, claiming to be your grandmother's daughter and swearing up and down that there were only girls and none to inherit. And so we were free, but the dark magic of the drum had come full circle."

"We had to get rid of them, of course," Ginnie explained. "So that very night, we loosed the Hounds of Hell upon the Evans brothers. Those who have never known the work of hell hounds had little reason to believe that any supernatural elements were at work here. Surely, a wild animal of some kind had torn the two men to shreds."

"As they deserved!" Ginnie screamed with a wicked hunger in her eye. "It was their fate. And it is your fate to play the drum for the first time, and to glimpse into your own future. To look into the flames and read them; you play the instrument that knows the fate of all who play it. It is nearly time for you to pay, as I paid, the price for wielding this instrument and learn the day, time, and manner of your death."

"The hour, minute, and second of my birth anniversary is nearly at hand," Niecey crooned, tapping the drum mindlessly, without fear or thought. "Only then...when I make this ultimate sacrifice to divination, will I be able to wield its power. I am ready, Ginnie. I am ready for the divination spells and the darker incantations."

"Know this, then," Ginnie whispered. "Many believe that Lacey died on Juneteenth—the very day she was set free—and that Brynn was forced to kill her own sons that self-same day because of the dark magic they used to kill their father through this drum. Dark magic you now embrace."

"I know," Niecey solemnly swore. But she was a child, and a sheltered one. How could she know about evil?

"Very well," Ginnie said, finally prepared. "March 11, 1929 is the day of my death. I will be struck down by a metal beast. On wheels it moves upon no track, nor does it need any steam or coal to power it. I have always felt a deep guilt at the long date of my death. Further guilt and remorse as I do know that it was your father who died on the train tracks at the moment of your birth, and this dire secret I pass on to you. For your mother did curse him, and accursed, he was plowed down in his prime for what he took from her...her innocence, and nine months later, in childbirth, her life."

"So many dark tales and tidings," Niecey whispered huskily, shaking her head. "And as for I, dear aunt, I will die a far way off in years as well, in the year of 1957 and I will crash to the ground in a great metal flying beast."

"Flying machines?" Ginnie cackled. "That...that seems like madness indeed! Maybe the drum is no longer working, dreaming up these horseless carriages and flying machines in some strange and unbelievable future."

Niecey grinned. "It sounds like madness. No sense in worrying about it." Ginnie smiled casually, but grabbed her niece's wrist just before the last slap struck the drum.

Then she saw it...bodies strewn across the grass, broken and mangled. Skulls bashed in and bleeding onto stuffed furniture of some sort, while large shards of metal poured out of the skies. A ball of fire rushed out of a circular chamber, and immersed her niece in it, just as fire had taken her great-grandmother on that Juneteenth. Ginnie frowned, and dropped her niece's hands. What a horrible way to die...even at such an advanced age!

Quickly, she assembled her face so as to not let her horror show. She went back to arranging the child's elaborate hair.

"Your hair is about done," Ginnie pronounced, distant and resigned. "Let's go visit the church for your birthday dinner and your

Christian blessing. Then, after the sun sets and the moon begins to rise, we will take the drum out back and call upon all of our ancestors."

"All?" Niecey asked, a dark look crossing her face that made her appear older than she was. "Great-grandma Lacey's father was the rapist plantation owner Delwyn Evans. I wouldn't want to be calling him up on any account."

Ginnie laughed. "They have no power over you now, child!"

"Do you think that the baptismal font will boil and spill over if I grace the church with my presence tonight?" Niecey teased, poking her aunt in the ribs.

"Of course not, wicked child!" Ginnie giggled. "After all, half of its congregation is Evans witches."

PALLAS' SWORD

BY SERENA TOXICAT

Pallas bodysnatched a capture of herself in the long bathroom mirror—she was dressed in a confident shade of nude, stood under an anachronistic lava strobe. She smiled, realizing she had attained something intriguing and special that evening—or whatever time of day it was. The sense of somethingness was nothing, really—nothing more than a feeling, at this point, and feelings aren't facts, or so her therapist said—but Pallas didn't much care. It was a welcome break from years of "What if?" and "Am I enough?" or "Am I too much?"

Other than this alien self-assurance, a full-being euphoric buzz, a steadily-ascending mood, and a queer excitement for what could be, there was little to distinguish this moment from a very good night at karaoke.

Maybe she should have played an important theme song from a movie hailing a champion to jerk her out of disbelief, or smoked an e-cigar with her bare feet propped up on a glass coffee table and crossed.

Pallas was wrong about her fierce nakedness, but she didn't much care. She was really clad in chartreuse polyester—not even the ironic, tacky variety from the 70s, just some mall crap. The mirror was cheap, like those screwed above hospital-room sinks, and the lightbulb high overhead was unpleasantly energy-saving. Was that a lucent dysmorphic disorder she harbored? Maybe, but if that's a disorder, she would take two. The catgirl had always had some variant of imposter's syndrome, and was wont to wonder if she was too much of an imposter to diagnose herself with even that. Not tonight, though, Santa! Tonight, she was a mirror *image*, not *the girl in the mirror*—and the image was that of perfection in the imperfect—perfection, because she glimpsed the acceptance of that which was less-than by the standards of the day: the poorly-toned arms, the flat ass, the pale marbled skin, some features that were deemed too feline to be human, and too girlish to be exactly cat. This magnificent, yet still nebulous, feeling, was in fact an early spark of gnosis arisen from that wrathful Goddess conceived from her vast Within. Those are three concepts to toss around over some midnight mouse or a couple poorly-mixed drinks in a dive bar with Michio Kaku, Lisa Gerrard—yes, the singer—and Deepak Chopra. These were constructs, possibilities, things that aren't things—*demi*-things that haunt dreams.

Pallas's esoteric sense of knowing and her prodromal enlightenment seemed rather unlikely at this juncture—but why the hell not? She had put her feline Goddess temple on hiatus due to the stench of cat spray and the need for a wet vac, even though her friends pointed out that it was the most appropriate of bad smells, if bad smells there must be. Everybody knew who the real temple queen was: She prowled on four paws.

Pallas had let her Tibetan Buddhist practice go, dog-years ago, when she found out it was a cult. The catgirl was aware that she had given up on attaining anything close to nirvāṇa, or even a good, stiff satori, and she was fine with that. Maybe it was the letting go that invited this occasion in.

The Wrathful Goddess is a guest who cuts our heads off for our good, not for Her pleasure, although She's got Her sadism like the rest of us have ours. She just owns it. What this head really is, is the business-end of Ego. When it's gotta go, it's gotta go; you can't hold it forever. No-one can. The Dark Lady's wrathfulness was really compassion. Who knew? As for this "vast Within," well, in and out are kind of moot at that degree of expansiveness. Might as well call it Oneness and get on with living.

Once Pallas was out the front door, away from the haze of the bathroom mirror and the daze of the overhead lights, and once her cattish eyes could become moons again, she was alive. She was a powerful, gentle lunatic under a big moon, and from those eyes projected more rays. Maybe she was in a bona fide peak moment, after all. It wasn't impossible, it just depended upon her believing in it long enough for it to take hold, and for her to rest assured that she wasn't just getting psyched up to be let down.

This "believing in yourself" stuff was what the catgirl *really* needed as a daily spiritual practice. Some say you must exalt the ego before you dissolve it. Others claim you have to annihilate the self before realizing the Self. The part of the ego that navigates life on the earth plane in order to let the body survive could surely allow for healthy self-development. The archetype of the Goddess who had come to visit Pallas from within her barely-tilled soil would certainly concur. There She was—a deity, a Godform, a hoped-for solution to what ails, a great etheric Being who is implored, written about, sacrificed to, and worshipped—standing in front of Pallas in all of Her—in all of *Their*—splendor.

There was nothing to believe in, no glory to be had, and nothing to be convinced of. She—It—the All—just *was*. There was no room for doubt, yet there was all the room in the world. Paradoxes ricocheted around the atmosphere just for kicks. It was the play of the Goddess, a *leela* that Pallas and the Divine were living out. The air became rarefied, just for effect.

Around the neck of the Goddess appeared a mala of skulls, just like Maa Kali's, brimming with blood, the water of humanity ascended from its collective core. The deity was ever consuming the errors of ego before they could hit the ground in the form of drops and create more karma.

We are not the body, not the finite mind, not the persona that ambles about this world, this incarnation.

From the Goddess's muladhara chakra at the root of her spine emerged the force of Shakti, a serpent awakening, uncoiling, riling the particles of Her into a harmonic assembly of winds, and a knowing heat from the embers. Pallas had heard about the *ida*, *pingala*, and *sushumna*. This was a kundalini awakening for sure that she was having, and once awake, the force takes on its own chaotic existence. The seeker is just along for the ride: one reminiscent of Disney's Mr. Toad's.

Pallas felt her energetic imprint in the great shimmering Above, and it really was shimmering. It was vibrating on other planets' moons, in the deep, deep unconscious waters, and, of course, in the frequencies of her inner-world stirrings. She had been awake in the life of early algae, in the mythic music of angels, in the chiffon-like folds of ether, in the rich, dark soil of a still-feral Gaia—in the whole of sentient life, in fact. And their imprints were in her. They were her as she was they. Funny how that works.

She saw amoebas growing up and forming scales—it was a rite of evolution. The fish were clad in iridescent skin, and above were forms taking off in unlikely flight. Pallas's dark Goddess lived in all the ages, and so did Pallas, she discovered—in the blooming and death of heliotropes, in colossal trees turned to rock, in the Mayan and Egyptian pyramids, in the glimmering marbling of minerals, in the great, vast waterfalls, in the artful works of living beings, in all of those testaments to life and time—and more—be they human-made or nature-spun, in the vibrating continuum of the All, and in its twin, the Empty, which is called the Pregnant Void.

The deity's scepter was now Pallas's sword. She didn't even know the Goddess was wielding such an object. She must have accepted it when her dimmer part wasn't looking. Perhaps that part never was. She couldn't recall ever having doubted herself—not her true self. She had tried to love herself in the past, but could barely get up the nerve to take herself out to dinner. What does a catgirl do with an imperfect hand clutching great responsibility? It sounds like words manifested from an online deepity generator, but it was the most appropriate phrase she could conjure. It's as if her thoughts had turned off, and all she could do was know. The thoughtless state had never been about thought*less*ness, rather, it was thought-free.

There was no *less*, because there was no lack.

The Goddess had done what She had come for; that was clear. She had initiated Pallas into her own mysteries at the dawn of her mind's transition, showing her that That was more than she knew, and that as small as she was, she was part of Its greatness. And so the deity slipped back into the astral plane and further, into the Feline Divinity system. Pallas did not return to the mirror. Vibrating with something that felt like ecstasy, yet feeling perfectly bushed, she tried, instead, for sleep.

ABOUT THE AUTHORS

Sarah the Black: Sarah the Black is an introverted California native hermiting deep in the Santa Cruz Mountains. Proudly multicultural, this primarily Sephardic Jew/Kaldresh Romani was raised in Southern California. A genderqueer, asexual, intersex disabled adult living with multiple chronic illnesses, Sarah opted for retirement off-grid with a fiercely independent private contractor/writer companion and neurotic female feline minions. "She" is an unapologetically voracious reader with a healthy appetite for street tacos, good beer, and Hello Kitty.

Felix Flynn: Felix Flynn is a writer who has always had a love of horror. Raised in the South, he has always found himself out of place, a feeling compounded by just generally being different. He was diagnosed as autistic late in life, but after he was, he was relieved to know that most of his perceived oddities were normal in his community. His other works can be found in *The Third Corona Book of Horror Stories*, *Black Rainbow Vol. 1*, and on the *NoSleep Podcast*. When not writing, he spends his time with his loving fiancée playing video games or coddling their two fur babies.

Kat Fury: Kat Fury was born in Albuquerque, New Mexico, and began telling stories as soon as she could speak. She has been a member of Toastmasters International for most of her adult life, as well as the Society for Creative Anachronism where she honed her storytelling skills both on the page and with an audience. She has also done advocacy work since her diagnosis with Ehlers-Danlos Syndrome at the age of 17. This work includes mental health advocacy, rare disease advocacy, and advocacy to raise awareness of the needs of disabled persons who experience domestic abuse. Her advocacy work was further shaped by her autism, spinal cord injury, multiple traumatic brain injuries, and visual impairment.

Omewenne Grimoire: Omewenne began as a writer in the Bay Area of the 1980's and 90's with poetry, short stories, and plays. Her theatre credits as playwright include *Visitations by Death*, *Nico...My Empty Pages*, and *Grimm Guignol*. Her chapbooks include *Slipped Out Under the Door*, *Cold Eye Blind Window*, and *Nekrosurrealia*. In 2019, she published a book of short stories on Amazon called *Amduat*. She is also known for her music which can be found on Bandcamp, and as an actress in independent cinema. She lives with her husband and black cats in Cornwall, England, now by the ocean. Her works are dark, and eerie in nature like she was as a child and continues to be into her old age. Omewenne was diagnosed with schizophrenia in the previous millennium and has dealt with mental health issues since her childhood. Her works reflect this.

Karen Junker: Karen Junker is widely regarded as the Most Powerful Witch on the West Coast. Having published in a professional capacity since she was 8, "Bloodstock" in the Iconoclast Productions anthology *Wickedly Abled* is her first professionally published short story. She lives in the Pacific Northwest, where she is the administrative assistant for Readerfest.org. She amuses herself by getting writers into a room with other publishing professionals who will help them with their work and their careers. So far, it's working.

Seruus Ualerium Tristissima Liber: Merlin Monroe, Kaleidoscope Eyes, Seruus Ualerium Tristissima Liber, Pope Uncommon the Dainty, Skunkheart, etc., has 15 names. Fey is an Autistic, transfeminine genderqueer whose science-fantasy space opera "Aduality {0≠2;100=108}" stars Autistic, Deaf, and wheelchair-using queer characters of a variety of races. Fey's a muppet, wannabe nun and aspiring trophy wife, longing for both a family and a temple to tend. Identifying as a toy, fear primary sexual identity isn't gay, straight, bi, or pan, but submissive. Fey mostly writes RPG material, poetry, and graphic fiction, and is currently writing a book about DD/ss (Divine Dominance/sacred submission) with one of fear Dominants.

AJ Martin: AJ Martin is a speculative fiction writer and community educator living in central Connecticut. As an epileptic writer, she uses her work to disrupt and dissect ableist stereotypes both in literature and society at large. In "The Last Book," AJ explores the relationship between genocide, disability, and the importance of reclaiming one's own story through the perspective of Damien, a young man haunted by the loss of his people and the story that he never had the chance to finish.

Jef Rouner: Jef Rouner, formerly known as Jef With One F and Jef Withonef, is an award-winning journalist and musician, as well as a short story author with *Crushing Hearts* and *Black Butterfly*. He lives in Houston. After a brief, moderately successful career as a pop artist in *The Black Math Experiment* and *The Ghost of Cliff Burton* as Jef With One F, Jef Rouner turned to pop culture commentary and journalism in outlets like the Houston Press, the Houston Chronicle, OutSmart, Free Press Houston, Cracked, Green Label and Your Tango. After a chance encounter with author Carmilla Voiez in a professional capacity, he began penning fictional short stories including "Just a Kiss Away" in *Broken Mirrors, Fractured Minds* and "Sleepers, Wake!". His first collection, *The Rook Circle*, released in 2015, features illustrations by Dori Hartley.

Carolyn Saulson: The author of *Living A Lie: Tales of Intrigue, Homelessness and Telepathic Power*; the comic book *Living A Lie*; and the plays *The Strange Case of Dr. Henriette Jekyll* and *Song of Solomon: A Love Story*. Her works have appeared in *Writer's Muse Magazine* and *Tale of an Iconoclast: The Carolyn Saulson Story*. Co-Author of *Profiles in Black* published by the Congress of Racial Equality in 1978, one of the first Black Who's Who guides in America. She was the lead singer of the Afrocentric gothic band Stagefright, and co-founder of the media arts non-profit Iconoclast Productions, the San Francisco Black Independent Film Festival and the African American Multimedia Conference.

Sumiko Saulson: Sumiko Saulson is a cartoonist; science-fiction, fantasy and horror writer; editor of *Black Magic Women* and *100+ Black Women in Horror Fiction*; and author of *Solitude*, *Warmth*, *The Moon Cried Blood*, *Happiness and Other Diseases*, *Somnalia*, *Insatiable*, *Ashes and Coffee*, and *Things That Go Bump in My Head*. S/he wrote and illustrated the comics *Mauskaveli*, *Dooky* and the graphic novels *Dreamworlds* and *Agrippa*. S/he writes for *SEARCH* Magazine. The child of African American and Russian-Jewish parents, a native Californian and an Oakland resident who's spent most of hir adult life in the San Francisco Bay Area, s/he is pansexual, polyamorous and genderqueer.

Stacy Schonhardt: Stacy Schonhardt is an author and artist from the Pacific Northwest, where she lives with her partner and their dog. She is a founding member and participant in Vaginomicon, an annual one-night event in February celebrating women in horror. She has fibromyalgia and related disabilities. She graduated from the University of Minnesota-Duluth with degrees in philosophy and studio art. Stacy is also a freelance editor with nine books to her credit, and has some pretty strong opinions about the Oxford comma. When she's not writing, Stacy is often painting or making jewelry. "Believe," is her first published short story, and is based on real events that happened when she was a young child. (Hi Mom!)

E.F. Schraeder: Semi-finalist in the 2019 Charlotte Mew Chapbook Contest, E. F. Schraeder is the author of *Ghastly Tales of Gaiety and Greed* (coming in 2020 from Omnium Gatherum) and two poetry collections, most recently *Chapter Eleven* (Partisan Press). Dr. Schraeder's fictional stories and nonfiction essays have also appeared in journals, blogs, and anthologies including *Mobius: the Journal of*

Social Change, the *Intellectual Freedom Blog*, *Radical Teacher*, *Mystery Weekly Magazine*, *Subliminal Realities*, *Pulp Modern*, *Literary Hatchet*, and others. Schraeder holds a Ph.D. in interdisciplinary studies, emphasizing ethics, and is at work on a full length manuscript of poems.

Graham Swanson: He studied English at the University of Nebraska. While Living in Lincoln he started Castleswanson.com to post horror stories on. His work has been published in Midnight Magazine and Midnight Tales. After school he started writing novels and is now working hard to finish them. He believes the horror genre offers a unique perspective on the events of the world, and the problems happening everyday. The provided story is a love letter to the delights of horror.

Serena Toxicat: San Francisco-born and -bred Serena Toxicat scratches out dark fiction, lyrics, plays and poetry in English and in French. She sings in a Black Catwave band called Protea, and her parallel recording projects include Starchasm. An actor, model-turned-designer, former-pro Domme, NLP life coach, and literary translator, Toxicat leads a scattered, sketchy life and delights in showing her paintings, taking part in LGBTQ+ and kink-focused activities, traveling and collecting tattoos. Serena is a psychic reader, healer, priestess and feline Tarot deck creator. She lived almost 8 years in Paris and traveled to Egypt, where she recorded vocals in the King's Chamber.

www.ingramcontent.com/pod-product-compliance
Lightning Source LLC
Chambersburg PA
CBHW030816310726
48980CB00006B/512/J
9781794833142